# FOUNDING STONES

ABBE ROLNICK

GENERATIONS OF SECRETS, BOOK 3

*A Novel of Cultural and Environmental Conflict*

# FOUNDING STONES

**ABBE ROLNICK**

*Founding Stones*
Generations of Secrets, Book Three


For permission to reproduce selections from this book or to order copies, write to Sedro Publishing, 21993 Grip Road, Sedro-Woolley, WA 98284. http://www.sedropublishing.com or http://www.abberolnick.com.

Design & Prepress: Sally Dunn Design & Photography (www.sallydunn.com).
Copy Editor: Ariel Anderson (www.arieledits.com).
Cover Images: iStock//Toltek, iStock//Orbon Alija, Big Stock//Wavebreak Media



Library of Congress Control Number: 2019902603
Rolnick, Abbe
ISBN: 978-0-9995291-4-0 (Trade Book)
ISBN: 978-0-9995291-5-7 (Electronic Book)

Other Books by Abbe Rolnick:
*River of Angels*, 2nd edition, Book One in Generations of Secrets (2018)
*Color of Lies, Book Two in Generations of Secrets* (2018)
*Cocoon of Cancer: An Invitation to Love Deeply* (2016)
*Tattle Tales: Essays and Stories Along the Way* (2016)

Forthcoming:
*Bubbie's Magical Hair*

***Dedication***

*To Abraham Javodick, my grandfather. You came to the United States from another country and found a home, a fulfilling life. I never met you, but your essence has guided me for my entire life. I carry your name and all that you were.*
*~Abbe*

## ACKNOWLEDGEMENTS

The idea for this book came to me on our camping journey across the United States—Sedro Woolley, Washington, to Duluth, Minnesota. Fascinated by the geology, the industries of mining and farming, the fauna, and the flow of life different from that of the Pacific Northwest or the Caribbean, I contemplated the essence of the earth. From there, I began with characters and discovered their essences. A thread that pulled the emotions together was the stories each rock told. Blending history with the present, I brought the characters back. No one lives in isolation from this essence.

I thank Jim for his biological bent and for his great skills at finding off-the-beaten-track campsites. He is my grand adventurer as well as my first reader.

A special thanks to Mary Gillilan from Independent Writers Studio, who has led my critique group for more years than my fingers can count. Thanks also to Janet Oakley, Janet Bergstrom, and Stephanie Hopkinson, who have read more than a few revisions.

# CONTENTS

## Prologue

*What Defines Us May Kill Us*

Records Group F-444 documents of the Jewish emigration from the area of "Pale":

1905 Kiev, a year and place young Abraham would never forget but refused to remember. He ran from gaslight pole to gaslight pole, milepost to milepost. His breath slowed to that of a hibernating bear, and his legs grew muscular from running. Gone was the panting, the aches of despair. Now, after months of rigorous nightly forays, he could travel twenty miles in an evening. His city, awash with fabricated anti-Jewish riots, forced family after family to leave southern Russia.

He left behind the city of his birth and traveled by dark to Hamburg, Germany. Too dangerous and expensive to use the train system, he slept at safe houses till he reached port, where in seven weeks the Bulgaria set sail. He abandoned the pogroms and with them his seven dead siblings, his feeble and tormented parents. If all went as planned, he'd emerge in the Americas, someone new.

Besides food and another pair of shoes, Abraham's haversack held falsified papers. Clean shaven, he looked less like an Abraham, more like an Edward or Eduardo. His practiced English and Spanish sounded passable to the uneducated ear. For the last time, he reviewed the Torah. He covered his head with a rag he found in a darkened alleyway, lit a candle, and slid out the miniature scroll. He didn't need to see, just feel the sacred words. He had them memorized, as he would never speak or read them again. From now on he'd be a Christian. May God forgive me and save my life for a good purpose.

As Abraham ran through the night, hid among the trees, under rocks, and in barns, he gathered fragments of stones, pieces of the world he knew. Who would question a slice of rock or the stains of dirt? He kept them as evidence of a lost world—earth blood. Nothing he took could identify him. He memorized smells, the movement of the wind. He foraged mushrooms, ate roots. Practice kept him from the poisonous ones, restraint shrunk his stomach, and patience turned into resilience. He learned the secrets of the fungi cells, their healing and destroying properties, and used them to absorb toxins on his inflamed skin.

After seven weeks of running, he boarded the ship. He used the last of his savings to travel steerage, rested for a week, and emerged from the transcontinental voyage as Eduardo, not the Edward he had hoped for. Storms blew the ship off course. Instead of New York, he had landed on the coast of Costa Rica—a nobody to become somebody.

# CHAPTER 1: *Sensual Stutters*

Hannah stared at her closet. Everything looked outdated. Her mother's taste in clothes didn't reflect the new century, let alone the year 2016. She chose what she thought her mom would approve—a short-sleeved navy A-line dress. The anniversary of her sister's death was hard enough, but attending a ceremony in front of the town made it worse.

She thought of Luis instead. He was an unintended secret. A friend, a boy, and someone she could talk with. If she closed her eyes, she could still see the rivulets of sweat that slowly rolled over his muscles. They had gone to the beach, and their dancing seemed to naturally flow with the sounds of the ocean. She could hear the music, a background of rhythms that rippled over the sculpted stomach, the flexed thighs that quivered with strength. Words had always stuck along her tongue, until the music came. If she concentrated on the beats, she spoke without the stutter, almost normal. Otherwise she kept her thoughts sealed.

Now as she remembered watching Luis, she not only heard the music but saw the rhythms of life move along his body. Her friend danced with unspoken words. He became the rocks, the rain, the anger of abandonment, the sweetness of morning birds, and the speed of an eagle swooping down on prey.

She felt tears along her cheeks. Her lips parted, and she tasted the salt of understanding.

*So this is what it was like to desire.* This was what it meant to love. Even now her body trembled with his imprint. Upon Luis's insistence, she had danced alongside him. With each leap she had leaped, with each lunge she had lunged. They had circled one another, bending at the waist, rolling on the sand until, breathless, the music ceased. The only rhythms left were those of their hearts. One finger along her lips, tracing her unspoken thoughts.

Even the hum of her house couldn't release her knotted words. Slowly she tapped *dah-dah-da dah, dad-ah*, repeating over and over. In the mirror she watched her lips slowly open, her tongue tip along her palate as her fingers repeated their tapping. Her blond curls shook along with her head. She took her brush and unraveled the curls, then formed a long braid down her back. She walked out her bedroom door, letting the swish of her braid deliver the message she could only stutter: "I-I-I'm coming, M-Mother. We won't be late."

Hannah took the stairs two by two, still tapping on her leg. She flashed her mother a smile and got the once-over, the review of her clothes, her hair, her lack of makeup.

"Good choice. The dress color isn't too bright or dull. You'll blend into the background, and no one will notice you. I wish you would wear hose, but at least you pulled your curls back."

Today, June 23, was the memorial for Jenna, Hannah's twin sister. Cancer separated them forever. Hannah still missed her. Four years felt like two lifetimes. Jenna's absence echoed in her every thought, tripping up her words. Hannah doubled her efforts to make up the loss.

She watched her parents walk arm in arm down their driveway to her father's 4x4 pickup. He had spruced it up, waxing the midnight-blue paint so it looked like a moonlit night. They drove by their blueberry fields. Acres and acres of bushes lined the long paths. Hannah watched field-workers picking bushels for market. She tapped her leg, sensing the wave of arms and heads as music. Lost in thought, she snapped to attention when she heard her mother's voice say her name.

"I don't suppose the dedication will take long. I know we are doing this for Jenna, but it is just a formality, a public relations event. Our money funded the new cancer wing. Hannah won't have to speak. I can do it instead."

Hannah became a shadow. She tapped along her legs, feeling the tires roll over the bumps and potholes, the up and down of a road well-traveled.

Skagit County had always been her home. She loved the fields of tulips and daffodils in the spring and the blue tint of their berries, the open skies, and the mountains to the north. Invisible to her parents, caught now in readying for the public, she smelled the air, which was mixed with the sweetness of late-blooming flowers, hay, and salt from the bay.

Hannah thought about Skagit Valley, her home, the home Jenna left behind. She wondered if Jenna would talk for her if she had lived, or if she would have been silenced by the farm's problems, which hid the beauty of the land. Hannah concentrated, widened her mouth and lifted her tongue to form the *S* of *Skagit*, then placed her teeth along her lip for the *V* of *Valley*. Inherited land worked its way into her bloodline. The other home Hannah knew was that of their cabin upriver. Jenna had died before her parents had bought the retreat.

Her mother turned and smiled. "Hannah, did you say something? I thought I heard you whispering."

Caught, Hannah tapped one syllable. "No, I am o-o-only th-thinking."

"Well, don't worry, you won't have to talk at the ceremony. You and your dad can cut the ribbon, and I'll make the thank-you speech."

Hannah nodded, not wanting to expend the effort of talking. She only talked upriver at the cabin and only with Joseph—and now with Luis.

## CHAPTER 2:
## *Musty Mushrooms*

Joseph raced through the woods, hurrying despite the frequent tangling of his feet among the roots, toward his cabin. He ran faster and faster, knowing he had stayed too long spreading wood chips and sprinkling spores. Mentally he calculated the time he needed to shower, change clothes, and drive from upriver to the dedication. Not enough to arrive on time, but just enough to make an appearance. He knew only Hannah would notice or care.

The smell of decaying duff and dirt lingered in the air. The woods held the aroma of fallen trees, crumbling leaves, and insects. Here with the Pacific Northwest rains, his mushrooms flourished. Joseph concentrated on transitioning from his experiments to becoming part of Hannah's world. The sight of his home helped. Built with sandstone from the Chuckanut Mountains and the yellow cedar trees of his woods, the cabin lumbered along like a river. No steps to mount or stairs inside, Joseph had created ramps to connect rooms instead of walls and entryways. The gradual incline up or down signaled a purposeful attempt to equalize settings. His kitchen dipped, his living room rose. Bedrooms and bathrooms fell to where the windows hid or exposed a view.

As he approached, he listened to the music of the entranceway. The gurgle of water, the plunk of droplets from dripping leaves on the stone path. He lived alone. The stones set in hardened clay changed not only through weathering, but by presents his friends left for him, or by the absence of stones taken in exchange. Even now he sensed an alteration, a hole to the left of the path. The flat piece of sandstone with a fossilized imprint of a palm frond had been exchanged for a small heart-shaped soapstone deposited at his doorway. Joseph accepted the exchange, neither wondering nor judging the purpose or fairness.

His thoughts rested with Hannah. Her visits over the years meant so much to him. He smiled picturing the first visit. He had been dismantling an airplane engine at the back of his house when he heard a rustling of leaves in a tree. The smallest of yellow fuzz peeked out beyond the greenery as Hannah's head appeared at the top of the branches.

Joseph had pretended he couldn't see or hear the child. Instead he went to his entranceway where his view was aided by reflecting pools. Occasionally he'd plunk a small rock into the pools or turn on a hose, releasing a flow of water trickling down the pathway. Each plunk elicited an ooh from the tree, and then an aah, until they had secretly created an alternating pattern of plunks and oohs and aahs. These weekend rituals always ended with frantic calls from Hannah's mother, "Hannah, don't hide from me. Come out from wherever you are. Don't get me angry." Within seconds he'd watch the yellow fuzz scurry down the tree and run home.

Weekends turned into years until Hannah came down from her post. Joseph let her roam, paying no attention to her wanderings. Hannah became his shadow, following his every action. Her silence echoed the patterns of the outdoors—no words, just the syncopation of nature's voice.

Today she would need more. The dedication of the cancer wing was a public coming-out for Hannah. Joseph thought of rituals that marked adulthood. Every religion or culture seemed to have one. Sweet sixteens meant maturity. Why confuse this special time with the death of her sister?

Dressed in black slacks that had seen more years than Hannah, Joseph found a collared shirt and a handkerchief for his pocket. He slipped his feet into polished shoes that allowed for his wide toes. Without a mirror to verify that he looked presentable, Joseph hoped that he could slip into the crowd without being noticed. His trips into town were few and far between, only out of necessity.

His latest refurbished car, a swayed-back royal-blue '50s Oldsmobile, sat in the driveway. The finishing touches would come later, but the engine purred, and the car would get him to town and back. Joseph made one last stop in his garage, to check that he had turned off all the equipment and to leave Luis a note, before he headed out.

He knew Luis would ignore the dedication, preferring to hide from the community. The least he could do was leave him work to challenge his mind. Nothing good came of idle thought, thought that circled back to nowhere and, in Luis's case, often landed in Ecuador. Joseph thought of *nowhere*, a place without connections. Everyone needed to be connected. He rolled down the window and let the smells of the woods fill the car. As he headed down his driveway and entered onto Highway 20, fresh air from the river valley replaced the damp smell of the woods. Soon the smells of the burger joint wafted in and then the chemical odor of plastics melting from the local composite factory.

Joseph had lived upriver for so many years that he had become a fixture. This made him smile. His idiosyncrasies didn't matter, as no one questioned a fixture. He didn't envy Hannah or Luis their youth, particularly the insecurity of internal and external questions. He hoped they knew that they still had time to write their stories, that some questions didn't have answers.

# CHAPTER 3: *Blueberries to Market*

Luis drove slowly, just a notch below the speed limit. Being Hispanic, he worried about getting stopped by the police. He worried his hair gleamed charcoal black. He worried that his skin shone too dark. And he worried that his dark eyebrows and wide brown eyes told his story. *Not a story worth hearing.* The pickup truck belonged to his parents. He paid the license fees, and the insurance, but the registration was in his father's name, Thomas Lozano. Thomas and his mother, Ria, no longer lived with Luis. Luis drove a car belonging to an undocumented immigrant. He didn't know if this, too, was a crime. For the last two years, Luis had walked the line between being a Dreamer and the son of undocumented parents. Now he walked alone, since his parents had lost the battle with immigration officials and were deported.

Luis rode past the blueberry fields and watched the pickers. He knew most of them from when his mother was in the fields. When he was a baby his mother carried him on her back, where he sat swaying with her arms, reaching, plucking, and carrying. After he could walk, he ran alongside her picking the dropped berries, and by the time he turned ten he had his own two rows to pick.

With his parents deported to Ecuador, he felt more like an outcast than a son of immigrants. The fields he had picked all his life represented a trap, a risk for his compatriots by association. He chose to leave, shutting out all that he knew.

Music and Hannah kept him sane, and he drove thinking of how his sanity made no sense and that his brain must be really screwed up. As he turned onto Highway 2O, he caught a glimpse of a midnight-blue pickup, a snatch of blond hair in the back seat, and his old boss and wife in the front. *Trouble.* He didn't wave or acknowledge Hannah. Instead he turned up the radio and concentrated on the music, the beat of drums, the shake of maracas, and the ding of the triangle. This was the language he understood. His left foot kept the rhythm, and his thumbs alternated taps as they cradled the steering wheel. The truck danced its way away along the Skagit River's edge up toward Sauk Mountain—so much for driving inconspicuously. Prudence set in, and he turned the radio off. *No sense in getting a ticket.*

Luis held on to his memory of Hannah, at first just watching her and then the thrill of her dancing with him. Her words so softly spoken: *I feel like a bird let out of a cage, free of expectation. No boundaries, no limits, just me.*

By the time Luis arrived at Joseph's cabin, those words had become his whispered mantra. He parked behind the stone wall that over the years grew taller and taller. Moss between the crevices and the dampness of the woods created a mosaic of time. The latest edition to the wall held dark-green stones, lines of white, and blue. Luis repeated the mantra: *No boundaries, no limits, just me.* He felt free here, hidden behind this wall.

Luis noted Joseph's absence, a hush beyond the normal rustling of leaves, the uninterrupted trickling of water. Even the birds held their songs. Curious, Luis made his way to the metal-pole building at the back of the property. The building extended Joseph's workspaces—a metal shell with an oversized roof where Joseph could store all his projects. Luis jiggled the handle of the door, and just as he suspected, Joseph had left the door unlocked. Engines from cars, tractors, and planes lined the benches, each one in various stages of repair. A large note with his name lay beside an airplane motor:

*Luis,*

*Please degrease this engine. On your next visit, I'll let you experi-*

*ment with the welding. If you have time to work in the garden, the beans need picking, and there are way too many for me to eat. Take some as well as the corn and carrots. I'm at the dedication.*

*—J*

A lump formed in Luis's throat. He hadn't forgotten about the ceremony. When he had passed Hannah riding with her parents, he knew where they were going. It wasn't his place to help Hannah. Shaking his head, he put on gloves and began the meticulous work of breaking down the engine and soaking each part.

Despite Joseph's note, Luis felt something amiss. He had never known Joseph to travel into town. Granted, Luis didn't know everything, but people visited Joseph, not the other way around. He rationalized that Joseph knew he'd be here and could hold down the fort while he supported Hannah. Luis hoped that Hannah knew he cared as well.

Luis forced himself to concentrate on the engine. He worked until the engine shone, then cleaned up the workbench and headed over to the sink to wash his hands. Three large soapstone sculptures that Joseph had carved stood in the corner. One already had a cover, and the other two awaited Joseph's inspiration. Tempted to peek, Luis stared at the canvas cover. Temptation took many forms, and if he looked, he wouldn't be able to trust himself. More than anything Luis needed trust. If and when Joseph wanted to share, he would.

Tired, Luis headed to the garden. At least he'd have food for tonight's dinner, thanks to Joseph. He always seemed to look out for his friends, and that gave Luis some comfort.

His day would be long. He still had to attend the grounds at the Concrete Airport, study for his classes, and try to practice his dance routine. Staying busy kept him safe from the streets. His parents would want him safe.

# CHAPTER 4: *Train Tracks—Which side are you on?*

Slowed by the flashing lights and the honks of the BNSF train, Joseph revved the Oldsmobile's engine. He counted the 120 freight cars that rolled past before the crossbars opened. Each was packed with black gold, the latest cargo of controversy. Joseph remembered the silk trains, another forgotten time when politics and economics clashed.

He parked the Oldsmobile behind the Food Co-Op. So many of the customers had old cars that his fit right in. Again, Joseph leaped along in his traditional deer-like run. Within minutes he'd mounted the hill and was in earshot of the hospital. A crowd of dignitaries surrounded the Hendersons, as well as the owners of the larger local farms in the area. Hannah stood between her mother and father holding oversized scissors, readying to cut the ceremonial ribbon to the cancer center. Joseph noted her paper-thin skin, so pale that the purple veins of her forehead created waves along her brow. Yet Hannah held her hands steady even if her lips remained sealed. She stepped back as her mother began her speech.

"My daughter Jenna died at age twelve, but she remains here with us in our hearts because of all of your donations. We are a rural community with an adequate local hospital that now has a state-of-the-art cancer center. She died because we couldn't help her. She remains because this new center will be able to help others. Thank you for helping to change the world for others."

Mrs. Henderson turned to face the crowd, her arms raised high, welcoming applause. Hannah and her father snipped the ribbon and melted back among the donors. While the officials from Skagit Valley Hospital and all the donors made their own speeches, Mrs. Henderson shook hands.

Joseph noted two teenaged boys hanging off to the right, walking up and down the line unengaged. In a matter of seconds, he witnessed a handoff of a wallet and then a quick exit. Joseph followed from across the road, outpacing each of their steps. Shorter than either of the boys, Joseph used his slight build to sandwich himself between them, then grabbed each of their arms.

Joseph didn't play dumb. He turned to each of the boys and hissed, "I saw you, and I will remember." But it wasn't his words that made the boys turn away. Joseph's eyes penetrated through their cockiness with a fierce stare. Joseph snatched the wallet and deposited it inside the open window of a nearby patrol car. The officer touched his hat, acknowledging Joseph's effort.

Joseph searched the crowd for Hannah. He found her sitting on a bench away from the group. He didn't approach, just whistled a high-pitched rhythm, *da-doot*. Hannah looked up and smiled. Satisfied she had seen him, he headed back to his car. He'd been in town too long. He needed his solitude.

Back at the parking lot, Joseph's upriver neighbor Ralph and his wife, Sharon, waved a hello as they entered the Food Co-Op. Joseph figured they had made the trip down to pay their respects to Hannah and run some errands. Neither of them knew Jenna or the other Hendersons.

Before Joseph could pull out, Ralph ran out of the store and stopped him. "Wait up, Joseph. I wanted to catch you and say thanks for the advice with the mushrooms. Sharon is feeling better, but she's still tired. We only came out today to give Hannah support."

From the corner of his eye, Joseph spotted the boys again with more merchandise. Impatient, Joseph nodded his head. "We can talk later. I got to go."

Ralph waved goodbye and called out, "Oh, you were right. We had a bumper corn crop, just like you predicted. We had enough for ourselves and plenty to sell to the co-op."

Joseph revved the motor, turned his head toward the window, and called out, "You're my neighbors, whatever I can do to help." Within seconds his car peeled out, headed toward Riverside Park, hot on the chase of the two teenagers he had just busted. He wouldn't have bothered, but the leather purse dangling from the boy's shoulder didn't match their style. The purse looked a little too familiar. He remembered Hannah being so proud of buying her mother a gift.

Joseph's head pounded with the old sensation of anger, a past addiction just as bad as any drug. This is why he avoided coming to town. He saw too much—an affliction passed down from his father's migration to seek an income and grandfather's flight from the pogroms.

Families filled Riverside Park with picnic baskets, bicycles, runners. He slowed his car down to a standstill, turned the motor off, and forced himself to walk along the Skagit River. Within minutes he spotted the boys behind a tall stand of rhododendrons, smoking a joint and drinking beer.

"I thought we were busted by that old guy with the freaky eyes. We lucked out with the dedication."

"Yeah, but then the sucker just let us go. What do you think he was playing at?"

"I don't know, but at least we were able to grab this purse without anyone noticing."

Joseph stepped out from the bushes and planted himself between the boys. In one sweeping motion, he knocked the beer cans out of the boys' hands and grabbed the purse. His curled knuckles held the bag against his chest. "I noticed and will always notice. Worse yet, I can do something about it."

Frozen, the boys stared at Joseph's fists, then at his eyes. Stoned, they rose in slow motion, waiting for Joseph's penetrating gaze to burn through their haze. The taller of the two towered a foot above Joseph, but the little man still met his eyes.

"From where I stand," Joseph said, "you are digging yourself into a hole without a shovel. One more encounter like this, one more incident of taking advantage of others, and I will meet you on my terrain. That's a promise." Joseph held out his hand and motioned for the boy who remained seated. "I'll take the credit cards and money."

With trembling hands, the boy riffled through his pants. He came up with a knife, a wad of bills, and four credit cards. Joseph looked at him again and breathed his last request: "And the photos." One picture of Hannah standing at her cabin, one of her and Jenna, and one of Hannah's mother in a bathing suit. Joseph shoved them all back into the purse and walked off.

## CHAPTER 5:
## *Ceremonial Blinds*

The crowds from the dedication dispersed into a reception area inside the hospital adjacent to the new Henderson Cancer Center. Hannah stood in line with her father and mother, shaking hands and smiling, until her handshake withered and the room spun. "Dad, I'm going to take a break, walk for a bit. T-tell Mom w-where I am." With his nod of approval, Hannah escaped to the sanctuary created for worried family members, a sunroom that faced the Skagit River and gave a glimpse of the railroad and bus station outside of the business district.

Here Hannah found a woman whose skin shone with a mixture of olive and cream, auburn hair that tumbled in waves, and a body that barely filled the cushioned rocking chair. She sat with her hands folded in her lap, eyes closed, with legs crossed at the ankles. Her feet tipped up and down, alternating a beat Hannah couldn't hear. Toe and heel and then the woman's hands answered in a clapped syncopation. Finally, the woman opened her eyes and smiled at Hannah. "Don't worry. I'm working out a dance routine in my head. I have to do something while I wait for my daughter's treatment."

Even though she knew better, Hannah stared at the blend of colors and textures, fascinated by a skin foreign to her own. She studied the woman's calf muscles as they flexed with rhythms. Two words stuck in her head: *dance* and *daughter*. Extending her hand, she tried to relax and introduce herself. "Hi, I'm H-Hannah H-Henderson."

Taking Hannah's hand in both of her own, the stranger smiled. "I'm Shelly. I'm so pleased to meet you. Your family helped build this center, right? Thank you."

Hannah wasn't sure how to respond. She liked the warmth of Shelly's hands, the way she looked Hannah straight on, and how her smile took over her face. Hannah didn't see the creases of worry or the anger of an anguished mother, though she remembered the sobs from her own mother as Jenna had treatments. "H-how old is your daughter?"

Shelly motioned for Hannah to sit down next to her. "How did you know I needed to talk? Not everyone can listen. My daughter, Robin, is young but older than most kids her age. I sometimes wonder at how wise they can be at twelve. I'm blessed to have her. She is the most beautiful dancer. They found the cancer after a fall at practice. Funny how that works—a fall might just save her life. At least that is what we hope. We're trying some experimental procedures."

Hannah sat quietly and let Shelly's story lie between them. She noticed a tear form in the corner of Shelly's blue eyes, quickly wiped away. She knew better than to ask too much, to focus too deeply on the cancer. Robin was more than the sum of her disease, just like Jenna was. "What kind of d-dancing does Robin like?"

At this Shelly jumped out of her chair and lifted her arms. Somehow her legs followed—quick steps, a lift, a lunge, and a spring into the air. They both laughed as Shelly, out of breath, landed back on the floor.

From across the way, Hannah heard a familiar clearing of the throat. She turned to see her father, stern faced, marching toward her. "There you are," he said. "Let's go, your mother and I need you."

Immediately she backed away from Shelly, stumbled, and then turned to face her father. She tried to talk, to get the words out, but even her stutters held back. Thankfully, Shelly stepped forward.

"Hi, I'm Shelly. You must be Mr. Henderson, Hannah's father. Hannah was kind enough to make me laugh while I was waiting for my daughter's treatments to end."

All his bluster dissolved as he focused in on Shelly. Hannah watched his stern face soften. His fierce approach dismantled, he seemed a gentle man. "I'm sorry that you have this burden. Our Jenna died four years ago, and my wife, relives the loss over and . . ." Mid-sentence he stopped, as if the mention of his wife set him on another path. He turned to Hannah. "Say your goodbyes to Shelly. Your mom is distraught. Her purse was stolen during the ceremony."

As he hurried out, Hannah stared at his hunched shoulders, the familiar quick-paced walk. When the corridor emptied of his image, she slowly turned to face Shelly. "My f-father isn't always like that. He used to laugh more. M-my mother needs me, I have to go."

Shelly rummaged through her pockets and pulled out a business card. "Here, take this. I liked talking with you, and I know Robin would like to meet you. Maybe you could come to the dance studio. I'm there most days, if I'm not here." To ease the situation more, Shelly stood on tip-toe and raised her left leg high, well over Hannah's head, then put it back down and bowed with a flourish.

Hannah found her legs answering the rhythmic pull. She twirled and lifted her right leg out behind her, leaned forward and then toward the floor, letting her leg reach toward the sky. By the time her head rose to meet Shelly's face, Hannah lost her balance. Only Shelly's quick reach saved her from falling. Hannah caught her breath and Shelly's arms. Without hesitation she said, "Thanks, I'd like that."

Not waiting for a response, Hannah raced down the corridor, back to the reception area. She knew she should feel guilty. That is what her mother felt about cancer, about Jenna, about death. Instead, Hannah felt the same lightness and ease as when she had danced with Luis. Not exactly the same, but not the sense of burden her father mentioned to Shelly.

. . . . .

Hannah found her mother surrounded by security guards. The returned purse lay on a table with its contents spewed. Hannah imagined an operating room where the sterile instruments lay strewn across the tray, displayed and ready for dissection. She watched her mother check the leather wallet for money and credit cards, the bottles of prescription pills to see if they were full, the family photos. Content that the essentials of her life were intact, Hannah's mother looked up. "There you are, Hannah. They found my purse. Some kids ran off with it and got all the way to the park. Weren't you watching it?"

There it was, the accusation asked in the form of a question. Red faced, Hannah inched her way toward her mom. She hated the stares, the sense that she had let her mother down. The hospital security guards stepped aside, making a path for Hannah. By the time she offered her arms out for an embrace, her mother's demeanor had already switched from annoyance to her public persona. "Mom, wh-who found the purse?"

"The hospital security guards said a man with funny eyes claimed he found the purse in the hands of two hooligans. Their description reminded me of the little elfish guy who lives up near our cabin."

Before her mother said anything else, Hannah's dad stepped forward. "Connie, be grateful that Joseph was nearby and recognized the purse. He's a good neighbor."

"I didn't mean anything, just that it was an odd coincidence."

Hannah hated the tension, the unstated assumptions. It was one thing to overhear them at home, but not in public. So much for this day being dedicated to the Henderson Cancer Center and Jenna. "I t-think Joseph came to town for the d-dedication. He c-cares." The minute the words were out of her mouth, Hannah knew they were wrong, that her mother would pounce.

"Hannah, this isn't the place or time to talk about Joseph and what he cares about. I'm thankful that he found my purse. Let's not spoil the day."

Hannah's dad came forward and rested his hand on Hannah's

shoulder. She felt the familiar grip, the one that put her father between the lines of words. It told her to ignore what she didn't understand.

Hannah turned away and walked over to the window. One of the guards slipped back into her vacant space and took control of the situation. "Mrs. Henderson, we will file a report at the police station. Please let us know if anything is missing."

Hannah's mother gave a nod and a vacant smile. The silence that followed the security guard's exit filled the room. No one moved. Her mom finally spoke: "Jeff, do you want to visit Jenna's grave before we go home?"

Hannah closed her eyes. She hated the cemetery, hated the quaffed lawns and rows of coordinated orange and red flowers. Jenna had always been messy, a kid romping outside, putting rocks in her mouth. Hannah could hear the old reprimands from her mom, when she and Jenna had come inside with mud dripping from the corners of their mouths.

"You two will break your teeth, choke, or die from worm germs," she had said.

Her dad had always laughed. "Connie, as long as the rocks are big, let them play. You know the kids will find another to replace it. They won't choke, and besides they've already cleaned it, no new germs. Just look at their precious brown faces."

From the window, Hannah watched a pigeon land on a sidewalk bench and peck at the remains of a stranger's lunch. Another pigeon arrived to share the spoils. Together they took flight, dropping pigeon shit behind. Nature's presents. Hannah smiled at the absurdity of appearances. No one cared. Pigeons came and went as they pleased. Two boys, with baseball caps turned backward and shorts that hung like sacks, plopped down on the dew-sprayed bench. The one that looked like a giraffe pulled a black purse from inside his pants. Hannah saw the ruse. She knew that these were the boys that had stolen her mother's purse.

Hannah didn't care.

Already her father had roused her mom. His right armed hooked inside of his wife's elbow, as his left waited for Hannah's. She took her place next to her father and forced a dog smile. Unconsciously she tapped her thigh with her free hand. They walked as a unit down the new cancer center to the old hallways of the hospital. The smells of medicine lingered even with the ammonia-washed floors. Here the weariness of illness clung to the aging walls where Jenna had stayed. Hannah recognized nurses and doctors, faces memorialized from old childhood fears. The staff, absorbed in the cases of the day, paid them no attention. All but one older gentleman, who winked as she passed. Hannah thought she recognized the man from one of her visits to Joseph's house.

She remembered him dressed in jeans and holding a shovel, coming from the wooded area beyond her family's cabin. Joseph and the gentleman conferred over some paper, and he had left with a sack of mushrooms. Tempted to say something to him, Hannah slowed her steps. The moment passed when, from the opposite hallway, Shelly appeared with Robin seated in a wheelchair. The two talked with a small woman whose wild black hair filled the space with electricity. Her hands waved words, and her eyes looked deeply into Robin's. Hannah thought for a moment that Shelly had spotted her walking and waved. But the wave was for the older man she had seen in the woods, the one now in the hallway, a hospital employee.

Hannah stumbled with the tug of her father's arm and her mother's command: "Pick your feet up, Hannah. Keep up with us."

Hannah obeyed, tapping the pace precisely so that she now marched in line with her family. But as she passed the conclave, she turned her head. This time Shelly saw her and gave a wave. Hannah lifted her tapping hand in answer. As they walked out the hospital door, she heard Robin tell her mother, "Rosie thinks she can make me feel better. She knows a man named Joseph who . . ."

# CHAPTER 6: *Poker Faced*

Luis stood naked from the waist up, a red bandana wrapped around his forehead to catch the sweat. As he spread the compost and turned the soil, he counted the hangars and the flower beds left for him to plant: fifteen hangars, and then the center food garden. It was good to be using his body again. Different muscles than when he danced. Dancing freed him; digging in the dirt grounded him. The weight of each shoveled patch, heavy with moisture, worms, and life, strained his back and his arms with a sense of worthiness. This was a different freedom, one with purpose.

Only two small planes had landed on the runway in the last two hours. Luis figured that the mountains and the isolation kept pilots away. The soft runway only a stone's throw away from the hangars, the views of Sauk Mountain, and the solitude suited Luis. He'd had enough of the farmhands in the fields. Concrete Airport's smallness expanded his horizons. What really mattered was that someone was paying him to landscape.

As an older gentleman, dressed in baggy jeans held up with suspenders, approached with a shovel in hand, Luis averted his eyes and bent his head. He quickened his pace, turning the black compost over and over until the brown and black dirt blended. Luis needed to blend in, to be part of the landscape. He wished the man gone. The nervous flip-flop of his stomach persisted, the same pressures from the fields to meet the daily quotas. The *or else* hung in the air. This was his job. No one was going to take it away.

Without a word, the older man took to spreading the compost.

He angled the wheelbarrow forward so the point faced the flower bed. Throwing a shorter distance with less on each blade, the shovelfuls went farther than Luis's. After ten throws, the old man tapped the tray bed, and the compost shifted toward the point.

Annoyed but curious, Luis finally looked up. "Thanks for the help, but you don't need to. It's my job." Luis put out his hand. "I'm Luis. I've been hired to plant flowers around the hangars."

No hand followed, no introduction, just the shaking of the old man's head. Luis loaded up another barrow of compost and headed over to the next hangar. To his annoyance, the old man shadowed. This time, Luis lined up the wheelbarrow point tipped downward, acknowledging the lesson just learned. The two shoveled in silence. Luis knew better than to ask questions. If he asked a question, he had to be prepared for the answer. That's why so many of the farmhands pretended they knew no English—they didn't want to be misunderstood.

Exactly one hour after the old man appeared, he disappeared. Returning from a short break, Luis spotted the old man walking with the shovel slung over his shoulder to a hangar near the museum hangar. He could hear his father's warning: *Don't follow the tail that wags. Stay in front.*

Without knowing the old man's name, Luis dubbed him Mr. Poker Face. Poker for short. Sure that he'd encounter Poker again, Luis packed up his shovels, filled the wheelbarrow with the empty flower pots, and headed back to the garden shed by the museum. There he found a sheet on the wall where he posted his hours and the work done.

Joseph had arranged this job for Luis through the museum's director. The only qualifications for the job had been to be an honest man and to get the garden planted with flowers and food by the end of the summer. No instructions, just the honor system. Luis wondered if Poker's help violated the honor system. Just in case, he knocked off a half hour of time and wrote down, "with Poker's help."

Chilled as the sun lowered, Luis rinsed off by the hose and put his t-shirt on. He knew that Hannah would be home now. He knew that most families would be eating dinner. Back at his truck, he found his pack and pulled out a carrot from the stash Joseph had left for him. His mother often said that the hungry weren't picky. Luis knew that the tired weren't either. With the windows rolled down and the radio turned on, Luis listened to the beats within the beats. His mind danced as if it were his body, choreographing steps that tip-toed light and feathery, others that rolled, and those that landed solid, only to crumble. He envisioned the rocks along the Chuckanut shoreline, the stones of time.

But now he had to find a place to study, eat, and sleep. He drove slowly, feeling tired down to his bones. He passed the hangar into which Poker had disappeared. The door remained open, the inside lit up with lamps along a workbench. Poker stood at the center, dressed in bib overalls, tinkering. As Luis passed, Poker raised his hand and motioned for Luis to stop.

Why now would this man want to talk? Why, after an hour of silence, would he want to speak with him? Luis circled his truck around so that his window was by the hangar door. Whatever the old man had to say, Luis would be polite and listen, then be off. He waited as Poker shuffled up to the truck, still carrying the wrench he had been using at the workbench. "You're not a bad worker, Luis. Don't worry about your job. I'm just doing community service. Today was your lucky day."

"Thanks, man," Luis answered to be polite, somewhat confused by the backhanded compliment. Why even bother to stop him? Good manners prevailed, and Luis again reached out and offered his hand. "If I'll be seeing you around, I should know your name."

Poker ignored the hand and shrugged. "Call me what you want. Folks around here call me Frank."

Luis stuck his head out the truck's window and yelled out, "I already made up your nickname, Poker. Will that do?"

Frank turned away, shaking his head and this time waving. "Suit yourself."

Luis guessed that he had just made friends with a troubled man. Better a friend than an enemy. He realized that he had acceptance into a world where few were given the honor.

# CHAPTER 7: *There Is No Money in This*

Joseph took down an old notebook, one his father had passed along to him from his grandfather. Two names appeared on the inside; Abraham had been crossed out and Eduardo written next to it. Joseph learned from his father that they were one and the same. The book codified oral traditions for the future. This tattered notebook held studies of mushrooms from Russia and Costa Rica, with spore prints, scribbled drawings of plants, and the discoveries of how to live with the gifts. One entry described the forest as his grandfather ran:

*When you run through the forest, they keep up. The mycelia know you are there. I can hide from the police, but the mycelia show themselves. I ate what I needed to survive.*

Joseph waited. He knew from experience that moving when his heart raced faster than his mind would lead to errors. His grandfather's instructions, etched in his brain, warned of fragility. To rise from the latticework of fine roots, the fruiting body of the mushroom needed energy. His experiments in the woods were harder to replicate indoors. Still shaking from his encounters in town, Joseph chided himself not for his self-righteous display of justice with the two insolent teens but for losing his temper.

Joseph worried not about the boys, nor his exposure to folks in town. His worry came from the fungal mind-set. One of his grandfather's cardinal rules was that in order to understand life, one had to treat everything with the same sensitivity as that of the mycelia. The network of roots absorbed nutrients from its surrounding environment, but they also absorbed the surrounding energy. The cells of the mycelia adapted to the processes of decomposition, knitting together, absorption, and creation. Joseph believed his arrogance, his impatience, influenced all that he touched.

Carefully he removed the sterile bowl covering the white paper. He studied the spore prints with a magnifying lens. Always at this juncture, the beauty of patterns caused him pause. He waited. He waited for the art, the patterns that mimicked the inner gills of the fungi, shapes and forms of nature replicated, fossils from long ago repeated even in the stones.

So much of his personal history followed him. Secrets, the silence between the trees and the mushrooms, and the shared space, all created a relationship based on necessity. Even Joseph's home belonged to the valley. He lived here by the grace of wiser people. His stone path acted as a reminder of the worlds that brought him here.

Joseph's calf muscles twitched. He curled his toes upward to halt the urge to run. His grandfather's athleticism skipped his own father but haunted him. He forced himself to stand still, to concentrate on the importance of propagation. Even with the precise temperature, the exact moisture level, growth of the spores couldn't guarantee success. The internal trigger to bear fruit could fail. His grandfather's notebook warned of the dangers of misidentifying the mushroom fruit:

*I lay still for hours, the world coming in upon me. I could hear my heartbeat but couldn't move. Do not eat the caps found near landslides or near sugared soil.*

With care, Joseph transferred the network of fuzzy growth onto sterilized petri dishes dusted with grain. He had high hopes for this strand. Not the hallucinogenic high, but the high of healing. Joseph ignored edible mushrooms and psychedelics. He sought fungi that solved human problems. Even as his grandfather ran to save his life he wrote, "Step lightly on this earth. Move with healing grace." Since the death of Hannah's sister, Joseph had concentrated on curing cancer.

Joseph covered the petri dishes, sterilized his equipment, locked the door, and headed back to the house. Tired and still unsettled, he looked forward to the quiet of his kitchen, the seclusion of his home.

On the kitchen table he found a basket of fresh lettuce, onions, and Sharon's homemade corn bread. Joseph smiled at this kindness. Ralph and Sharon must have stopped in after their trip to the Food Co-Op. He lived tucked away in the hills of Skagit Valley where favors never went unnoticed and were always returned.

As he sliced and diced onions, his eyes teared. He took a chopstick out of the drawer and placed it between his teeth, and within seconds his eyes stopped weeping. The sizzling of spices muffled the music of the stone path. The water droplets created the background beat with the frying pan juices popping as a counterpoint. He half expected to see Luis appear, dancing his way through the trees. Just in case the boy landed back here, Joseph threw more vegetables into the pan and opened another vacuum pack of smoked salmon.

Twenty minutes later, smells of fried potato cakes filtered through Joseph's cabin. As he set the table, the droplet rhythm changed when the stone path accepted the steps of a visitor. Three knocks on the door and then the call: "Joseph, it's me, Luis. Can I come in?"

Joseph smiled for the second time. "Come on in. I hoped you'd be back here for the night."

The door swung open, and the smile slipped off Joseph's face. His lips tightened as Luis stumbled inside. Joseph noted the split lip, the buffed right eye, and the torn t-shirt. Luis favored his left side, wincing as he walked to the sink to wash his hands and then over to the kitchen table. Joseph ignored the pulsing in his temples. He kept his eyes on Luis, looking for signs, searching for the *why* behind the attack. "I expect you're hungry after a long day of work. The word is that you did a good job at the Concrete Airport with the flower beds."

Luis bent his head down. He folded his hands together as if in prayer. Joseph set the food on the table, took his place, and bowed his head. His own custom of pausing before eating was to savor the abundance. He had no allegiance to religion, only to be thankful for the bounty.

Joseph waited until Luis raised his head to pass the potato cakes and say, "Do you want to tell me what happened? Go ahead and eat—you must be hungry. We can talk afterward, if you want."

"I don't have anything to say." Luis scowled. "You can see I got beat up. Yes, I'm hungry if that is what you want to hear. I'm surprised you didn't know about the beating already, if you heard about my work at the airport."

"Ah." Joseph nodded. "If you want to be angry, you better eat. Anger wastes energy, and you'll need yours. While you decide, let me tell you about potato latkes."

Luis's face reddened. He ate as he listened.

"One day when I was really young, my father came home from working at the railroad yard. He welded the rails whenever maintenance required a quick turnaround due to the silk trains passing through. There must have been a fight between the workers, the ones brought in from Costa Rica and the regular employees. My father sat in the corner of our one-room apartment for what I thought was an eternity. Finally, he got up and started chopping onions, grating potatoes, adding eggs and bread crumbs. He formed patties, and the kitchen filled with the aroma of herbs and fried potatoes. All he said to me was, 'Potato latkes come from the old country. Not from here, not from Costa Rica. Don't waste energy on what you can't change.'"

Luis waited for the punch line. None came. "So did the potato latkes fix the problem at the railroad station?"

Joseph dished up his food and shook his head. "No, of course not. They just reminded my father that he was better off than his father. Potatoes triggered an old memory of persecution and salvation. More important, they tasted good."

Luis smiled despite his anger. "Okay, I'll eat one more, and then I'll tell you what happened. Not that it matters. I can fight my own battles."

Joseph let that thought linger. Who was he to discuss battles? His own history had been to avoid fighting at all costs. Each day he rose knowing that his life had been gifted. Still he felt the shadows.

Luis finished off the last of the salmon and latkes. Before Joseph could jump up to clear the table, Luis scooped the plates together and headed to the sink. "Thanks for the meal and the story."

Joseph followed. "I've got lots of stories. Stories are from the past. I'd rather hear your version of the day. You didn't think by washing the dishes, you could avoid the telling?"

Luis shrugged. "Washing dishes is when my mom and I talked. No matter how crazy our life was, she'd find the energy to talk. I wasn't avoiding. I was just getting ready for your interrogation."

At the word *interrogation*, Joseph paused. Here was another trigger, a shadow word that lurked across borders. "What makes you think that telling me about your fight will cause me to cross-examine you?"

Luis shrugged. "Some of the workers got into trouble fighting in the blueberry fields. Everyone hid the truth to protect themselves. The management even tried to stop personal fights. You didn't want to be in the rows that witnessed the fight. No matter who was right, you'd lose wages."

Joseph thought back to the journeys of his father and grandfather. "It takes a toll to stand up for one's rights. Sometimes it is better to walk away."

Luis stopped scrubbing the frying pan and faced Joseph. "In my world, that would seem cowardly. Besides, I was just in the wrong place. I don't even know who attacked me."

Questions flooded Joseph's mind. He held on to the dish towel, waiting for Luis to hand over the frying pan. "Well, if washing dishes is the best place to tell stories, continue on, or else I'll bombard you with questions. But don't forget to wash and keep the flow going."

"After I finished up at the Concrete Airport, I went to the rocks along the shoreline on Clayton Beach to practice dancing. Usually no one is around after the sun goes down."

Joseph interrupted, "You practice in the dark?"

Luis smiled. "I wanted to be alone with just the waves, so I climbed along the rocks to perform lifts and jumps. Some guys must have been watching me. When I landed on the beach, one came from behind and held me down. The other one searched me for money. Who knows what they really wanted."

Joseph waited for more. He dried the last of the plates and finally spoke. "These aren't questions, just my rambling thoughts. Sounds like the attack was opportunistic or maybe done to scare you away. Are you sure you didn't recognize them?"

Luis shook his head. "No, when I tried to get up, I had my back turned, and they ran off when a man yelled at them."

Joseph kept silent. He sensed that Luis had left something out. Now there were three people besides Luis on an isolated beach, mid-week, late in the day. He filed the information away, knowing that circumstances explain themselves over time. "I'm glad you made it back here in one piece. It's a long way from the Concrete Airport to Chuckanut Drive."

"I didn't have anywhere else to go. You don't mind, do you?"

Joseph didn't, and that surprised him. "No, I don't mind. I can't say I'm used to having someone around. I've been alone longer than you are old. With you working at the airport, it would make sense to sleep here. Frank stopped by to tell me you were an okay worker. That's a compliment, in case you didn't recognize it."

Luis scratched his head and touched his swollen eye. Mimicking

Joseph, Luis continued, "I'm not asking questions. These are just my rambling thoughts. Is Frank an ex-con or spy for you? Even though he helped me shovel, he acted as if I was in his territory."

Nodding, Joseph agreed, "You were. Frank's got a past like we all do. He lives at his hangar. It's against the rules, but the owners thought it best for him and the community. If you're thinking that Frank had something to do with your fight, you're wrong."

Luis picked up his backpack and headed to the back of the cabin. "Good, I liked him. If it's okay with you, I'm going to hit the sack. I still have to study for my GED."

"Okay. Looks like you know where the bed is. There are extra towels in the bathroom. Help yourself." Joseph waved him off. Tired from the day and the evening, he gazed out the window. Darkness, the blanket of comfort, surrounded him. His running legs twitched, muscles overused. He felt too old to be needed. There was no money in being needed. Laughing to himself, he realized that he had no use for money. He was off the grid. His ancestors' legacy forged his life. His grandfather paved the way, and his father, even though he sought to better his life by following the money trail of the silk trains, opted to remain unencumbered.

Joseph picked up Sharon and Ralph's basket and set it on the table by the door, to return later in the week. If what Ralph said at the Food Co-Op was true, Sharon would need more mushroom extract. Old healing techniques befuddled the scientific community. Without money from grants or the big bucks from the pharmaceutical community, science stood still, but Joseph couldn't. It wasn't in his DNA. He didn't care about patents. His debt to the world had nothing to do with money. Sharon and Ralph kept his vision real.

He opened the door and listened to the darkness. The night sounds echoed off the stones. Water flowed, and the wind rustled in return. Tree talk. Joseph closed the door, knocking down the basket and a sheet of paper from inside. He read, "A man named Miguel asked for you. He has news about your niece, Carmen."

Joseph smelled trouble. Trouble with Hannah's parents' reaction to Luis and Hannah's newfound friendship, and the stench of the past he thought he'd left behind. He refused to worry. Family choices, family worries—family finds you even when you are hidden in plain sight.

# CHAPTER 8: *Rhododendron Café*

Frank drove slowly, squinting at the sun reflecting off the road, the mirage effect of puddles where there were none. His stomach growled in anticipation of Sunday brunch. Usually he'd hit the local diner along Highway 20, but today he journeyed through the sleepy roads of Skagit County over Bow Hill Road to where an old landmark, the Rhody, welcomed hungry customers for the last time. Frank came to pay his respects before the new owners of the restaurant made their transformation.

Instead of feeling the aches and pains of his seventy-five years, Frank acknowledged the magic of illusions. He felt younger. Time seemed to reverse itself, and his happiness grew as his past disappeared. He didn't worry anymore. He kept to himself. Did what he needed to do. He listened.

He parked his truck at the far end, past the small art gallery, past the lines painted for cars. This corner connected two counties, Whatcom and Skagit. Chuckanut Drive slithered around the edge of the bay, a road for tourists to gawk at the islands in the distance, the sparkling water, and local kayakers. Frank noted the cars outside of the restaurant. Those that came from Chuckanut shone with the polish of city folk. But Bow Hill Road turned into the Farm to Market Road, a road for farmers, trucks, and tractors. The cars lining this side held the dust of the fields. No matter, the Rhododendron had served everyone equally for the last thirty years.

Although a line of customers stood in the entranceway, Frank made his way to the back corner of the café. Meant as a serving counter, the owners let the old-timers eat without waiting—their sense of courtesy for patrons of another era. Frank nodded at Don and Carol. Usually Don stayed in the kitchen while Carol fussed over the patrons. Not today. Both hugged and mingled with the customers, the last stand before they became outsiders, freed from the work.

Frank didn't order. The waitress automatically brought him the special: a ricotta waffle with caramelized apples and cinnamon butter. He ate slowly, watching another patch of history be buried to sprout anew. Even before the Rhododendron Café transformed the small town of Bow into a destination spot for an organic restaurant, Frank had made his way to the old Kalistrom Palace for a plate of homemade fried chicken. The idea of eating fresh eggs, fresh chicken, and fresh vegetables from the garden wasn't new. Wholesome food, homemade, authentic—these buzz words came and went.

From his eating spot, Frank watched regulars as they walked in. Some left gifts. A few vendors paid their respects. Years back, Frank had been the designated vendor for organic lamb. Drinking his cup of coffee, his hand shook slightly at the memory. He missed the contact, missed the hard work. The loss of his sheep farm happened; it didn't matter why. Blaming his greedy sister didn't change or excuse his actions. He had new freedom now. He thought of his hangar at Concrete Airport. There he had his solitude and work.

Frank studied the chalkboard menu. Each month had a theme, usually too exotic for his taste, but he'd find the good stuff buried in the fancy descriptions. Tonight, they'd be serving oysters from Taylor Shellfish, as the red tide restrictions were absent for now. Just like his farm, the ocean had been prey to toxins. At least the fancy cheeses from the local creamery were still safe.

Seated by the windows, the Henderson family ate their brunch. Frank never had the pleasure of meeting the family, even though they had a cabin not too far from his friend Joseph. Some families made you feel welcome; some kept you at a distance. Frank figured they deserved their solitude just like everyone else. Recent problems in their berry fields and the death of their daughter years ago gave them rights. Frank took his fork and swirled his waffle in the caramelized apple. He wondered if the Rhody's owners had had a spat with Mr. Henderson or if blueberries wouldn't have been better than the sweet apples.

Mrs. Henderson's voice rose above the din of the restaurant: "Hannah, stop waving across the table to that family. It's rude. Let them eat in peace. You don't even know them."

"I do kn-know them. I m-met her at the hospital."

Frank didn't have to stretch his brain cells to see a tug-of-war between the mother and daughter. Mr. Henderson squeezed his daughter's hand and then gave his wife a look. A look that warned but, as Frank witnessed, held no power, as Mrs. Henderson continued, "I don't care how you know them. You look like a puppy dog, drooling for attention. We met lots of strangers in the hospital. They don't count as friends."

With that statement Frank felt a chill run up his spine. He learned the hard way that you must grease your body and soul so that when stinging words fly at you, they simply slip away. The alternative would chip apart your heart. He smiled as the woman across the way waved back at Hannah. After she paid her check, she walked toward the Henderson table. "Hannah, so nice to see you again, and Mr. Henderson, this must be your lovely wife. I'm Shelly. Your daughter was so kind to offer her ear. You are lucky to have her."

Frank studied Mrs. Henderson's face, flesh gone cold. "Shelly, you are the kind one. Hannah seeks out the wounded."

Even with Mrs. Henderson's sweetened smile, the icy reply left darts dangling in the air. Shelly recovered quickly, and turning toward Hannah, she winked. "Don't forget to stop by the dance studio."

Frank drank the last of his coffee and picked up his bill. Before he could make his exit, he saw Rosie, the woman who had turned his life around. He hesitated, but it didn't matter—Rosie had spotted him and waved at him to come over. He made his way to her table. Neither spoke as Rosie peered into his eyes and smiled.

"Frank, good to see you. I wondered if you'd remember me. Dr. Knobs told me you had made a complete recovery and that you had worked out an arrangement with the Concrete Airport."

Frank knew how conversations were supposed to go. One spoke, the other answered. He remembered Rosie, but he couldn't figure out why she would keep him in her memory. He wasn't her patient. "The years have been kinder than I could expect. What brings you back from Puerto Rico?"

Pointing at her table guest, Rosie flashed one of her caring looks. "My friend, Miguel, is here with me from Puerto Rico. Each of us is on a different mission. He is hunting down the renowned sculptor Joseph, and I'm after Joseph the mushroom man."

Frank turned his face away from Rosie. She had a reputation for reading one's thoughts. All he could think about was his friend Joseph. His need for privacy, his generosity to strangers. He wondered if Rosie and this Miguel were bringing trouble back into Joseph's life. He forced himself to remain calm. "Your missions must be important to travel so far. Good to see you."

He didn't wait for a reply and headed for the door. Rosie's friend Miguel stood up. For some reason, Frank panicked, but Miguel passed him and went to talk to Mr. Henderson. Part of their conversation floated by as he made his way out.

"Hi, my name is Miguel. Didn't I see you painting among the sculpted rocks at the beach the other day?"

Mr. Henderson shook his head. "I think you must be mistaken."

## CHAPTER 9: *Windows Reflection*

The few hours between the ringing of the school bell and the bus's departure to take her home belonged to Hannah. She'd broken her mother's annoying habit of chauffeuring her to and from school when Hannah discovered that the Skagit Transit bus passed her house before dark. Usually she'd go to the library to study, but since Luis no longer attended classes and worked upriver, she roamed.

Even though the air temperature hovered near seventy degrees, Hannah pulled an old red hooded sweatshirt over her school clothes. The hood concealed her wild blond hair and let her feel, for just a moment, anonymous. Today she walked along the streets past the kitchenware shop, which was her mother's favorite store, past the Food Co-Op where her father had his blueberry outlet, and finally past the county jail. She stared at the bars on the windows. Her eyes squinted, she tried to see beyond the lines. Since she had met Luis, she noticed prisons. Luis never complained, not even after he told her of the beating at the beach. She envied him his ability to slip out from behind the bars placed along his way. Somehow, he'd either physically disappear or he'd go to a place in his head to escape. If she closed her eyes, his thoughts entered her mind. She blinked, and the image of his half-naked dance along the beach—fluid motions that followed the waves—dissolved.

Hannah dug her hands into the sweatshirt pouch, fists clenched. Her feet pounded the pavement. *Who would be so vicious to attack Luis for dancing? Why was Luis so silent on the issue?* She buried her nose deeper within the hood so that only her eyes showed. A faint chemical smell of ammonia came from the sweatshirt. The smell reminded her of paint and lighter fluid. Her stomach churned as she remembered her father's face at the Rhododendron, when one of the customers seemed to have recognized her father from his wanderings on the beach. He had stared at the stranger with narrowed eyes, and his skin turned gray like the ashes from a spent fire. Polite and firm, her father shook his head. *You must be mistaken. Someone else must look like me. I don't paint.*

Rattled, her family had left immediately after that encounter. Hannah took another whiff of the sweatshirt, realizing it had come from her father's giveaway pile. No holes, no stains, just this weird smell of ammonia. She found herself walking in circles, lost in thought. On the second loop, she noticed the sounds of feet behind her. She quickened her steps, and the pattering quickened. She peered in the window across the way to get a glimpse of her followers. Recognition flashed through her—the pickpocket duo from the other day. She slowed her pace to a deliberate halt. The two crashed into her just as she turned around.

Her hood fell backward, and her blond curls sprung out. The two boys jumped back a step, not prepared for a confrontation. Hannah waited for them to pass. All three stood still. For once Hannah felt silence worked in her favor. The taller of the two boys towered above her, but Hannah worried more about the shorter guy. He smelled of marijuana, and his eyes gleamed with a stoned glaze. She'd seen the look of passive disinterest before. She didn't trust herself to remain silent for long. The boys passed, and as she watched them go, she made a decision.

Instead of continuing her stroll, Hannah waited a few minutes and then reversed her course. She followed the boys to an alley, watched as they lit a joint. When both were distracted with smoking, she sat down next to them. No one spoke. Hannah pulled the hood over her hair; she smelled the paint, the lighter fluid, the lie her father had told. When the shorter guy smiled and handed her a joint, she took it in her hand. Studying the slow-burning paper, she let the smoke filter up to her nose. One puff and she handed the joint to the taller guy. After two more rounds, Hannah got up to leave.

She felt a tug on her sleeve, someone grabbing. The short guy smiled. "Not so fast, Blondie. You have to give us something in return."

The haze lifted, and Hannah's heartbeat doubled. She glared back. "You need advice? S-stop stealing w-wallets."

The taller boy punched his friend in the arm. "Be careful, she could be a stool pigeon. Let her go."

"Hey, Blondie, are you a snitch or just a bitch?"

"Just a b-bitch who knows better than to snitch on two losers."

Inclined to run, Hannah forced her feet to stillness. With deliberate emphasis, she removed her red sweatshirt and tied the sleeves around her waist. She exposed her white arms, the shape of her torso. Hypnotically she stared at her confronters with a dare and a command to stay put.

As she walked back to the main road, Hannah heard their rants. First the small guy: "She's mine—I'll get her and give her more than she wants."

And then the giant said, "We don't need any more trouble, not after the other day."

. . . . .

Her feet felt lighter, almost as light as her head. Although she'd been down this road many times, the window displays caught her eyes. An overstuffed sofa in the antique store called out to her. She walked inside and sat down. She stared at the embroidered fabric and the small grandmother clock that sat next to an ordinary grandfather clock. She wondered if they were mates from another time.

She listened to the tick and tock and then the chime of the hour. The voice of the owner startled Hannah out of her reverie. "Well, Miss Hannah Henderson, to what do I owe this honorary visit? I haven't seen you or your mother in ages."

She stood up slowly, walked over to the parental clocks, and softly touched the varnished wood, ignoring the Do Not Touch sign. "I was just looking for a Mother's Day gift and liked the miniature clock."

The owner stared and put her hand under her chin, acting as if Hannah had made a perplexing statement. "Miss Hannah, I sure hope you've already given your mother a gift. Mother's Day was last month. I don't think you could afford it on your allowance, but we could put it on layaway for next year."

Hannah's thoughts shifted back to the alley. For some reason, her comfort level diminished here at the antique store. She found the owner a more formidable obstacle than the potheads. "Th-that's okay. I'll keep it in mind for her birthday." The clocks synchronized their chime to mark the half hour. Suddenly aware of the real time, Hannah waved and ran out the door.

Just as she approached the bus stop, the Skagit Transit bus pulled away. It would be another half hour before a bus going toward her home would pass. She meandered along, gazing at the displays. Window-shopping meant you looked inside, perusing merchandise from afar. Hannah looked at her reflection as she passed. Ever since Jenna's death, she avoided mirrors and windows, always seeing her sister attached by a string. Her own image grew larger as her sister stayed the same size, small and vulnerable. Today only her silhouette fleeted along.

She quickened her pace to a run, watching from the corner of her eye, as her reflection hurried along. As the building ended, her figure dissolved into the wall, and once again Hannah walked alone.

In the middle of the block she noticed a hand-painted sign of dance figures arranged to spell out *Dance for Delight*. Without realizing it, Hannah had stumbled upon Shelly's studio. Half expecting to see Shelly walk out the door, she approached the entrance and peered inside. The room shook with life. She counted twelve leotard forms bending and stomping in a choreographed chaos. With her nose pressed against the glass, Hannah felt the rhythms. Pings, pows, pats were patterned with feet and arms moving as if their hearts beat on the outside. Wide-legged, knees bent, jumps high and low, back and forth, imitating jungle animals as they roamed. Hannah felt the beastly calls. Wild echoes of battles old and new, primal taps on the floor, and all the while the forms danced with smiles smeared across their faces. Hannah walked away as their feet rested.

Almost at the end of the block, Hannah turned when she heard Shelly's voice call out, "Don't leave, Hannah. The class just finished. Come inside and tour the studio."

Hannah felt trapped. Still in her anonymous mode, she hadn't realized that anyone could see her from inside the window. She untied the red sweatshirt and pulled it over her head, covering her arms, torso, and hair. She faced Shelly and forced her lips into a smile. "You startled me. I didn't see you in the room."

Shelly took Hannah's hand in hers and pulled her along. "Oh, I often stand behind the students to give them more freedom of interpretation. I got excited seeing you in the window. I apologize for running out after you. Is something wrong? You look distracted."

Hannah felt Shelly squeeze her hand, felt the warmth of her concern. "I missed my bus to go home, and if I'm not careful of the time, I'll miss the last of the line. My mom gets angry if I come home after dark. But I loved watching the class."

Shelly eyes brightened. "How about I give you a ride home? I just have to run back and close the studio. I don't have to be at the hospital until dinnertime. Robin is with her dad."

Shelly's enthusiasm lifted Hannah's mood. "I don't want to bother you. I'm sure you have better things to do."

Shelly shook her head. "No, in fact I wanted to find you. The cancer world is so consuming. I thought, because you are closer in age to Robin, you might have some ideas on how to balance our lives. We're entering a research trial, working with a researcher from Puerto Rico, the University of Washington, and a local man who lives upriver and grows mushrooms. I think his name is Joseph. Robin will have the normal protocol for her blood cancer, but she wants to do this study as well. What do you think?"

Hannah felt a jolt. She knew that the only Joseph upriver was her neighbor, but she didn't know anything about his research. She chided herself for not being more observant when she had followed Joseph around his woods, gardens, and even into his shop, sneaking out of her house to visit. "Joseph lives up by my parents' cabin. I never knew he grew mushrooms for research. He's a mechanic and stone carver."

Shelly looked past Hannah at the two teenagers loitering by the light post. Shelly pulled Hannah closer to the dance studio while she locked the door. "Do you know those two guys over there? They're eavesdropping on our conversation."

Hannah stiffened, knowing even before she turned her head who was watching. "I had a run-in with them earlier. They like to steal and smoke weed."

Shelly maneuvered Hannah into her car and clicked the locks down. Hannah looked back to see the short guy make a heart-shaped sign and then stick his middle finger up. The taller guy looked away. Shelly pulled onto the road and said, "Good thing I spotted you. Seems like you walked here with trouble nipping at your heels. Tell me where you live."

Hannah noted the change in Shelly's tone of voice. She waited for a reprimand, probing questions. None came. "I thought everyone knew where I lived. We have the farm off Farm to Market Road, past the daffodil fields. Do you know the house on the hill that overlooks all those acres of blueberries?"

Shelly nodded and headed west out of Mount Vernon.

Hannah fidgeted with the window. Scraping noises filled the silence.

Shelly rolled down her window. "Sorry, Hannah, your side is broken. It only goes halfway down. I meant to get it fixed, but with Robin's medical needs, I'm putting our money where it counts more."

Hannah didn't detect any cynicism or regret. Her mother, who had enough money for anything she wanted, always found fault. "That's okay. I just needed a breeze. I like your car. My parents trade their cars in when something breaks."

Shelly laughed out loud. "I'm sure you are exaggerating. They are very generous with their money. Without their help, Robin wouldn't be able to afford the trial treatments at the cancer center. No amount of money makes the cancer journey easy. Cancer is an equalizer."

Hannah thought about her sister. Jenna had never complained, at least not to her. The memories from those years had shrunk away, just like Jenna's image in the window reflections. "I don't know how to ask you, but I'm curious about this experiment with mushrooms. Is there a risk to Robin's well-being?"

Shelly turned down the road and passed a field flooded by recent rains. Trumpeter swans lounged in puddles, a mass of white feathers feeding on grass. "There is nothing *well* about cancer. All the treatments kill. At least with the mushroom tinctures, there is a chance of removing the toxins left behind. The whole experiment was Robin's idea. My little biologist, even at twelve, looks to nature to help with science."

Hannah wondered what she could offer Robin. "My sister, Jenna, loved the swans. Before she had bone cancer, she used to chase the swans in our fields. Sometimes the swans ignored her. Jenna thought she was one of them. I had forgotten how we played together."

Neither talked for the rest of the drive. Finally, Hannah pointed to her house on the hill. "I'll push the button, so the gate opens. If you want to get back to the hospital, I can walk the rest of the way. I need the exercise."

Shelly glanced sideways at Hannah. "No, I'll drop you off at your door. After seeing those boys leering at you, I think it best to make sure you are home safe and sound."

Hannah silently agreed. She regretted getting stoned with those guys. She'd been selfish and jealous of their freedom and angry at their actions. Stupid, stupid, stupid—acting without thought. Of course there'd be consequences.

When they arrived at the head of the driveway, Hannah's mother stood on the front porch with her arms folded across her chest. Hannah thanked Shelly and quickly made an exit.

Shelly waved at Mrs. Henderson and called out to Hannah, "Do stop by the dance studio when you have time. I'll show you the African dance the students created. Also, I'd like you to meet Robin."

Her mother made no effort to wave back even as Hannah waved and mounted the steps to the porch. "That's the same lady at the restaurant. Why didn't you ride the bus home?"

Hannah took a deep breath. "I-I lost track of t-time. Shelly—"

"No excuses. Get cleaned up, you smell funny. Your father won't be here for dinner because of an emergency in the blueberry fields. Immigration issues and fights. For some reason, your father wants to work out new programs. I don't understand him. I don't know whose side he's on anymore."

# CHAPTER 10: *Trails*

Joseph drifted in and out of sleep, listening to what he assumed were coyotes howling in the wind and then the early-morning buzz of bees dancing their way home to their hives. Thoughts slipped in between the howls and buzzes. He called these waking dreams, powerful enough to shorten the night. One dream lingered, the image of a distant cousin knocking on his father's door. His skin prune lined, fingers knotted with burrs of hard labor. Waves of heat obscured the cousin's face, but not his words: "Some of us ran, some of us died, some of us stole our way through life. Freedom has a price."

By the time Joseph had made his first cup of coffee, sunrays had penetrated through the leaves. Ralph's note still lay on the table. The name Carmen meant little to him. He knew no one with that name, but not knowing didn't mean a person ceased to exist. The word *niece* meant more. Joseph had relatives, but each family had taken a different path. His father told stories of the pogroms in Russia, how each family had to make choices. He always ended the stories with a phrase that had puzzled Joseph: *You can stumble on your own feet. You must step outside of yourself to reveal who you are.* And then his father would smile and tell him not to step too far away, or he might forget what he already knew.

Not wanting to wake Luis, if he hadn't already left for the day, Joseph walked softly through the kitchen. The two hadn't spoken for a couple of days, each coming and going at different times. Luis, no matter how quiet and respectful he tried to act, left evidence of his days and nights. Joseph knew Luis had been working at the airport, not by his friend Frank's tales but by the mud and gravel tracked in on Luis's shoes. Joseph had hoped to see him this morning, but a cereal bowl lay upside down draining on the sink counter, and the last banana had disappeared. At least Luis had eaten.

Grabbing a handful of nuts and blueberries, Joseph headed out to his shop. Barefooted, his toes touched the worn stones of the pathway. He noticed another uneven area where a spot lay exposed. During the night the coyote howls had obscured his musical alarm system. The waterfall and rhythms of rainwater had been disturbed by a visitor with a calling card. Instead of a replacement stone, an oddly shaped piece of wood lay nestled in the space. Joseph dug it out and felt the hardness of the tangled wood, angled in a spastic cross reminiscent of the Nazi swastika symbol of hatred. His palm felt scorched with old anger and fear. His first reaction was to hurl the cross into the woods, but then he bent down and gently placed the wood back onto the path. He took clay dirt and nestled the muck in the spaces, so it fit snuggly. He pondered the visitor who left this contribution. Echoes of his father's words made him squirm. Could this be his past talking about the pogroms against Jews? Or worse yet, the ghost of his cousin, reminding him that sins follow family lines?

The door to the shop lay open. Music hummed in the background and Luis, adorned with goggles and greasy overalls, peered inside an engine. Joseph admired the concentration on Luis's face and the rhythmic movement of his feet and hips, two separate entities encased in one body. Joseph studied his young pupil with pride. His apprenticeship resembled that of his own with his father. Luis, straight from the fields, had watched Joseph's every move. Now after only a few months he acted like a mechanic.

Joseph put on his shoes and walked over to the truck engine. "Good morning, Luis."

Luis jumped at the sound. "You startled me."

"Apologies. You're up early. I thought I had missed you. I didn't expect you to work on the weekend."

"If you'd rather I wasn't in the shop today, I could leave. I just thought if there was work, I should do it. All the days are the same to me since I left school."

Joseph waved his hand, dismissing the idea. "Oh no, of course not. I assumed you were off having fun. I'm not used to living with anyone, let alone keeping up with their schedule. I used to have your energy, but when I was your age, I had to keep quiet. My father taught me to be a shadow. His philosophy was that it took concentration to learn a skill. He'd quiz me at night to see what I had absorbed. Don't worry, get on with your project."

Luis turned off the radio. He bent over the engine again, but without the music, he seemed lost.

Joseph walked across the room, to the clean section of the shop. He felt Luis's steady gaze. "I didn't mean for you to turn off the radio. The noise doesn't matter to me. You work how and when you want. There are no punch clocks here. Don't worry about time. That isn't my measure. Besides, I'm not working on anything with a deadline. I'm going to sculpt."

Luis raised his arms up in the air and then down in frustration. He stifled a laugh to cover his discomfort. Joseph waited for the punch line. Luis's face turned more serious. "I'm confused. I turned off my noise so you can concentrate. I'm trying to be useful. What do you mean by measure—getting paid, following rules? My whole existence is based on following rules, punching in on a time clock. I make myself fit in. I try to be a good citizen."

The edge in Luis's voice sent a shudder through Joseph. He watched Luis's face as the anger reverberated through the muscles of his cheeks. "Something bothering you this morning?" Joseph asked. "If so, tell me plainly. No use my guessing what ails you."

Joseph half expected Luis to turn away. His reprimand had the opposite effect. Luis's shoulders relaxed, his lips loosened, even though he ignored the question. Instead Luis came over to the workbench filled with soapstone and pulled up a chair next to the covered sculpture. "What are you working on?"

"I'm not sure. Some say the stones reveal themselves as you carve. But I believe you carve what is inside of yourself and the stones respond. Soapstone has a softness to it, which forces me to work without aggression or anger. This piece is different as I've had to put more energy into it. Luckily, I've got a hardier stone, alabaster. My marks remain as permanent extensions. Three years and still I'm in the midst of creation."

Luis touched the canvas covering the finished sculpture. "Can I take a look?"

Joseph shook his head. "I'm not ready. This is where time does count. Can't risk the piece being misunderstood. I think we are all sculptors in our own way, just that our mediums are different. You sculpt with your body when you dance. I've seen you take music into your soul and leap through the air with a story. Not everyone can receive what you are saying. This piece is still drifting, but when the time is right, the sculpture won't need an explanation."

At this Luis stood up and replaced the chair against the wall. Joseph wondered if he'd hit a nerve. Luis walked around the shop as if he was searching for clues. Finally, he stopped by another closed-off area where Joseph had a small loom threaded with silk strains.

"I don't understand," Luis said. "Not anything. Here you are up in the hills, tucked away from the outside world, and yet inside these doors you take apart the old, fix, and create new. You don't seem to need anyone. I'm not like you. I need my family, my roots. Working is all that I have."

Joseph felt the intensity of Luis's loss. He walked over to the loom and rubbed his fingers along the threads. "Did you know that silk is one of the strongest natural fibers? A tiny worm feeds on mulberry leaves until it spins a cocoon of fine silk filaments. My father came to the United States from Costa Rica to work on the silk trains. Funny isn't it, how such a small worm worked so hard to keep women dressed? Silk was in such demand all over the world. Who knew that their cocoons would create so much wealth? When the Panama Canal opened, my father lost his job on the silk trains. The work on the railroad dried up because ship travel was cheaper and faster. We had to start over. Poverty repeats itself if you let it." Joseph paused, lost in his memories.

Luis waited a moment for him to continue, then said, "I never heard you talk about your family."

"My mother died when I was a child. My father and I left Costa Rica for a better life. He raised me, and he passed away when I was about your age. When he died, I found out I didn't exist, an immigrant without a true home. My father's insistence on my silence not only helped me learn a trade but kept us safe. We didn't have paperwork. I was lucky not to be deported. My father's railroad buddies didn't tell the authorities. They buried my father on this land."

Joseph took hold of a chisel and jabbed the tip into his workbench. "I wish I could, Luis, but I can't bring your family back to the States. I just try to learn more, give more, adapt to nature. Think about the silkworm. We capitalized on the fiber's strength and lightness. Some of what we did benefited the world, and some exploited the worm, the workers, and the industries."

Luis pulled on the bib of his overalls, straightening an imaginary line. "Where is the fairness in all of that? My friends from the field shy away from me as if I'm trouble. But the trouble finds them with or without me. Exploitation goes two ways. My parents were deported, and I'm left here to wander like a Jew in the desert."

Joseph bristled at Luis's words. His good eye stared Luis down. "Don't you dare feel sorry for yourself. The comparison falls far from the mark. History repeats itself, but in your case, no one is being enslaved, killed, or forced to do unspeakable things." Fumes seemed to sprout out of Joseph's head. He bent down close to Luis's face and continued spewing his fiery diatribe: "We aren't the same people. You talk as if your parents were persecuted for a belief, that they were systematically executed. None of that is true. The laws in the United States might not be fair, but they are nothing like that of the old and new Russia with their pogroms or that of Nazi Germany and the Holocaust. At least now the government recognizes its prejudices. I isolate myself. I look for alternatives. I choose to live alone, but I can't escape the haunting past."

Joseph hadn't meant to rant, but Luis's alluding to the Jews had sparked painful memories. That and the note from Ralph left him unsettled. Joseph realized his mistake: he had let his irritation show, and that disobeyed his grandfather's cardinal rule. His emotions said more than his words.

In a whisper, Luis answered, "I didn't know you were so sensitive. I didn't mean to make you mad."

Keeping his face a blank mask, Luis studied the loom and the silk threads, each held taut in a complex weave. Blueprints of a wing lay on a table beside the loom. Another set of plans showed a hybrid plane. Distracted, Luis looked around the room again. "I've been here so many times to work on engines and never saw these plans. What are you working on?"

"Curiosity makes you responsible. If you're not careful, you'll be asked to solve a problem you didn't know existed." He glanced at Luis. "I'm working on layers, the crossing of directions to create strength and durability with a soft, light fiber. Even I exploit the silkworm. Every invention solves a dilemma while creating another."

Now that he had regained control, Joseph knew he had to guide Luis to a place where sense ruled, not anger. "What do you intend to do about your problem with the field-workers, your friends? You have made it my problem by being upset. As your friend, I'm responsible, just like you are responsible for helping me now that you have seen my projects." He waited for Luis to explain.

"I shouldn't have said anything about the pickers. This isn't your problem. You aren't involved."

"But I am involved. You are my friend, someone who is finding his way without his family, and you are upset. You were beat up last week, you are seeing the daughter of your previous boss, and you have witnessed some injustice. Can you keep all your various lives separate?"

"Do I have a choice, Joseph? The pickers are only looking out for themselves. They don't know any other way. Hannah told me things that confuse me. She worries about her father, she worries about me, and now she worries about you."

The last words jolted Joseph. "What has Hannah told you?"

Luis blushed. "Hannah drives now. Her parents bought her a car, and she has been driving up here to visit and dance. I don't want to talk about that, just what she said. A few nights ago, she told me about her dinner with her family at the Rhody restaurant. Hannah overheard Frank talking with a woman named Rosie. She came all the way from Puerto Rico to find you and talk with you about mushrooms. That part didn't seem odd, but she was with a man named Miguel. He was looking for you too. Something about you being famous for your sculptures. The coincidence bothered me. But it got worse. Miguel came over to Hannah's table and talked with Mr. Henderson. He said he had seen Mr. Henderson at Clayton Beach the other night, painting among the sculpted rocks. That was the same night I got beaten up."

Joseph watched as all color left Luis's face. Worried, Joseph made a mental note to talk with Frank. He pondered the relationship between Miguel and Rosie. He had been working with Rosie for a few years. Her knowledge of biology and her determination to find a cure for cancer inspired him to work on his mushroom experiments.

As far as Joseph knew, Miguel wasn't a stone sculptor and wasn't involved with mushrooms. Luis seemed more disturbed than on the night of the beating. "What upset you most about the conversation with Hannah?" Joseph asked.

"I don't know. To be honest it all made me feel like I wasn't aware. Maybe that other people knew your business better than I did. I've been coming here for months and didn't know that your work was noticed. You never talk about your projects. And the thing with Mr. Henderson. He must have seen me dancing. He witnessed the beating."

"Did you want him to protect you, or did you wonder why he didn't?"

Before Luis could answer, Joseph noticed a different rhythm in the background. He cocked his head toward the house. He heard the faint sound of water on stones. A warm breeze passed through the shop, rustling the cloth covering his sculpture.

# CHAPTER 11: *Black and White and Read All Over*

The wind picked up and with it came warm, moist air. Clouds darkened the sky, closing in on the day. Luis felt a superstitious foreboding, as if nature had turned against him. To enter the Concrete Airport, he drove under the high school through an oddity in construction that created a bridge of buildings and a tunnel below. He could practically hear his mother's warning to turn his shirt *de adentro hacia afuera*, but Luis never understood why she wanted him to turn his shirt inside out. Warding off bad spirits, balancing forces of good and evil, came from his culture, but Luis believed it came from misunderstanding and fear. Just in case, he turned his cap backward. Since his talk with Joseph, Luis felt less sure of himself. As if the world were rotating in reverse.

He left his truck at the entrance of the airport. The tarmac almost abutted the parking lot, and the five hangars were just fifty feet from the planes' landing. The garden beds filtered in between the hangars, and he approached them as old friends. Something about the repetitive motion of pulling out weeds satisfied his inner need. Today, the weeds caused him pause. They looked vital, not ornamental but edible. He bent down to get a closer look. Hairy fluffs of green protruding from the ground topped an orange root—carrots. Tall stalks with yellow lacey flowers rose as pillars, connected so tightly to the earth that the root could only be a parsnip.

Luis surveyed all the beds. He found purple cabbage leaves unfurling by the hosta plants, small lettuce leaves next to the poppy flowers, and sweet peas, wrapped around poles, hiding green beans.

Along with these vegetables, a handful of strawberry plants bordered the beds closest to the museum hangar. Luis's annoyance dissipated as he popped a ripe strawberry into his mouth. The sweet juice reddened his smiling lips.

For the last few weeks, Luis had concentrated on the fields surrounding the runway. With the upcoming fly-in scheduled, his boss had assigned him to field maintenance. He felt a tinge of guilt that he hadn't come daily to the gardens, but between studying and working with Joseph, the weeks flew by. He mowed twice weekly to keep the grass from obscuring the tarmac. His absence from attending the flower beds created an opportunity. He knew without knowing that his helper of sorts had revised the landscape to suit his own needs. Poker crossed the tarmac and stood just in front of where Luis weeded. A large carrot in Poker's right hand confirmed Luis's suspicions.

Luis nodded his greeting, not sure if Poker would talk on this visit or just stare. The crunch of carrot bites filled the silence. Luis wondered if he should change Frank's nickname from Poker to Bugs Bunny. Even as he thought it, the irony of his own sense of humor fell short. The joke smacked of hypocrisy.

Leaning over Luis, Poker pulled out a pair of garden scissors from his pocket and snipped a green bud off the top of the lily-like leaves. "I figured you'd get back to the flower beds eventually. I made the executive decision to make the space more useful. This here is garlic. You have to snip off the top bud, otherwise it won't send the energy to the bulb. Flowers may be showy, but the real show is in the fruit below."

Luis continued pulling the insidious weeds, the ones with thick succulent knobs that crept into the soil and now covered the dirt. He concentrated, ignoring Poker's crunching, ignoring Poker's advice.

"You're working real hard there, boy. Don't you have the time of day for me?"

Luis tugged at the roots of another weed and then looked up.

"Just call me Luis. I am not your boy."

Poker smiled and extended his hand. "Yes, and I'm Poker to you. Seems to me that you're attacking the weeds as if they were people. Are you mad at someone?"

Luis stood up from his crouched position, uncomfortable with looking up at Poker. Mad meant he was out of his mind, and in a way that is what he felt. Anger had a target, but madness consumed his body. Poker's garden was the only thing that had made him smile all day. He ignored Poker's question. "Tell me about these parsnips. The stalks are taller and harder than anything I've seen."

"They are old like me, leftover from years ago. Woody and probably taste horrible. Most likely they came in with the compost. No use pulling on those stalks, they're as stubborn as I am. That is, unless you're mad at me. Then by all means, attack the parsnips."

Luis stared at Poker. Poker irritated him, called him *boy*, but he had nothing against the man. He had nothing against anyone. So why was he so mad, pulling weeds with a vengeance? He still felt spied upon. Knowing of Joseph and Poker's friendship somehow tainted their exchange. He wondered if he had underestimated this old man. He tried to soften his mood. "No, thanks, I'll leave the parsnips alone. Did you plant anything else I should be aware of?"

Poker shrugged. "Oh, nothing illegal if that's what you're getting at. But if you want some of my bounty, stop by my hangar when you're done."

"Will do, if I have time."

Luis watched Poker slowly make his way along the tarmac. He realized that this was Poker's job, the unofficial guard of the airport. What he had interpreted as prying and spying had nothing to do with himself. For whatever reason Poker hovered, he watched over his territory with a loyalty that kept him visible and focused.

As Luis finished weeding the last of the beds, dark thunderclouds covered the skies. Only a couple of planes had landed while he worked, and each pilot mentioned the changing wind, a brewing storm. With a sudden clamor of thunder and an answering flash of lightning, the skies opened. No need to water the plants. The storm hovered just below the mountain. The downpour soaked the soil, bounced off the tarmac, and cleansed Luis.

Packing up the garden tools, Luis hurried to dry off. The sudden rain surprised him, and he worried about the berry fields. Usually rain at this point of the growing season fortified the berries. Only a sustained rain could do damage. None of this mattered to him anymore. His only charges now were the beds around the hangar. With time to spare before he met Hannah, Luis pulled his truck in front of Poker's open hangar door.

As promised, Poker greeted Luis with a plastic bag and a wave. "Come in. I offered a bounty, and here it is. I know you could use some feeding. Not sure if my friend Joseph can keep up with you."

Luis didn't know whether to take offense or accept the generosity. What was the difference between looking out for someone and prying? Joseph's words this morning had left an impression. Once Luis shared his concerns, they became Joseph's. Somehow it appeared that Luis had become Poker's concern as well. "You don't need to worry about me, Poker. Joseph shares what he can. I hope I help enough around his place to deserve his kindness. Unless Joseph has told you something different?"

"Worrying is an activity I'm used to. Might as well worry about you, as I've got nothing better to do. Has Joseph told you anything about me?"

Luis shrugged. "Only that you two are old friends. What should I know?"

Poker walked off to the back of the hangar and brought out a stack of newspapers. "Most people know my history. No need to listen to rumors. I'll just let you read about my older sister, Molly, and my actions. This is my history, but the newspapers tell the story fair enough. You can read in English, can't you?"

Luis felt the familiar insult hit him in his gut. He wondered if Poker wanted to provoke him. He answered the question in a flat voice: "I can read in two languages. I was top in my class until I dropped out. Now I'm working on my GED."

Poker didn't react. He just dropped the pile down and wandered off to the back of his hangar.

A front-page headline read, "Toxic Waste Dumping: McCain's Hidden Fortune," and in the accompanying picture, an older obese woman stood in front of a sheep farm. Luis skimmed through the papers, searching for Poker's face, and buried within the stack was a picture at the Concrete Airport in front of the museum hangar. The article said, "Concrete Fly-In pilots save the Skagit Valley from a fraudulent plot of trafficking in nuclear and medical waste. Molly McCain and her brother, Frank, have pulled the wool over the eyes of the community."

Luis's Adam's apple moved up to choke his throat. Sweat accumulated in the small dimple of his chin. He dared to look further. Finally, he found the newspaper that told him why Poker remained at the Concrete Airport:

*After Miss McCain's death, Frank McCain's sentence has been reduced. The courts found him guilty but said that he had acted out of duress from a lifetime of abuse. Frank McCain will serve his sentence as the guardian of the Concrete Airport and must find ways to enhance the community of Concrete for the rest of his life.*

Luis restacked the newspapers, putting the oldest at the bottom and leaving Frank's sentence on the top. For some reason, this mattered. He waited for Poker to return, and when he didn't, Luis wandered, taking in the bare walls, the simple cot neatly made with squared corners, a small kitchen set up by the sink with a toaster oven and camping cookstove. The only picture he found was of a woman in a wheelchair in front of the museum hangar. As he held the frame, Poker suddenly appeared.

"Don't go messing with that picture. As bad as I was back then, Miss JoAnne saved me. Please put the frame down. I don't care about much else in this world but living up to her belief in me."

Luis obediently replaced the picture frame on the counter. Curiosity caught ahold of him, but he stopped himself from asking anything more about the woman. "Those articles are the first I heard of any smuggling or your part in it. I must not hang in the right circles to hear the gossip."

Poker smiled. "I guess not. Especially if your circle just includes Joseph, me, and the girlfriend you hang out with. Local folk simmered for quite a while. Health Department meddled in, but Joseph took a lead with his experiments. Hooked up with a lady named Rosie, and they seemed to be working miracles."

Miracles. Luis stared out, lost in thought. Here it was again, the great works of Joseph, topped with everyone knowing he had a girlfriend. He must have stood that way for some time, because Poker was staring back at him, holding a bundle of vegetables.

"Sorry," Luis said, "I spaced out. I've got to leave now. Thanks for the food."

Poker handed him another stack of more recent newspapers. "Not so quick. I thought you might be worried about the blueberry fields."

Luis shook his head. "The blueberry fields aren't my concern. I don't work there anymore."

Poker shook his finger at Luis. "Worry doesn't let go that easily. It tends to linger. Take these papers, you might find them interesting. Just bring them back. I keep track." He didn't wait for an answer and left Luis standing alone.

Luis gathered the newspapers and headed to his truck. The rain belted down, hard pellets following him. Soaked again, Luis mopped his head with a rag. Curiosity got him, and he sat in his truck to read.

The front-page photo showed Mr. Henderson standing in the middle of his blueberries. He towered above the orchard with his arms extended, almost in an embrace of his land. To Luis, he looked pained, stern, defeated. A group of pickers surrounded him, and behind the pickers, Luis recognized the troublemakers. The caption below the photo read, “Henderson Farm struggles with crops as pickers bicker. Negotiations fail for unknown reasons.”

Another newspaper article featured a violent thrashing of a group of young migrant workers, who were hauled off to the county jail to sort out the assault. Luis sifted through the pages and found yet another article on a robbery at the migrant workers’ camps. He stared at the scenes. He felt the familiar distress of the camps bubbling inside his stomach. His mouth tasted metallic, as if the machetes used to keep back the weeds swung in front of his truck. Machetes, knives, fights, violence, bickering, all set off an alarm.

Luis tossed the newspapers onto the seat and pulled away from the airport. Now he would be late to meet Hannah. The downpour continued. His windshield wipers whooshed at top speed. The downbeat of the rain, the swish of the wipers, and the thumping of his heart rushed into the worry he thought he had escaped.

Luis abandoned his normal caution and sped down the highway. Out of habit he scanned the shoulders of the road for police cars. The rain made the highway slick, so despite his sense of urgency, he downshifted. Just a little too late. Luis’s truck swerved to the right; he corrected to the left and hit a pool of water. The truck stalled. He cursed in Spanish and banged his fist on the dashboard. The spirits taunted him. Luis should have turned his t-shirt inside out when he drove under the high school. Even the potholes caused him trouble. By the time the motor had dried out, the rain crawled down from the sky, long slow drops that plopped on his truck. He pulled up by the library an hour late. Hannah stood under the eaves, drenched and crying.

## CHAPTER 12: *Permeable*

Hannah knew better, but she couldn't help herself. She had made a grave mistake. It was like a toothache, the kind that doesn't hurt too much until she touched it. Just to make sure it was still there, she would probe the spot with her tongue, and then the pain would come. Crazy thoughts. Why would she do that, inflict pain?

Tears fell, but they couldn't wash away hazy images of herself smoking a joint with the two boys. Hannah intended to visit Shelly at her dance studio. But her feet hadn't followed that route. Regret from the day before didn't stop her. Shelly had used the word *seedy*, but Hannah knew that was too nice of a word for the guys who had shadowed her. Deep inside, she believed she could give then a scare, punish them for stealing her mother's purse.

Hannah had found the two creeps in the alley, smoking and bragging about their exploits at the migrant camps. Too high to notice her, she listened to the small guy talk about another raid on the camps. How stealing was easy there and no one cared. His filthy mouth described the women as pieces of meat, carne asada, marinated and tender for the taking. Invisible, she became the spy. Every word from this punk's mouth attacked all that she was.

But of course she wasn't invisible. The tall guy spotted her and nudged his buddy. They both came after her. This time there was no offer of a smoke. Hannah's ears still rang with their rants. "Hey blond bitch, we're coming for a piece of you." She ran and leaped over trash cans, until she tripped. She held her breath as a hand grabbed for her foot.

"Miss Blondie, rich bitch, Mommy and Daddy can't save you now."

Adrenaline kicked in just as a downpour of rain coated the sidewalk, drowning out the voices. The rain caused the hand to slip, and as her foot pulled away, Hannah pushed up on her arms, lifted her feet, and half cart-wheeled herself back down on the pavement. Gymnastics had finally paid off.

Hannah sprinted from the alleyway to the main road, then zigzagged from one side of the storefronts to the next. Their breathless gasps followed her crossings. Afraid of what she'd see, she ignored the reflections in the windows. She ran faster than she'd ever run at school. Rain drowned out the sounds of the cars, but not the tremors and pounding of her heart. She headed to safety. Exhausted, drenched, she waited for Luis under the canopy of the public library, next to the No Loitering sign.

Nearly an hour later, Luis's truck sped into the parking lot as if it were on fire. Startled, Hannah held back. She felt soiled, ugly, dirtied by what she had done and what could have happened. She worried that Luis would be angry. But as she shivered under the eaves, Luis jumped out to escort her to the truck.

"Sorry I'm late. Hannah, you look frightened. What happened?"

Hannah tried to explain, but her words were trapped within her halted breath. Thankfully Luis knew her well enough not to force her voice. He handed her one of his soiled t-shirts, and she contorted her body so that the t-shirt covered her as she slipped off her wet top. "Can we leave? Go someplace where I can erase the bad?"

They drove in silence. Hannah slumped down in the seat and took Luis's cap and placed it on top of her head. Luis kept his eyes on the road, but looked at her from the corner of his eye. Then, for some reason, he reversed the bill of the cap to face backward. Hannah slid her hand across the seat, and Luis's hand folded around her fingers.

As they left town, Hannah scanned the sidewalks. Luis drove below the speed limit, more guarded than usual. Hannah found herself pushing down on the floor with her right foot, as if she could force the gas pedal to accelerate. And then she saw them. The creeps stood in front of the Food Co-Op, where the windows held signs proclaiming, "Boycott Henderson Farms: Unfair Wages, Unfair Housing. Support the Migrants."

"Luis, g-go faster. Please get us out of here." Hannah read her family name on the posters. She felt exposed, as if being a Henderson made her dirty. She looked over at Luis. His hands shook. She reached for his arm, but he pulled away.

"Why the hurry now? Are you embarrassed to be with me? You know I can't risk being stopped by the police."

She shook her head and looked out the window. Hannah felt shame in her own last name, that it defined her in ways she had never understood. Luis represented more than just a boyfriend to her. It didn't matter that she saw his spirit, his grace, and intensity; she still worried that her parents would be angry. She didn't care where Luis came from.

Relieved that Luis kept driving, Hannah stared out at the fields as they went along Highway 99 and over the Bow Hill Road. They passed the Rhody and continued winding down Chuckanut Drive. As the scenery changed to seascape and hills, Luis's fingers searched for Hannah's hand again. She inched her way over until her thigh almost touched his. Gradually, she told her story without tears, without stutters. Her voice steady. Luis listened to Hannah's explanations as he focused on the curves and edges of the road.

He didn't speak until they had parked at Clayton Beach and climbed down to the sand and rocks. He sat atop one of the boulders. "I hope this will do, a place to erase the bad."

Hannah watched kayakers paddle off in the distance, seagulls circle in the air, and the bottom duffs of duck feathers as they bobbed for food below. "Luis, I'm sorry about what is going on in the fields.

I hate that I am a Henderson. I can't erase that. I think I tried to be someone else by confronting those guys. I thought I'd try it on, being from the streets."

"You don't *try on* being from the streets, as if it is a game. Those guys aren't migrants. They aren't boycotting for better wages or even better conditions. They assaulted you, they robbed your mother's purse, and they are pilfering the migrant camps. I saw their pictures in the newspaper. You were gambling with your life. I don't want you to be in my world, at least not that part."

Hannah grabbed her stomach, as if she had been punched in the gut. Her eyes stung with the spray of his words. "And what part of your world can I be in? I don't want to be in a world of privilege if it means that my family uses people. My mother made a comment about my father, wondering whose side he was on. Lately he's been acting like he doesn't want to be a farmer anymore. Since my sister died, I've tried so hard to make it up to them. I thought my father at least wanted me in his world."

Hannah sat down on the rocks and let her feet dangle. Luis sat behind her, encircling her body so that she felt his chest rise and fall. She let the waves do their job, steadily cleansing the beach, depositing gifts of shells and driftwood in their wake. Luis's silence allowed her thoughts to wander. She hadn't expected answers when she was just forming the questions. Lulled by the rhythmic natural melody, the patterned sweeping of waves, her brain rested, and her ribs pressed outward as her heart expanded. If she didn't think, she could feel. She liked feeling Luis, his sculpted body, his quiet power.

And as he had done before, Luis rose, stripped down to his shorts and began to dance. He watched the wind and used the breeze as wings, allowing his leaps from one rock to the next to float and roll. Sure-footed, he fell into the curves of the sculpted rocks as if he were elastic, malleable. And when he reached his arms out toward her, Hannah stood on her toes as her upper torso rolled like the waves.

Her arms stretched till their fingers touched. Her long legs answered in an arabesque, one foot holding her to the rock, the other extended behind her. The two leaned forward, pirouetted, and then Luis held her hands and led her in a chase where they galloped with straight legs and pointed feet, finally leaping onto a flat rock. Spent, Hannah sat upright and watched the ocean as Luis wrapped his body along the smooth edge of the rock. He seemed etched into the stone, shimmering with beads of sweat.

Hannah heard the *qua, qua* of the seagulls, the lapping of waves along the rocks. Dance had drawn her to Luis. The sounds of water on stones had drawn her to Joseph when she was very young. The rhythms of both calmed her and let her voice be heard. And yet here, where both water and rock met, everything washed away. Permeable or permanent. Salt spray clung to her skin, and with it came a memory of her twin sister playing in their crib. It was a silly memory, but still she had it. Her sister's cries of pain upset her. Hannah had licked her tears to take the hurt away. Salt, sand, rocks, waves.

The memory of Jenna vanished with a more persistent crash of water from the waves. The sprays mixed with new rain, teardrops from heaven. Hannah wondered if the droplets were *replenishers*, the true purpose of crying, to fill the skies and oceans. Dark clouds returned. Hannah scrambled down from the rocks. The serene scene morphed into turbulent crests, foaming waves and pellet drops of water moving sideways. She took refuge under the dark-red trunk of a madrone, a scaly, robust tree that survived with its waxy evergreen leaves despite the beatings of the wind. She watched Luis peel himself off the rock and run toward her. His skin shone like the maroon bark, a contrast to the gray skies and dark waters.

As they scurried to gather their belongings, Luis turned. His body stiffened. Hannah searched for what he sensed, the trigger that readied Luis for action. "Luis, what is it?"

He held his hand to his lips. She remembered that this is where he had been attacked. Just an hour earlier, Luis had lectured her on not putting herself in harm's way. She guessed that he didn't follow his own advice. They crouched behind a boulder and peered from the side. One lone beachcomber ignored the rain and gathered large irregularly shaped driftwood in a pile.

Hannah grabbed Luis's arm, pulling him forward as she whispered in his ear, "I recognize him. That was the man at the Rhody who wanted to speak with Joseph."

# CHAPTER 13: *Protocols*

Mounds of papers, journals, and books lay neatly stacked on the kitchen table. Joseph's head protruded above the circle of official documents. His face scrunched as he tried to read between the lines, searching through data of his work on mushroom properties and the connection to the immune system. The next step loomed large. He rubbed his eyes, absorbing years of work. Even the pen in his hand, made obsolete by the digital era, felt heavy. How could he possibly consolidate all this information to fit neatly into the grant forms from the University of Washington's Science and Technology Department? Shaking his head, he hoped his friend and collaborator Rosie would take over. Determined to share, Joseph wondered about the consequences of giving out so much truth.

Needing a break from the tedious work, he pushed aside a space on the crowded table and pulled over a mishmash of old newspapers. Most were yellowed with age and, to the casual bystander, appeared as a random collection of local news. Just yesterday Frank had dropped off the latest publications highlighting events at the Henderson Farms. Joseph skimmed the articles for facts but found only opinions and speculation. The farm's problems splashed across the front-page headlines, but the crucial pieces of the puzzle lay within the folds of the newspaper. Joseph felt the familiar tightening of his stomach as he read of violence, petty theft, and fear. Discontent at the farms, as Luis had tried to tell him, stemmed from many issues. Not all of which were farm related.

Joseph glanced at the rest of the paper. He found world news on the inside, distilled down to mere paragraphs. A plane flying over Ukraine shot down by Russian insurgents; the Israel and Palestine skirmishes on the Gaza Strip. Discouraged, Joseph searched for an old binder that his father had left him. A map of the world, almost a century old, lay inside. With care, Joseph unfolded history. Eastern Europe, the Middle East, the old and new countries, all shifted names and divisions, yet still the battles over sovereignty remained. His grandfather had landed in Costa Rica and raised his father, who brought Joseph to the United States when he was ten years old, but the threads of hate spun a tight web. No one people could claim innocence. His father had kept track of the past as a reminder. Joseph held his pen over North America and circled the borders on his father's old map. A tear fell from his long-ago injured eye. Out of focus, all lines blurred. *If only the boundaries dissolved. If only humanity prevailed.* Joseph closed his eyes. Nothing had really changed in the world.

Knocks at the door jolted Joseph back to the present. Before he had the chance to walk to the door, Rosie had already made her way in. A smile and a head of electrified curls greeted him. Joseph's spirits soared at the sight of her. "Rosie, your energy precedes you. All these forms and protocols lull me to sleep. I need you to save me. Come sit at the kitchen table, if you can find room among all my research."

Joseph felt the effects of Rosie. She drew out the best in all her surroundings. He watched Rosie take in his home, the walkways, the absence of walls, the nooks that held specifics, the windows that met the outside world. He hadn't realized he cared until Rosie spoke.

"I love your haven. I had no idea that you lived so secluded here in the woods. You never mentioned the windows and views in your letters. What a perfect place to work with mushrooms and have peace and quiet. Nature is your lab."

Her comments seemed to have come straight from Joseph's mind. Joseph's good eye focused on Rosie's face. "I'd forgotten that you read peoples' thoughts. I'll have to be more careful. I suppose you realize that you dazzle any room even when you aren't trying. What worries me are these statistics and formulizing my experiments for the larger world. I'm computer illiterate and want to stay that way."

Rosie seemed undaunted by the grant forms that lay on the table. "My new research position at the University of Washington and the Cancer Alliance needs your results. Your data will make a difference. Quantifying results is the only way we can benefit a wider population in the cancer world. Without verification of your findings, you'll be questioned to death, and you will fail. I've been down that road too many times. Computers allow us to share information, tabulate quicker. Besides, I have the sweetest young girl excited about being the first patient in our trial. I know the cancer protocols will wreak havoc on her system. Mushroom tinctures may be the answer to cleaning up the toxins. I'll take your research papers and have interns at the university plug in the statistics."

Joseph searched the room for a box. With his back to Rosie, he stacked the notebooks by mushroom type and date, binder label in front. He felt her eyes, her gentle yet firm intensity. "I think it best that all my experiments be done in the lab at the UW from now on. My woods may prove to be a problem. You said it yourself—we can't let this project fail."

"Oh, I didn't mean for you to bow out now, if that is what you're saying. I'm the scientist, the one who has to make sure all the results can be repeated, that patients are monitored in a controlled situation. I never expected you to be so sensitive."

He couldn't help but smile at Rosie's misunderstanding. "I'll make us some tea, and we can discuss my sensitivity. You may be able to read others' thoughts, but you don't always know why they think those thoughts."

By the time Joseph had prepared the tea, Rosie had settled herself at the kitchen table, nose buried in the old newspaper stories.

He sat beside her and waited until she had read the entire stack. "I'm afraid I only have tea and some homemade dessert to offer you. I inherited an old recipe for mandel bread, or dunking cookies. You bake them twice, so they are hard and last forever."

Rosie took a bite and let the crumbles linger on her lips. "I remember my grandmother baking this. I don't know if it was an old wives' tale or if it was true, that when the Jews were forced to leave their homes, they ran with their cookies half-baked, or was it that they needed rock-solid cookies that wouldn't crumble. Who knows for sure? I have a question for you. Why did you leave these articles out for me to read?"

Joseph felt like he had met his match. He chuckled to himself. "I'm too transparent for my own good. Perhaps that is why I'm reluctant or, as you say, sensitive. Last night I had some intruders up in the woods where I do most of the mushroom propagation. I ran after them. I know who they are, hooligans but not so innocent. I fear, and I use the word *fear* for emphasis, that they have been put up to this by one of the gangs."

"Tell me exactly what happened."

Joseph stared out the window as if the answer lay in the woods. "I caught these two boys in town, stealing my neighbor's purse. We had words, and I cautioned them that I'd be watching. They must have found out where I live. The intruders not only damaged the flats of mushroom spores but also destroyed the locks on the outbuildings. I chased them through the trees, but they got away. They left empty handed, but I recognized them. Why would they turn the flats of mushrooms over? Why dump everything? It would have been easier to come into my cabin and wreak havoc or steal. Someone knew about my work with the mushrooms and its importance. When the boys didn't show up with the credit cards, their bosses sent them here."

Joseph paused, not sure he had made his own thoughts clear.

"Something in the newspaper articles made me think that last night's tormenters sent me a warning. I see the threads of past atrocities, power in the hands of the weak. I don't want my work compromised because I'm a target due to my family's past. I need to be free to act separately and not have my experiments fall into the wrong hands. So, by all means, legitimize all this research by tracking results, applying laboratory controls, and giving it the stamp of a PhD."

Rosie sipped her tea and ate another piece of mandel bread. Joseph watched as she faded away from the present moment, her thoughts going inward, and then her brightness returned. Her voice filled the room, soft and strong. "We can't let old ghosts haunt us, stop us from giving fully. My father's legacy is why I do what I do. Some other time, I'll tell you about jungle warfare and the wars of proprietary invention from the pharmaceutical companies. But that's my old story. I have a new one. I research, I connect. I'm really just a means to an end. I must confess, Joseph, that I'm here for another reason. I don't want to upset you. I don't want you to think I've tricked you in any way."

Joseph listened to the water dropping on the stones outside. He heard the plunk of a missed beat. He stood up. "Rosie, don't say any more. I want to take you out to my workshop, and then we can talk about your other reason for visiting me." Joseph's ears perked at the sound of a car door. "I assume that'll be your friend, and if I'm not mistaken his name is Miguel. He's welcome to join us."

Joseph opened the door for Rosie. Undaunted by his observation, she walked out the door and touched his arm. Joseph mused that only a gap of a generation, twenty-some years, held them apart. The two walked in silence. Both understood the folds of history, how the past crept into present moments.

Miguel stood peering at the stones. Joseph considered the man. He noted Miguel's hands, thick fingers, muscled arms. His legs bent as if he were a runner. A pose that allowed him to leap into action, pivot if a directional change seemed prudent. Joseph approached slowly, allowed Rosie to step in front just in case he had misjudged the stance.

Miguel seemed transfixed by the stones. He shivered as goose bumps rose along his arms.

Rosie held her arms out in opposite directions, one arm opening toward Miguel and the other toward Joseph. "Miguel, this is Joseph, a researcher, sculptor, inventor, and peacemaker. Joseph, this is my friend from Puerto Rico."

Amused, Joseph chuckled. "Rosie, I'm not sure I could live up to your description of me. I don't have a choice but to welcome Miguel into my home, as you declared him your friend. Miguel, you must be dazzled with all the labels Rosie has given me. Come with us to my shop, and you can tell me what made you shiver."

Miguel stepped forward and grabbed Joseph's hand with a firm grip. "Your walkway tells many stories. It is hard not to feel the weight of them all."

Joseph, shorter by a foot, recognized Miguel's strength and exuberant greeting as a show of sincerity. Sun lines etched his face, remnants of frequent smiles. Eyes that remained wide, brow that furrowed when confused. Joseph's initial reaction to pull back subsided, and he returned the handshake by grasping Miguel's hand between his own. "You must be a kindred spirit. My friend Frank told me that you have a message for me."

Miguel looked to Rosie and then back at Joseph. "Small towns are the same everywhere. Word travels fast, especially to those who listen. I'm not sure what message I have, just information that will cause you pain and maybe worse."

Joseph heeded Miguel's tone, the simple words and all their import. He listened to the woods, noted the lack of birdsong, the still air, the quiet before the storm. So many years had gone by while he ignored, waited, pretended that the past remained silent.

Joseph opened his shop door and headed over to the mushroom stations. He found three chairs, which he faced toward the open door. "I hope you don't mind the musty smell."

Rosie said, "These walls encase so much power. You have harvested dreams with a vision. Not an easy task. Don't let what Miguel tells you hinder your creations."

Joseph sighed. "I'm too old to squander my dreams. I do what I do by choice. I believe we met for a reason. Frank's friendship binds us, and I'm thankful that you could help him get out from under his sister's spell. Her death wouldn't have been enough unless someone could see his goodness inside. I doubt that Miguel's news will change what I do. I suspect it will only change how I do it. So, let's get on with it. Just tell me."

Miguel slowly wove a tale of drugs and prostitution and illicit smuggling. He talked about Puerto Rico, his and Rosie's home, as if it were a foreign country and not part of the United States. Joseph listened to the sordid story of a woman named Carmen, a woman who denounced her Costa Rican family, who sold her life away for money, and who killed anyone who got in her way. This woman was a daughter of a cousin on the side of his family that had been left behind in Costa Rica. So distant and so present, why did it matter if she were already dead?

Joseph barely remembered his life in Costa Rica. He had no memory of a distant cousin named Carmen; he doubted she had even been born when he lived there. "What else is there, Miguel? How does this affect my work with the mushrooms?"

"After the explosion, we tried to find Carmen's family. She had told so many twisted stories about her past, but we felt that no matter what she had done, her family should know. Her friend Monica found what we think is a hit list inside her satchel. Your name is on there with lines drawn to names that go back to Russia. *Lyosha—Joseph.* I know it sounds bizarre, but I think someone is hunting down old Russian immigrants to settle a vendetta. I tracked you down because of your research. You have become famous and visible."

Joseph felt the pain in his stomach, a historical blow so powerful that lifetimes delivered the message in a one-two punch. "Yes, Lyosha was my Russian name. My father told me it meant *one who helps people*."

Joseph stared at the spilled mushroom experiments. He'd have to begin them again, sterilize the medium for the spores. He tried to draw the lines back to his family past. He had never met this person, Carmen, yet her actions had targeted him. The words from his dream came back to him: *Some of us ran, some of us died, some of us stole our way through life. Freedom has a price.* His grandfather Abraham had transformed his life from Russia, hid his identity by changing his name, learned Spanish, and then denied his religion—all for freedom. But still the tentacles of Russia's power reached out. What claim did Russia have over his research, his family's past? Carmen was of his blood.

"Rosie, we have to work fast. I thought something was strange with those two boys. It was how they spoke English, just like my grandfather. Those two hooligans are of Russian descent. I may not be able to help you for long."

## CHAPTER 14:
## *No One Is Spared*

Hannah lifted her chin, pulled her shoulders back, as her heart echoed in the tap of her heels and toes. Tears hung in the corners of her eyes. As she walked through the halls of the cancer wing, she refused to give in to the urge to peek inside the waiting room. She wondered if the walls remembered her cadence, how her feet had dragged as she came to visit her sister so many years past. Jenna had always waited for Hannah to come visit after school.

Hannah would sit on Jenna's bed, between Jenna's legs, so that Jenna could comb her hair. Jenna's bald head shone, and her eyes, naked without brows, appeared as dark holes filled with mica. Jenna had refused Hannah's offer to shave her own hair, wanting instead to feel the silky curls like she'd once had. They'd sit without talking, a mantra of combing meditation.

In these last four years, Hannah's ponytail had grown to reach her waist. Long enough for a wig, long enough to fulfill her unspoken promise. She took her place in the cutting room. Tenth in line, she compared hair. A man with a charcoal-black ponytail sat stiffly in the chair. His slanted dark eyes shone like his glossy locks. Two snips, and the pony disappeared. He smiled in the mirror as the cutter trimmed what hair remained. Next came a woman with spring coils, woolly tufts that framed her face. Her skin shone as polished ebony. Hannah watched as the cutter sprayed water until the coils unfurled and the curls straightened. Unraveled, the woman's hair hung below her shoulders. Once wound in a new elastic, the cutter snipped it.

Piles of ponytails lay on the table by the time Hannah's turn came. Her blond hair seemed naked, void of the rich darkness of pigment. The cutter studied Hannah's face, turned her around, and felt the strands of hair. "I'll cut your hair shorter, if you don't mind. You'll look like a pixy for a while, but that way your hair will make two wigs."

Hannah stared in the mirror as the cutter snipped. The tears that had hung in the corners of her eyes fell. Her lips caught the edges of salt, the spray of cancer's toil. Unashamed, Hannah let the sadness pool. Years of unshed sorrow fell in silence. Here she felt the safety of cancer's cocoon. A place where no one had preferential treatment, a place where she could express loss, change, and resolve. As she stood up to leave, she made a decision. "Do you think since there are two ponytails, one of the wigs could be made for a friend of mine, a new twelve-year-old patient?"

The cutter handed her a piece of paper. "Write her name down and place it on the pony."

All smiles, Hannah left to find Shelly and Robin. As she walked through the halls, she unconsciously pulled her fingers through her hair. What had been waves weighted down by length now curled into wisps of budding springs. She zigzagged through the maze of hallways until she found the floor marked Infusions.

Hannah took long strides, her eyes intent. She knew that if she walked through the doors with a sense of authority, no one would question her presence. Without a second thought, she hit the handicap knob with her elbow, and the doors to apheresis, transfusions, and infusions opened. She studied the line of cubicles and veered left to the apheresis section. Robin sat like a robotic princess. Two tubes extended from the porthole in her chest to a machine that whirled and swirled blood. Robin's eyes rolled around and around. Hannah listened to Shelly laugh and say, "If you keep that up, you might pop out your eyeballs. I don't think that will help your stem cells any."

Robin stuck out her tongue and pointed toward Hannah.

Shelly turned from the edge of the bed where she held Robin's hand and faced Hannah. Hannah's words caught themselves in a mélange of memory and momentary panic. She tried to distinguish between her recollection of Jenna's ordeal and Robin's joyful enthusiasm. She had come to be helpful, but Robin seemed more than okay. Slowly she backed away, mumbling an incoherent goodbye.

Shelly stood and held out her arms. "You aren't going anywhere, Hannah, with that new haircut. We're in need of some special fairy dust to bring good luck. Robin and I were just playing a game of pretend. Please sit here next to Robin."

Hannah sat on the other side of the bed. Robin took her hand just as the machine's swirling ceased. A nurse came in and adjusted the knobs. Robin squeezed Hannah's hand. "They're harvesting my stem cells to reboot me. I'm not supposed to worry about the blood-sucking machine. They say that chemo didn't just eat my hair but devoured my cancer cells. I'll be brand new. Just think, I'll have two birthdays. We're going to have a party."

"Well, if you don't mind having blond hair, the salon downstairs will make my ponytail into a wig just for you."

In her excitement, Robin jumped up to hug Hannah, and alarms blared from the apheresis machine. Nurses from every direction ran into the room. Shelly and Robin stared as blood spilled from Robin's chest. Hannah froze. She remembered the panic, the lights flashing, and the code blue call when Jenna's heart had stopped. Hannah felt faint, and before she knew what had happened to Robin, she collapsed on the hospital floor.

. . . . .

Hannah woke in slow motion. She tried to move her hands, but the tingling sensation felt like needle pricks on her skin. Her eyelids refused to open. "Hannah, Hannah, you're in the emergency room."

Voices called her name. Distant echoes of music, dancers flew across the sky. Again, the call: "Hannah, wake up. You fell." The voice belonged to her mother. She didn't want her mother to worry, to know what she had done.

Another voice whispered in her ear, "You're okay. Robin's okay. No one's angry with you." This registered as good news, and Hannah tried to recall who had that voice. She flashed back to her recent dinner at the Rhody. Yes, the voice belonged to the lady who worked on the cancer study. Her name belonged in the garden. Roses, yellow, white, red. One black rose with curly petals. Hannah's eyelids popped open. The curly petals morphed into hair.

"Oh, it's you," Hannah mumbled. "W-Where am I?"

"Good, you're awake. Your mother just stepped out to call your father. You had everyone worried. You weren't unconscious for long, but you have a nasty knot at the back of your head. I don't think we've met. I'm Rosie, a friend of Joseph, and I am working with Robin and her mother, Shelly."

Hannah pushed herself up to sitting. She rubbed the bump on her head and found a sticky goo clinging to her hair. Embarrassed, she stood and stumbled forward. "I-I've got to get out of here. I-it's my f-fault."

Rosie caught Hannah by the shoulders. "Not so fast, Hannah. You hit your head hard, and the hospital needs to make sure you don't have a concussion. Besides, I need your help."

Hannah sat down, closed her eyes, and repeated in her head the letters of the alphabet. Time seemed to be playing games. Counting never worked for clarity, but the alphabet held images. If only she could erase the image of blood, cancer, Jenna, and now the letter *R* for *Robin. J* flashed into her head, *Joseph*, and then the letter *L*, *Luis*. Finally, she came to *R* again, and this time she opened her eyes. "Rosie. I remember that you were supposed to help Robin with her cancer treatments. I messed that up, didn't I?"

Rosie nodded. "Ah, yes. Hannah, do you believe that you embody the all-powerful, the all-knowing, and control the universe? Nonsense, I don't think you could mess up too much. If you are worried about Robin, you needn't be. The nurses hooked her Hickman line back into the apheresis machine and cleaned up the blood. You made Robin happy, that's all. There's no fault in that. In fact, you took away another of her fears. She's so happy to have your hair as a wig. She says it'll be like Samson's hair and give her strength. Maybe your gift to Robin will lighten your path, give you freedom."

Hannah stared at Rosie as if she were crazy. She looked around the room, a makeshift cubicle in the emergency room. Noises from the hall pounded in her ear. A flash of her sister appeared. Same hospital, same smell. Hannah had felt free once but not now, not after her sister's death, not after she felt the weight of her mother's demands and the hypocrisy of the family farm. She no longer understood her father's behavior. She wished she could change her appearance, dissolve the past. She wanted to dance away with Luis.

Hannah swallowed these thoughts and challenged Rosie. "What do you know about freedom? All I see is loss, greed, and rules. The more I see, the less I understand. Giving my hair to Robin doesn't bring back my sister. And once again I've upset my mother."

Rosie waited until Hannah's anger lost its steam. "That sounds about right. You've nailed all the problems in the world to fit within your life. What do I know about freedom. Well, freedom starts with seeing that the world isn't fair, that bad things can happen to good people, and that you don't know everything. I said I needed your help, and I mean it. I want you to be part of a study."

Hannah closed her eyes, shook her head no. "What kind of study? I'm not a scientific person like you."

"There's no science involved, just the careful eye of observation. Joseph told me you were his neighbor and friend. He trusts you. The two of us have a research project with the University of Washington.

Recently two uninvited guests, two boys, caused some damage to his garage and his mushroom propagation room. Joseph wants me to take over the experiments at the lab because he thinks his work could be jeopardized."

Alarmed, Hannah stared at Rosie. "What does this have to do with freedom? Shouldn't you be calling the police?"

"Would you call the police if you saw someone pickpocketing wallets, or if your boyfriend, Luis, was beaten? Sometimes more is at risk than you know."

"How do you know about that? Now you're scaring me."

Rosie sighed. "I listen and watch. It's a talent and a gift, if I use it wisely. Even you know more than you aware of."

Hannah bent her head and exhaled ever so slowly. She knew without knowing. Luis had told her it was impossible to be him, to live within his skin. She thought about her father, his problems at the farm. She wondered about Joseph. He seemed so powerful, so independent, yet the last person he would call would be the police. She dug her nails into her arm. Pain—why did she want to feel pain? Maybe Rosie's idea could stop the pain. "If you think I can help Joseph, I'll help you out. But I should warn you that my mother doesn't like Joseph, and she forbids me from going to his house."

"Don't worry about your mother. She and I talked. I have a feeling that she'll be your advocate."

## CHAPTER 15: *Boundaries*

Luis sat on a log at the edge of Joseph's property line. He heard a truck pull up, a door shut, and the voice of Mrs. Henderson. "You're late again. Dinner is cold. You promised me that you'd try—" The cabin door slammed, cutting off her reproaches.

Luis waited. He had rushed home from his job at the airport to meet Hannah. He threw imaginary darts into the darkness. Something in Hannah's tone of voice when she had called made him hurry, made him worry. Why would Hannah be asked to look out for Joseph? Anxious, he counted the rooms lit up in the Henderson house. Finally, the lamp in the far window, the one where Hannah slept, went out.

Hannah appeared within moments. Luis heard the snap of dead branches under her feet and smelled citrus from her wet hair. She came breathless, eyes asparkle. His hand reached out and pulled her down to share the log with him. Their fingers entwined. Hannah's lips brushed his with a whisper of a kiss. Neither spoke until an owl swooshed down and broke the spell with its *hoot-hoot-hoo.*

Luis fidgeted with Hannah's hand. "Are you sure you won't get into trouble? I know your mother disapproves of Joseph, and I know she wouldn't want you here with me."

"I told her I was coming here. I don't know what this woman Rosie said to her, but my mom suddenly sees me differently."

"Maybe it's your haircut. You look older."

Hannah put her hand up to her wet hair. She smiled. "I don't think so. I didn't even tell her about donating the hair to make wigs.

I guess when I collapsed at the hospital, she feared she'd lose me. Maybe not to cancer, but by smothering me."

Luis nodded as if this made sense. He thought about his parents. He hadn't spoken to them in months, but each night he made a promise to the stars that he'd find them a way back to the United States. "Does your father know you are over here? I heard his truck."

"I didn't tell him, if that's what you're asking. I passed him as I left. He gave me a hug. Didn't even notice my hair."

Luis had heard rumors about another boycott at the farms. That Mr. Henderson had made lots of concessions with working conditions and rate of pay. "I think your dad still has issues with the workers. Some of them are getting greedy. What bothers me are the rabble-rousers who don't really work the fields. They're those boys who gave you trouble. If I were your dad, I'd be worried about the crops not getting picked and the vandalism. He's already given lots."

Hannah looked back at her family cabin, a mansion compared to Joseph's rambling home. "That is why I needed to meet with you. I think those boys came here to make trouble for Joseph. Rosie told me that two people had messed with his mushroom experiments. Why would they do that?"

Luis stood up and drew Hannah to his chest. His heart pounded against her thin shirt. Gripping her hand, he started to lead her toward Joseph's workshop. But she tugged Luis back, and said, "You're acting funny. Why are you so angry, so pushy? What do you know?"

"Maybe these guys know you live next to Joseph. They know you are Mr. Henderson's daughter. They're mad at you. Maybe this is about you, and not Joseph."

Luis wished he had kept his mouth shut. He had never seen Hannah's rage. She stomped past him to the entrance of Joseph's shop. Luis followed. When he was within earshot, he whispered, "If we want to protect Joseph and look out for his property, then we need to be quiet. I know a spot where we can hide and see everything."

Luis didn't wait. He made his way over to a mound of debris, a combination of broken branches, moss, fir needles, and Joseph's compost pile. In one corner Luis had set up a makeshift bench with fallen tree rounds. He pulled out a knife from his shoe to clean off some bird droppings and bowed toward Hannah. "Not the most elegant watch post, but we'll be out of view and comfortable."

Luis noted Hannah's dimple, the one that appeared when she smiled. Relieved, he sat beside her and waited. The two held hands in a comfortable silence. The swish of an owl overhead, the rush of water from the creek, lulled them, until they heard raised voices deeper in the woods. Luis put his finger to his lips and motioned for Hannah to follow. They scrambled through the trees, Luis leading by the light of the moon. The voices became louder, a shouting match of three: Joseph and the two boys that had stalked Hannah. As Hannah began to rush forward, Luis held her back. "Wait. They aren't speaking English or Spanish. By the looks of it, I think Joseph can hold his own."

Hannah stood behind a tree. She bent toward Luis and whispered, "I think they're speaking Russian."

Luis could kick himself. He felt like an idiot, so centered on his own situation, it had never occurred to him to ask Joseph why he kept to himself. Even their last conversation hinted at an uglier time. "Russian makes sense. The other night Joseph ranted on and on at me about the pogroms against the Jews in Russia. But he never said he could speak the language."

Luis and Hannah watched as if this were a scene from an old movie. Joseph held the smaller of the two boys by the collar. His giant friend circled Joseph, switching a knife from one hand to the next. Joseph ignored the knife and its owner. He spoke to his captive with a voice that bellowed. The words had less significance than the tone and sternness. The giant stepped back, and Joseph put his friend down. The three stood in a circle. Joseph took a stick and drew in the dirt: first a large circle and then what appeared to be the continents of the earth. He traced lines across one area to another.

Baffled, Luis tugged at Hannah to move in closer. The squabble turned to what seemed like a lecture with Joseph's tone and volume muted. All three kneeled around the drawings as if it held the answer to the world's problems. Joseph stood up and shook both boys' hands. They had come to some agreement, and the smaller boy handed Joseph a piece of paper, which Joseph stuffed into his pocket without a glance.

Joseph led the boys down another path that crossed back toward the mushroom experiments. Luis stepped out from behind the tree and stared at the diagram. "What's so special about a map of the world? No hidden message, just lines."

Hannah kneeled in close and studied the lines. "I think the lines represent travel. Maybe it's a history of sorts. You know, Joseph said he lived in Costa Rica. There are lines from there to Russia, and lines from Costa Rica to here in the United States."

Luis felt his irritation rising. *Why would Joseph share his story with strangers?* He bent down with a stick and began to wipe away the drawing, but Hannah grabbed his arm and said, "Don't. Leave it. Joseph leaves all trails, all stones, and all messages. He doesn't erase anything. Just look at the pathway to his house." She stood up and faced Luis. "Rosie told me to watch out for Joseph, not to change his life."

Luis dropped the stick and took Hannah's hand in his own. "Joseph was right. He told me that my curiosity would make me responsible. Just look at me now." Luis threw the stick off into the woods and walked back toward the cabin with his head and shoulders bent. Hannah followed.

"Maybe you shouldn't be here with me, Luis. You act like caring is such a bad thing."

"I don't know. I worry too much and do nothing." Luis resisted Hannah's pull on his arm. His heart hurt. "Since when did you get so brave? These last few weeks, I thought it was me that had changed you. That our dancing together mattered. I thought it was because of me that you don't stutter anymore?"

Hannah's eyes shot out darts and then tears. Luis knew he'd hurt her feelings. He waited for her reprimand. Instead Hannah took a deep breath and spoke in the softest of voices. "I'll ignore that. There must be a reason you want to hurt me just when I'm feeling strong. Is it so I'll punish you because you couldn't stop your parents from being taken? I'm done with punishing myself for my sister's death, for my mom's meanness. Can't you accept what is?"

Luis let Hannah's words filter through his muddled thoughts. "I guess I don't have a monopoly on injustice."

Hannah nodded. "And you don't have a monopoly on me. Get that straight."

Luis couldn't help but smile. He looked sideways to see Hannah's grin. Hannah stuck out her tongue, then started running. Luis took pursuit. He finally caught up with her outside of Joseph's cabin. Out of breath, they stumbled through the door and into Joseph.

"'Bout time you two came out of the woods. I'm surprised my newest intruders didn't hear you in the brush. Were you spying on me?"

Luis and Hannah stood with their mouths open. Each blurted out a different excuse as Joseph looked on. Then he said, "If you're going to lie, your stories should be the same. So, who's going to speak the truth?"

Luis stepped forward, but Hannah pulled him back and said, "We were watching out for you. Rosie told me about the damage to the mushroom experiments. She asked me to come around more and observe."

Joseph picked up a broom and swept the cabin floor. "So now they call spying *observing*. Do you want to tell me what you saw, or is that just for Rosie to know?"

Hannah looked over to Luis, and he looked out the window. He tried to reason his way out of the trick question. "I don't know what we saw. You spoke in Russian, and you were clearly angry. Was it a fight or a planned meeting? If you hadn't seen us, I doubt you'd tell me."

Joseph swept the last of the mud and dirt out the door. He turned to face Luis and Hannah. "Odd, isn't it, how friends can easily become enemies? I'm trying to avoid that, but old mistrusts have a way of seeping in. I'll make us a pot of coffee so we can talk. But you're right, I wouldn't have told you about the boys."

Luis shook his head and put the water on to boil. Joseph took the coffee beans from a tin can and ground them by hand. Hannah found Joseph's stash of dunking cookies and set them on the table. Luis had eaten two cookies and drunk his coffee before Joseph began.

"Those boys are troublemakers in town. They have no alliance to anyone, just greed. They're the ones who stole your mom's purse, Hannah."

Hannah nodded. "I know. I followed them and made a fool of myself. I thought they wanted to get back at me."

Luis cleared his throat to speak but thought better of saying anything when Hannah kicked his leg.

Joseph continued, "I think the boys have bigger fish to fry. You're just an annoyance to them, and they won't forget it. But I'm the real problem. You heard us talking in Russian. They're just puppets in the grand scheme. Russian puppets. So many of the Russian immigrants left family behind. Their government still has a hold on them. Sends them out to do their dirty work, or else they'll hurt their loved ones."

Luis felt the hair on his arms rise. He interrupted Joseph's story. "Does this have something to do with that man, Miguel?"

Joseph looked tired. He took a sip of his coffee and ate a cookie. "Miguel is a messenger, but he has no affiliation with the Russians."

Luis waited for more, but Joseph seemed to have mentally left the room. He stood and refilled Joseph's cup before saying, "Come back from wherever you were. I've never seen you this distracted."

"Maybe that is the problem," Joseph said. "I'm not who you thought I was."

"Now you're really scaring me," Hannah said. "What did Miguel tell you? What does Russia have to do with you and those boys?"

"Miguel came with Rosie to give me some news. Apparently one of my distant relatives died a horrible death in Puerto Rico. Her name was Carmen. I didn't know her, but Miguel found my name among others on a slip of paper, which he believes is a hit list. It goes back to a family dispute from Russia."

"And those Russian boys?" Luis asked.

Joseph began clearing the table. "Those boys have names. The smaller one is Vladimir, and the taller one is Yuri. Never talk about anyone without a name. It's so easy to make someone a villain when you don't know names. Vladimir and Yuri have family in Russia that might be harmed. Whenever they're approached by their gang leader, they have to respond. But now, they're more afraid of me than their gang leader."

Hannah interrupted, "Should they be?"

Joseph stared past Hannah and whispered, "When fear gets ahold of you, you lose your power. They don't know who to fear."

Luis studied Joseph's face. His one good eye had dulled, and the crease lines around his mouth had deepened. His soft demeanor, gone. "You didn't answer Hannah's question. Should Vladimir and Yuri fear you?"

"Yes, they should fear me. Not because I'll hurt them, but because I faced them. I became real to them, like they became real to me. The anonymous enemy no longer exists. In fact, I invited them to help me with my mushroom experiments."

"You did what? How could you invite vandals here?" Luis stood and shoved the chair beneath the kitchen table. He looked at Hannah in disbelief.

Hannah stood as well, but instead of challenging Joseph she stood next to him and whispered back, "I've never feared you. What do you need from us?"

Luis felt the tension lift. He'd been holding his breath and his annoyance.

Joseph smiled at them and said, "Now we are getting somewhere. You two aren't spies, and Vladimir and Yuri aren't enemies. Get to know them. The oldest wisdom I gained from my grandfather's notes was to befriend those you don't know so the differences disappear."

In disbelief, Luis blurted out, "What differences are you talking about? People, who you don't know, who live across the ocean, want you killed for something a family member did a lifetime ago. And your answer is to make friends and not war, like turning your cheek?"

Joseph ignored the comment and pulled out an old binder. He opened it to a map. "Come and look. This was the old world. Same land, different boundaries. Still everyone fights. No one will be safe if we don't eliminate all boundaries and see that all of our ancestors came from somewhere else."

"We can't even cross the Mexican border safely," Luis argued. "How do you think we can change anything in Russia? I don't understand."

"And yet Vladimir and Yuri did. I drew them a map. Created the world in the dirt. They saw themselves outside of the lines."

Luis understood the concept of imaginary lines. He placed his hands on the table. "Okay, so say we befriend them, help with the mushrooms. Then what?"

Joseph shrugged. "I don't know. Maybe we stop something bad from happening here. Maybe we go beyond tolerance. Maybe we learn. Vladimir and Yuri must feel connected to us, or they will act just like Russian puppets and not worry about the consequences of their orders. Now at least I've planted some doubts in their minds. It could help me figure out the endgame. My grandfather's connection to Russia can't be the only reason I'm a target. The Russians want something I have. Or maybe they're setting me up as a decoy. Either way we learn about them and keep them in our vision. They won't be working in the shadow."

Hannah took Luis's hand. "I've got to go home. Vladimir and Yuri are the troublemakers out at the farms. I should try and help my dad."

"I'll walk you back."

As the two left, they heard Joseph mumbling to himself, "The boundaries are in the mind and heart, not on paper. But greed and power are everywhere."

# CHAPTER 16: *Know What You Ask*

Sweat dripped into Hannah's eyelashes. She ignored her blurred vision and plucked two fistfuls of ripe blueberries and dropped them into a white bucket. Each picker had their assigned rows. This was her fourth pint bucket in an hour, almost nothing compared to what the other workers had picked. At this rate her hourly production would be of little help.

The woman in the row next to her hummed a tune as she picked. Her hands rhythmically plucked and dropped without a pause. Hannah smiled at the blueberry arm dance, silently wished she could use her feet, give her tired arms and shoulders a break. As she stood up to stretch, the woman paused and motioned with her hand to come over.

"*Señorita*, take this headband. At least make it so you can see."

Hannah took the orange bandana and wrapped it around her head. "Thanks, I've never picked before. My name is Hannah. What's yours?"

The woman shook with laughter. "Yes, I know who you are. Mr. Henderson's daughter. They say you are a spy, but I don't think so. You'd have worn a hat and shirt to protect yourself from the sun, but here you are, blinded by your sweat and with arms the color of tomatoes. My name is Estella. You can call me Stella."

Hannah hadn't noticed her sunburn. She shrugged. "Tomorrow I'll be better prepared."

"So you'll be here tomorrow too? Does your father want you out in the fields with all that is going on?"

Hannah shook her head. "No, he doesn't know I'm here."

As Hannah turned back to her row, Stella called out. "You wouldn't have made much money anyway. Somebody needs to teach you how to pick. If you come back, I'll show you some tricks."

Hannah beamed. "If you teach me, then you can get my pay."

The laughter from Stella made Hannah realize how silly her offer sounded. The rows of blueberry bushes went on for many acres. At least half of the blueberries would be wasted if her father couldn't convince the boycotters to come back to the field. She had overheard her parents fighting. She knew that their troubles seemed unfixable. Her father's last statement to her mother was said with sad resignation: "Even if there wasn't a boycott, even if I could do more, it wouldn't help. We need more people. There are too many berries and not enough workers."

Hannah had been in the fields since sunrise, so she hadn't noticed the supervisors hovering at the entranceway where a line of boycotting workers held signs. Hannah looked for Vladimir and Yuri, but they weren't among the crowd. She saw a group of young men she knew weren't from the area. She had seen one at the school job fair, a representative from the university. His sign stated, "Solidarity with Labor, Solidarity with the Common Man." Hannah wondered who this *common* man was. Certainly, the protester wasn't common, not with his designer sandals and Patagonia pants.

Many of the pickers tried to walk past the line of signs. Boos and taunts made some turn away. Hannah kept her eyes focused, kept a dog's smile on her face, and waved at the supervisors. She hadn't been down to the field in years, but the workers had recognized her as the owner's daughter. Wrinkled streaks of time framed their dark eyes. Their mouths showed surprise, but no words followed. Hannah knew their loyalty to her father by their silence. Not knowing the procedures, she had watched the others and finally picked up a stack of buckets with assigned row numbers. At least the lady, Stella, had talked to her.

At day's end, the supervisors counted the worker's buckets, weighed them, and wrote the number of pounds in a blue book. When Hannah brought hers to the scales, they shooed her on. When she didn't move, the most senior supervisor whispered, "Miss Henderson, just take your buckets. No need for us to count your takings."

Confused, Hannah moved to the side with her ten buckets. The other workers ignored her and rushed to get their pickings tallied. They disappeared within minutes, a swarm of tired workers heading home to their lives. Hannah marveled at the bareness of the harvested blueberry bushes, the sum product of the worker's energy, and the silence they left behind.

She approached the supervisor who had pulled her aside and said, "You know, I'm not here to take these berries home. I'm here to work."

He shook his head, and his smile disappeared. "Miss Henderson, it isn't allowed. You're not employed here. You have no documentation, no paperwork for the authorities. I let you in because I thought you wanted to take the berries home or to your friends. There are strict rules we must follow. Especially now with all the problems your father has."

"You mean I can't work in the fields? With the boycott, I thought my help would be welcomed."

"Please, Miss Henderson, don't make a problem for us. You don't know what you are asking. The workers will see you as taking their jobs, just like the guest worker program. I beg of you to leave before the protesters make an issue."

This was the last thing Hannah wanted. She realized now why the pickers had disappeared so quickly. They weren't just tired and hungry; they wanted to avoid the protesters. Normally the supervisors had them head out the same way they came in, but today the workers had scattered through the fields to avoid confrontations.

Hannah didn't have a choice. She made her way to the front office, but the supervisor ran after her.

"Follow me, the back way. I'll take you to your car. The press is out front taking pictures of the protesters."

Hannah nodded. As she followed, she racked her memory for the supervisor's name. Something about his walk reminded her of when she used to come to the fields with her father before she went to school. One time there had been an accident, and a picker had fallen from a ladder. Her father had taken the injured worker to the emergency room. She had stayed there with her sister and father as they waited for the man to come out of surgery. "Thank you. I didn't mean to be a problem. But tell me, are you Zapato? I can't remember your real first name, but I remember when you got hurt. I called you that because you couldn't wear a shoe for months after the operation."

The supervisor laughed. "That was a long time ago. No one calls me that now. I wondered if you'd remember. I'm Rubio."

"My father used to talk about you at the dinner table. Something about your son going to college and studying to be a doctor because of your fall."

Rubio motioned for Hannah to go through a gate. She caught a glimpse of the front parking lot where the local television and newspaper reporters all clustered around her father and the man she had seen at the beach. Curious, she waffled between walking on and stepping out to be with her father.

Before she could decide, Rubio called out to her, "Don't make it worse. Your father wants you protected. He is a good man, and he will find a way to make things right. Go, get something to eat. Stay away from the protesters and the press."

Hannah slipped out behind the office entrance onto a trail that led to one of the housing clusters. The aroma of tortillas, beans, rice, and sweet bananas brought back another set of memories. This is where her father would take her and Jenna after work. An older lady would always give them hot tortillas and fried batter smothered in powdered sugar to take home. As if on cue, an elderly woman came out of her house with a steaming plate and a tall glass. "Missy Henderson, *ven aca*. I've got your food. Rubio sent one of the workers to tell me you'd be here, and I figured you'd be hungry."

"Thank you. Please call me Hannah. Are you Rubio's mother?"

"Eat, you must be hungry to say something so funny. You don't remember me, but I'm Rubio's grandmother, Maria. You can call me Abuelita, like you used to."

Hannah sat down on the stoop outside of Abuelita's house. "I don't want to intrude. Rubio thought it best I stay away from all the protesters."

As Hannah ate and drank, she looked at the houses where the workers lived. Painted in vibrant colors, lawns mowed with small gardens, the neat pill boxes framed out a space called home. "Abuelita, are you happy here? Is your life too hard?"

"Eat, relax. You ask too many questions just like you and your sister did." She laughed again. "You both came in to see our toilet. Back then we only had outhouses, not like now. We missed you after Jenna died. Life is hard for everyone, especially for your mother and father."

Hannah waited, but Abuelita didn't continue. She had never thought of her own life as hard, just misunderstood. As she finished the last of the sweets, Hannah saw a group of young men running through the rows of houses. Vladimir and Yuri were among them. "Abuelita, do you know those two boys?"

Abuelita frowned. "They are our troublemakers. Everyone knows them. They don't have parents or a home. They try to make our children do bad things. Ah, but we are not stupid."

"What do mean?"

"We are kind. We give them food, try to show them a better way.

Who knows what small kindness will help? They need lots of help. We watch."

Hannah thought about Joseph's philosophy of keeping his enemies close. She stood up to leave, but Abuelita motioned for her to sit down again and said, "Your father will be here soon. Rubio wants you to wait until he gets here. Your father walks a narrow line. He can't have you upset the balance."

Maybe this is what her mother had meant about not knowing whose side her father was on. It didn't appear that Rubio or Abuelita had this worry. Maybe that was her father's position, not to take sides. The more she knew, the less certain she was about her own life.

Abuelita said, "Here comes your father and his friend."

Hannah rose from the stoop. Her father strode toward her with an unexpected smile. The nervous butterflies that had settled in her stomach disappeared when she realized she wasn't in trouble.

Her father embraced her. "I heard you were out in the fields picking today."

Hannah nodded, confused. She smelled turpentine, noticed blue paint on her father's hands.

When she didn't answer, her father turned back toward the man she recognized from the beach. "Miguel, remember Hannah. She was at the Rhody last week, when you had dinner?"

Hannah held her breath. The paint and the odor of turpentine reminded her of her father's red sweatshirt, a secret. At the diner, her father had denied seeing Miguel that night, denied being at the beach, and now her father introduced this man as a friend? The flutters in her stomach returned. She held out her hand to shake. "I remember you. Did you see my father at the beach again, painting?"

She expected a lie, that both would deny the beach, the painting. But her father laughed, and Miguel held her hand in between his own and said, "You have a good memory. We didn't meet at the beach. I was upriver talking with Joseph, and I saw your father. I hitched a ride into town, and he showed me some special spots on the beach. Good places to gather driftwood. I'm a wood sculptor."

Anger replaced the flutters. How could her father go off collecting driftwood when his farm was in jeopardy? Hannah counted to ten, then twenty, before she spoke. Even with her pause, her words came out hard. "I don't understand. Everyone is talking about how you need more people to pick. You left the supervisors with your problems, you abandoned the workers. I came to help you. Don't you care about anything?"

Her father's face turned crimson. His smile stiffened, and his shoulders sagged. Hannah immediately regretted her words. After what seemed like forever, her father spoke. "Don't judge me. It's my fault that you don't understand. Since your sister's death, I've been rethinking how we live. It wasn't fair that she died. For so long I've followed rules. I've discovered that the rules discriminate against what is fair both in life and in death. I've decided to make some changes on the farm. Rubio and most of my supervisors agree. They want a situation where both the farmer and the farmworker win. If they don't find this kind of a solution, everyone loses."

"So, what does that mean, Daddy? Are you just going to break rules, get arrested? I don't think this is a game."

Miguel held his hand out. Inside was the smallest of wood sculptures. On a thin piece of driftwood, he had carved a madrone tree, with a peeled sliver of maroon bark rolled together to appear like blueberries. The combination pulled the earth's cycles into one object: The ocean morphed a tree into driftwood, man felled trees to open fields, and the fields produced blueberries for man to eat.

Hannah gasped at the intricacy of Miguel's artistry. And Miguel noticed. Struck with the connection, Hannah shook her head and said, "This is beautiful, but art doesn't pick berries, or even change minds. I don't understand. What are you and my father planning to do to get more workers on the fields and keep the peace? I came down to help. I don't know why I even tried."

Her father looked straight into her eyes. "You're more like me than you know. Trust me. The problems on our farm aren't just about immigration. I wish I had talked to you sooner. I didn't want you to worry. I know how hard it has been for you these last few years. Forgive me for not trusting you."

Hannah spoke softly. "Well, it's not too late."

Her father shook his head. "Soon, but not yet. Not until I've worked out more of the details. Please be patient with me."

Hannah saw deep sadness in her father's eyes. She looked over at Abuelita, cooking tortillas. She glanced out at the blueberry fields. The tranquil scene hid the turmoil. She thought of Rosie asking for her help to protect Joseph, of Abuelita watching out for her children and feeding troublemakers. And lastly, she thought of Luis. Everyone had so much to lose. Her father just as much as anyone. There was so much she didn't know.

## CHAPTER 17: *As the World Turns*

Luis stood in front of the flower beds outside the airport hangars. Nothing registered. He failed to see the baby slugs curled below the half-eaten leaves, a clear sign that he'd be slacking off for a week. Distracted by his own thoughts, Luis barely registered a plane taking off or the double bump of a tricky landing. He felt the heat off the tarmac but missed the fact that he had watered the same flower three times. Even Poker's tomato plants, ripe with cherry miniatures, failed to tempt him.

Images flashed into his brain. Hannah in overalls, bandana on her head. Headlines from the *Skagit Herald*, "Henderson Farms stoops to a new low: Family first, workers last." Hannah's blue-stained fingers, her tired arms that held him tight, and her breasts, soft against his chest, heaving despair with each breath. Maybe they were too young to love like they did. But their frantic kisses lingered.

He had no answers to the questions that turned his own problems on end. With Hannah, his life became more complicated. Without Hannah, he'd be lost, drifting in an unfair world. His anger and passion caught him off guard. He looked up to see Poker twisting the hose, cutting the flow of water. "*Contra*, what the—"

"'Bout time you paid attention. You've been at that same flower bed for ten minutes, dumping all your worries. I had to get your attention somehow."

"Poker, cut that out."

"You wear your heart on your sleeve." Poker chuckled. "Except you're sleeveless. You better toughen up if you want to figure out your life. You aren't doing Hannah or Joseph any good festering with your emotions. Besides, Mr. Henderson sent a message. Seems you are in demand."

Luis studied Poker. Something about the ease in which he meddled in Luis's life both irritated him and made him feel at home. "No matter what I do, Poker, you are in the thick of it. I can't imagine anyone calling you by your given name, Frank. Poker suits you so much better. Is the message written down, or did it just suddenly appear in your brain?"

"I didn't read the message, if that is what you are asking. It's sealed in an envelope with your name. I just recognized Jeff's handwriting."

"I didn't know you were on a first-name basis with Mr. Henderson."

"You are too young to know everything. You have a job now that isn't just watering flowers. Get going."

Luis ripped open the envelope. Swirls of cursive made the words in the handwritten note appear formal, demanding, and hard to read. It didn't help that his hand shook, and the ink smeared from his wet fingers.

*Luis,*

*I need your help and special talents now. The farm and your friends' livelihoods depend on it. If not for me, then for Hannah. Meet me at your beach spot. It's important.*

*—Jeff Henderson.*

Luis wiped his hands on his pants and folded the note in three, making sure the creases were proportional. An odd plea, sent with urgency, and a sense of mystery. How could he not respond? His mother had taught him manners, respect. But he thought of Hannah and her reaction to her father's request.

He quickly weeded and watered the rest of the plants, taking care to remove all the baby slugs and wash off the mites. In record time, he mowed the grass adjacent to the tarmac. Poker disappeared into his hangar only to reappear with a lunch box, just as Luis finished his chores.

"You'll be busy for the rest of the day. This will hold you over till you have time to rest."

Luis took the offerings. "Thanks. Seems you knew I'd go help Mr. Henderson. Did he talk to you before he sent the note?"

"Does it matter? Stop asking questions. That's what's wrong with this world. Too much analyzing and not enough action. I'll see you next week. We can talk then. Glad you finished your job here before you left. Otherwise I'd have too much volunteering to do."

Luis left the Concrete Airport and headed west. His inclination was to pick up Hannah and find out if she knew what her father was up to. But he stayed on Highway 20 past the detour of the most recent landslide. He slowed as the vehicles took to one lane. Large boulders, pushed by mud, sat on the road. He thought about chance, fortune, vulnerability—all of these stood as rocks in his path. His parent's deportation, his friendship with Hannah, Joseph's kindness, even the beating at the beach, appeared by chance. He wondered how much was coincidental and how much was human nature? Even nature couldn't outsmart fault lines.

As he drove across town, his thoughts switched to the palm fossils embedded in the sandstone that lined the coastal road. He looked at the rough edges of another time as he zigzagged along. His life seemed so inconsequential, yet his old boss, his girlfriend's father, had reached out to him. Why?

Luis parked the truck and walked down the trail. He took off his shoes where the trail met the beach. His feet, used to the soft sifting of the sand between his toes, the cushion underneath, and the jagged pokes of the boulders, easily scrambled over the rocks. The sharp edges and then the smooth polish of weathered flat surfaces jabbed at him, like questions without answers. Luis forced them out of his mind, instead letting his feet guide him. Soon enough he'd find out what was needed.

Luis heard his name.

"I knew Luis would come. He's just around the bend. Are you sure he'll help?"

"Miguel, your hearing must be better than mine—that is, if you're right. I know how far he has to come from upriver. I'm patient. You don't need my reassurances. Luis will cooperate."

Luis stood quiet for just a second. Hannah had told him of her father's new friend, the driftwood carving, and their foolish notions of using art as a way toward change. Now he felt Miguel's power. Miguel heard the undercurrents, the wind within the rocks. Few could boast that ability. Luis came to these very rocks to dance with the salty breezes. He stepped out from the rocks and called, "I'm here. I'm surprised that the sound of the waves didn't hide my footsteps."

Mr. Henderson slowly climbed over the rocks to meet Luis. "Luis, thanks for coming. I've missed you at the fields these last few months. I'm sorry about your parents. You know that, don't you?"

Luis hadn't expected that. He kept his distance, not sure why he'd come. "That isn't why you called me out here, is it? Your note said you had a job for me. Something about my *special talents*. I'm not sure I can trust you after what happened to my parents. They loved the blueberry farm; did you need their *special talents* too?"

Mr. Henderson kept his voice low. "Hannah has talked about you. She has high regard for you."

Luis took note of his surroundings. He stared past Mr. Henderson, beyond Miguel. A large pile of driftwood lay across the beach. The pattern of the wood drew him in, reminiscent of some historical event. Even as he listened to the conversation, Luis picked up each piece of wood as if it were a piece of a puzzle. Miguel followed behind him, readjusting the wood in his precise design. Luis answered with another question: "This isn't about Hannah. What do you need?"

Miguel took a piece of the driftwood and tossed it toward the bay, just outside of Luis's reach. Luis leaped in the air and caught it just before the driftwood skimmed the water. Luis sensed that this was some sort of test. Mr. Henderson smiled. Miguel smiled.

Luis waited for an answer from Mr. Henderson, but none came. He felt like he was on trial, and old anger filled the silence before he said, "I know you both saw me dancing out here a few weeks ago. You saw the attack. Why didn't you stop them?"

Mr. Henderson walked toward Luis, but Miguel held him back with a raised eyebrow and a look of warning. Somehow Luis had caught them off guard. A full cycle of waves ebbed toward the driftwood, retreated and crept back to the shoreline.

Luis continued, "Mr. Henderson, I don't mean to be disrespectful, but calling me out here to meet seems odd. Why so far from home? If you needed my help, we could have met—"

Before he finished his sentence, Mr. Henderson interrupted, "At my farm, my house, at the Rhody. All of these places would have been uncomfortable for you. I looked for a neutral place, one where I, too, come for solace."

There it was. The common ground. Luis extended his hand to Mr. Henderson and then to Miguel. They walked to an overhang off the cliff face. A madrone tree protruded out at an odd angle toward the sun and the wind. Each man sat nestled in the shade, facing the waves.

Miguel said, "We should start over. You have more than your fair share of reasons to question this meeting. First off, I'm the odd one out, the stranger. I witnessed your beating but kept quiet. I thought it best to keep your privacy. When I saw you were okay, I followed the boys to see why they had attacked you. That is when I bumped into Mr. Henderson."

Luis nodded. "And you, Mr. Henderson? Why didn't you come forward?"

"Forgive me. I wasn't sure if you knew the boys. I was embarrassed because I recognized you and the group. I just didn't know if it was my business to interfere. I thought it better to remain hidden."

Luis dug his heels into the sand. "Better for who? I didn't know them. I wasn't ashamed that they saw me dancing. Dancing is what I do, even if it is private. Ever since my parents were deported, I've been living in the shadows. And if I'm in the public eye, I make sure I am on the right side of the law. I'm insulted that you thought I was friends with those guys. When I worked for you, did I ever do anything wrong? Did I hang with a bad crowd?"

Mr. Henderson took a piece of driftwood from the beach and drew circles in the sand. "Luis, I don't like what I did. The events at the farm have taken on a more sinister turn. I only realized that after all the boycotts. My longtime employees finally broke down and told me about the intimidation from an outside group. Some of those boys were in the group. When you left, I thought the worst."

Luis rubbed his eyes. A deep sadness overtook him.

Miguel stood up and placed his hands on Luis's shoulders. "I know what it means to live in the shadows, to walk that narrow line. I'm a political artist. I stir the pot whenever I can in Puerto Rico. But I hide in between each stir. There are two systems of living there. One exists with bribes, the other just exists. Here in the United States, the government listens, even if they are slow to react. We just have to make them see and care."

Mr. Henderson doodled with the stick in the sand, creating a labyrinth within a labyrinth. "Luis, look at my drawing in the sand. It's the same. I'm caught in a political maze and a criminal maze. I don't want to break laws, and laws have been broken. I need your help to get the public's attention. Too many of the laws backfire on hard workers. Your ability to dance and your honesty might be a way to share."

Luis smiled as it came to him. Hannah mentioned her father's plan with Miguel to tell the larger story. "So, you want me to leap, tell my story, because if we stay within the maze there is no exit."

"Yes, I guess I'm asking you to trust me. Take that leap of faith."

"Mr. Henderson, you do know that Hannah isn't a little girl anymore. She has a mind of her own."

"Yes, Luis. And you are on her mind most days."

Luis melted a little, relaxing his stance. "If I help, will you trust me enough to share your secret?" He moved forward and whispered, "You hid at the beach for another reason."

Mr. Henderson fidgeted, looked away, but finally answered, "Do you promise to be a gentleman with Hannah?"

Luis's face reddened. He felt Mr. Henderson's intensity—a glare rather than a stare. Finally, Mr. Henderson eased his look, broke the showdown, and turned toward Miguel.

Miguel took the cue. "Enough talk. I take it you will help us. Let's start with the driftwood."

## CHAPTER 18:
## *Dress Up or Disguise*

Joseph took the shortcut through the woods, where the worn path felt like cool clay. His feet had memorized the dips, and now his gait took on the hobble of the ruts. An observer would see him as a puppet bouncing between tree trunks, if they saw him at all. He had warned Rosie that he wouldn't appear at any of the university meetings. She was to be his voice. What had possessed her to check yes in the RSVP? Some emergency meeting about validation, a crisis of interpretation of the study. He shouldn't even know about the meeting.

If only Frank hadn't left a note on his truck, if only he hadn't visited with Ralph and Sharon. The note read, "Rosie needs you to meet her at the research center." By the time he opened his cabin door, his anger had dissipated. There was no use complaining about "if only." He chuckled to himself hearing his grandfather's voice: *If only I had seen what I saw, before I saw it, I wouldn't have sawed it in two.*

Joseph had devoted most of his day to teaching Vladimir and Yuri the fine art of mushroom hunting. For the two city slickers, this meant a new way of walking and seeing: a soft touch of the foot, a search for hidden shapes. Joseph had sent them on their way after a few hours of foraging, but he was no nearer understanding the threat on his life than before. The two were not really part of the Russian Bratva, just their messenger boys—puppets to the infamous Brotherhood. Joseph wondered what strings the Russians wanted pulled after so many years of silence. He'd find out soon enough. At least he had been able to gather enough mushrooms for Ralph and Sharon's farm and make another vat of detox for the soil. After a few years, their other plot of soil would be okay to use again for their corn crops.

Frank's sparse note meant Joseph had to go into town. *Poor Frank.* He still felt responsible for Molly's transgressions. His punishment saved his soul. The buried waste had leaked all over the valley. Now Frank was a zealot with a mission to correct all his transgressions. The community had embraced his new attitude and with Joseph's studies, mushrooms had become the unofficial cure to absorb toxins in the soil.

All this meant that Frank had become the confidant of Skagit Valley and also the local busybody. Joseph suspected that Frank knew more about the meeting at the university than he had indicated in the note. It didn't matter. If Joseph couldn't predict the future, he could at least be present. He wouldn't let the offenses of his ancestors or that of his unknown niece, Carmen, hold him hostage. Time to dress the part of a scientist.

Joseph took a white short-sleeved, button-down shirt from his closet. Almost never worn, it looked brand new. Black trousers and a leather belt made him look ordinary. He found a pair of glasses from his father's stash of mementos and fooled himself into believing he looked respectable. As he headed out, he glanced in the mirror. A flash of a shadow passed behind his image. His father appeared and dissolved. Joseph found he was staring at his own reflection.

The image left Joseph unsettled. He sensed something amiss, a warning. Within seconds, Joseph had slipped outside and circled back to his shop. Footprints in the clay took him to his mushroom experiments. All the flats had been turned upside down again. This time Joseph smelled kerosene. Anger rose and receded. He stood in silence, his mind clear and attentive.

He found a can of oil emptied and a box of matches. The tracks ended here, too large to be that of Vladimir or Yuri. He didn't pursue the intruder. Instead he found a box of salt in the supply cupboard and dumped it over the kerosene. Someone had left him a message. The salt took the shape of the drizzles. An outline appeared in the shape of the Star of David and an X.

Joseph flexed his fists, released his rage. The warning wasn't enough to scare him. This was more a taunt than a threat. Fire wasn't the intent. Someone knew that Joseph would throw salt on the kerosene. Someone from the old country knew this was what he had learned from his father and grandfather. The intruder had left his calling card.

Joseph arrived at the hospital just before the shift change. Still dressed in his finest, he smelled more like a mechanic than a scientist and looked like he'd just run a marathon. From habit he avoided the main entrance and ducked in through the service door. The fewer people he had to see, the fewer questions he had to answer. He walked the staircase up to the fifth floor and then waited at the elevator to go up another flight. Only authorized staff were allowed on the sixth floor. Rosie stood by the elevator door with a sour face. Joseph smiled and said, "Good thing you don't play poker. Your face tells me whatever is going on isn't good."

Joseph had never seen Rosie's eyes so stern. They held an iron will of control. He waited for Rosie to slip her badge over the keypad. Finally, she swiped her badge, and they took the elevator to the university's research lab.

Rosie's words rushed out. "The lab was broken into last night. The only work messed with was the mushroom experiments. Not the university's secondary test, the blinds, but ones that had already been verified. The paper files are gone. I haven't brought in anyone to investigate yet. I wanted you to know first."

Joseph felt a chill in the air, and he looked up to the air conditioning vent. "Whoever wanted to destroy the experiment knew how to get around security. The culprit came in the old-fashioned way. You have any salt?"

"Why salt, some magic formula?" Rosie went to the cupboard and brought out a container labeled natural iodine. "I brought you here to discover why and who, so go ahead, show me something I don't know."

Joseph shook the iodine on the floor below the air vent. Rosie waited by Joseph's side for the symbols to emerge. The outline of an eight-pointed star and a spider became visible.

"Rosie, this is bad. No need to investigate. The answer is already here."

Rosie said, "I know what the star represents—Russia and the mafia. But what does the spider mean?"

"Since the spider is in the web, facing upward, it means that person is active, ready to harm. The Russian star symbolizes solidarity with the underworld of gangs. Old ways worn as a badge of prison honor."

"You don't seem surprised."

"Someone left another message at my shop, a warning they knew only I could understand. I think you and Miguel unwittingly brought Carmen's demons with you."

"You're scaring me." Rosie grabbed a handful of paper towels and began wiping up the floor. She sprayed a degreaser over the spot and wiped again. "We can't erase the past, can we?"

"No, but it's about time that I acknowledge it exists."

"Then while you do all this acknowledging, Joseph, I suggest you figure out what needs to be done. I don't think Carmen's demons are yours. There is a difference between you and Carmen, isn't there? You two may be related, but you're nothing alike. Carmen killed people. She used and abused her situation. Her vendetta came from a path gone awry."

"I can't speak for someone I never met. I don't know what my grandfather did to trigger this. Maybe it's simply that I exist, that I'm Jewish, that vendettas are transferable. Am I still needed at this meeting?"

Rosie's eyes softened, and the stiffness Joseph had sensed earlier was replaced with a sly smile. "Frank has turned out to be a great advocate for the community. I needed you here to answer the faculty's questions. The lab break-in happened after I sent the note."

Joseph sighed. "Ah, I see that I'm trapped by good intentions. My work has made me visible. I can no longer hide—I'm wanted for my knowledge and hunted down for my past. The world hasn't changed so much over the century. I worry that this meeting might not bode well for those needing a cancer cure. I'm more of a liability for the university."

Rosie leaned forward and waved her hands in front of Joseph's face, erasing his words. "To the contrary, the school needs you more now than ever. All their thinking is tied up in regulations and profit. They need someone who has no ulterior motive, someone who thinks with a history, who doesn't worry about his fame."

"Sounds like they should find someone else. My history may prove to be damaging."

Joseph followed Rosie down the hallway as he peered in the tinted windows on either side. Each of the lab rooms was pressurized, and the technicians inside wore disposable gowns and gloves. Contamination had ruined more experiments than those with successes. The protocols legitimized research, made sure that the science could be repeated. Joseph knew the necessity of proving an idea, but he was more the innovator than the technician.

As Rosie and Joseph entered the conference room, he wondered what value he could give the four scraggly men who sat at the table and the woman wearing a white lab coat who stood with her back facing the door. All eyes turned toward him as Rosie began the introductions. Four voices chimed in with questions, theories, and new ideas. He listened at the intensity more than the content.

Exasperated, Joseph finally broke in, "Excuse me, but none of these questions deal with my present experiments. What is it that you really need from me?"

The woman in the group walked over to Rosie and said, "I gather you haven't told Joseph who has employed us?"

Rosie shook her head. Joseph turned to Rosie. "You haven't been completely truthful, have you? I'll let you explain, before I walk out the door."

Joseph watched Rosie. Instead of her earlier tightness, she seemed transparent, almost ghostlike. Joseph could feel her heartbeat, her breath, and an energy that drew him in.

"I only just found out yesterday, after we spoke at your house, that many people are interested in your mushroom work. I say people because they aren't just scientists. They really aren't just people, but entities. Some are governments, and some are enemies of the state, profiteers. Apparently, the United States government wants to use mushrooms not only for their medicinal properties as antibiotics, antivirals, and immune-boosting compounds, but for protective uses. By that, I mean hazardous waste cleanup, space travel, and for use against threats." Rosie took another breath. Joseph witnessed a shiver run through her body. "These scientists work for the military now. Their paychecks don't come from the university anymore. I, luckily, don't receive a paycheck."

Joseph tasted metal in his mouth. He thought about the soil experiments that cleaned the toxins from Ralph's farm. He thought about his grandfather's journal that had led him to his new discoveries with cancer. The mushroom extracts used in food formulas and against viruses. Even the silk experiments were from ideas his grandfather had seeded. His design of the new airplane wings. Government and military, Russians, did it matter who wanted this information? Abruptly he made a move toward the door, but the woman in the white lab coat touched his arm and said, "I'm afraid that neither you nor Rosie can really walk away from here without a formal commitment."

Joseph glared at the group. "But I can, and I will. I haven't signed anything, and you already have my experiments and the results. Take them. I only have one commitment, and that is to do no harm and to make the world better. I'm out of here."

All four of the other scientists stood up. Rosie walked over to Joseph and opened the door. "Let's go together."

"Sir, could you answer one question? Why can't we find any evidence that you exist? You don't seem to have documentation."

As Joseph closed the door, he smiled and spoke so they could all hear. "You're the researcher, figure that one out yourself."

# CHAPTER 19:
# *Side Effects—"Closed due to illness"*

Over a week had passed since Hannah had cut her hair. She counted the days since Robin's stem cell transplant, remembered the fatigue and nausea Jenna had felt. Day four through day ten had been the worst. But that was so many years ago, Shelly had assured her that advances in science had made it easier for the patient. Besides, they were in a trial that helped with the side effects of the harsh chemo treatments.

It had been Luis's idea to come to the studio. He insisted that she take part in her father's grand plan to expose the community to an alternate view of what equality and diversity meant in this world. It had made sense when he told her to enlist Shelly, but now she had second thoughts.

Hannah stared through the blinds, past the handwritten sign that read, "Closed due to illness," and searched for movement. Shelly had told her that the studio was always open to the dancers for practice. The studio looked lifeless. She rattled the door, and to her surprise it opened. Dark and cool, the room echoed. Each footstep multiplied with a drawn-out tap. She called out Shelly's name, but the hollow room spoke back with only the reflection of her image in the mirrors that lined the walls. She couldn't help but twirl and leap just to see herself transported through air. As she turned to leave, Shelly walked in. Startled, Hannah jumped, and Shelly dropped her purse. They both talked at once until Shelly walked over to Hannah. Hannah noted the dark circles under Shelly's eyes, the slump of her shoulders.

"Sorry, Shelly, I didn't mean to intrude. I thought you'd be here, after I looked for you at the hospital. They said you had checked out. What's wrong?"

Shelly sat down on one of the benches that lined the windows. "Robin is at home. They don't want you at the hospital if they can't fix something. You know hospitals make people sick."

Hannah nodded. She knew the irony. Jenna had never left the hospital, so maybe this was a good sign. "You mean Robin is doing well, well enough to go home?"

Shelly shrugged. "Yes and no. She isn't dying. Her body is trying to regain strength from the stem cell transplant. She is so nauseous that food won't stay down. The chemo destroyed her insides."

"I thought the doctors had something to help with that?"

Shelly raised her hands in exasperation. "For some reason, the trial she is supposed to be on has been stopped. Robin was to be the first trial patient using mushrooms to rid her body of its toxicity. We don't have the money to pay for the trial without our insurance's approval. Rosie came to tell us that the approval by the FDA has been revoked. I've never seen her so angry."

Hannah sat down and wrapped her arms around Shelly. They stayed that way, swaying back and forth, until Shelly broke away.

"I came here to get some music for Robin. I've cancelled classes so I can be at home full time. My husband can't miss any more work. I have to get back." Shelly sighed. "But what are you doing here?"

"Oh, it isn't important," Hannah replied. "You've got too much on your plate to bother with my idea. It was just something Luis and I were working on for my father's project. Can I ask you a question without you getting offended?"

"Shoot."

"How much money do you need?"

"Don't go there, Hannah. I asked Rosie that same question, and she got funny on me. Normally she tells me the truth even when

I don't want to hear it. But I have a feeling that the insurance not paying isn't the only problem. She rattled off issues with liability and funding for research being cut off. She was pretty upset."

"Well, if it was just money, we could do a fund-raiser. I'm sure people would pay to see a dance performance. We could combine that with my father's project or something." Hannah pleaded, "You can't give up."

"I'm tired right now. But keep your idea for later. I've got to get back to Robin, but maybe in a few days you can come visit. She is so susceptible to germs, she can't be out in public. I gave you my business card, but let me write my home phone number and address down. Just close the door when you are done."

Hannah felt sick to her stomach. She had an odd feeling that the trial's cancellation had something to do with Joseph's experiments. Rosie had asked her to watch the property for a reason. Hannah asked herself, *What have I missed?* Joseph had convinced her that all was okay. So much for understanding.

Even when she tried to make a difference, it didn't work. She cringed thinking of the newspaper's headlines after the photographs had caught her picking blueberries. Someone would have a field day if they found her inside the dance studio, a burglar as well as a privileged owner's daughter, stealing others' jobs. She closed her eyes as she imagined another headline: "Henderson's daughter breaks into dance studio, steals dance steps rather than pay."

Shelly had been so hopeful at the hospital. Hannah hated the deflation, the helplessness. She took a deep breath and concentrated until she felt a mental push from Rosie and Joseph, as if they could influence her thoughts. Neither one seemed to care about obstacles. So what was her problem? Hannah looked around the studio as if the answer would come from the walls. She imagined all the dancers gliding across the floor. Maybe she *should* steal some steps.

Hannah remembered her first time sitting up in the tree above

Joseph's home, when she had listened to the water's rhythm on his stone path. Nothing else had calmed her, bypassed her anxious thoughts so she could talk without a stutter. Hannah walked over to the CD player and rummaged through Shelly's collection. Her first selection was from Africa, the next from Puerto Rico. Both had a steady drumbeat, similar patterns that collapsed in on each other. She followed with her body and elongated the rhythms into jumps and leaps. Next, she listened to some Russian music, which seemed more chaotic, frenzied. If her hair had been longer, it would have swirled out of control as she jerked her head. Then Native American music calmed her with drums again.

Hannah dropped back on the bench, overwhelmed with exhaustion from dancing. Over an hour had passed, and her brain and body vibrated with the codes of all these cultures. The expenditure of energy told her so much about what she didn't know. She gathered up the discs and wrote a note to Shelly:

*I've borrowed some music to work on a cultural project for my dad. If you understand peoples' rhythms, you'll understand them. Maybe this is the key.*

As Hannah left, she noticed Vladimir and Yuri on the sidewalk. She dipped back inside the dance studio until the two passed. She kept the urge to follow them in check as she tried to decide which voice she should listen to. Rosie's instructions were to watch out for problems at Joseph's home. Did his home include the town? Joseph viewed Vladimir and Yuri as innocents caught in a maze of issues. He'd push for caution. Luis would be furious with her for interfering.

She paused just long enough for them to cross the railroad tracks and for the traffic light to turn red. By the time the light had changed, the two were gone. Relieved, Hannah continued with her errands, ending up at the Food Co-Op. She meandered through the fresh produce aisles, checking the local fruit. Just as she feared, the usual bins filled with Henderson Farm's berries remained empty.

"Excuse me, sir, could you tell me where the Henderson blueberries are?"

"Oh, well, I'm not sure what's happening with the boycotts. They're experiencing some delivery problems. I can give you a map to the farm. Otherwise you can buy the local berries from Whatcom County."

"I'm just curious why the co-op would boycott the blueberries."

"Miss, I can't speak to that. I just know the Henderson bins are empty."

Hannah nodded, pretended that the answer sat well with her. She looked at the organic lettuce, the corn, and the potatoes. All the produce laid out in neat colorful rows had been picked by machinery. Machines can't boycott; they don't need to be fed, housed, or educated. Mechanize the world and the voices would be silenced. On a whim, she went over to the office.

"Can I help you?"

"Yes, I'd like to get an application for work."

"You can get that online. We have all the job openings listed, and our requirements. Just print it off and fill it out. There'll be lots of candidates. When you bring it back, make sure you look presentable, and you'll do fine."

Hannah thanked the woman and headed out the door. She thought of Stella working in the fields humming as she filled up her bucket with berries. Stella didn't have a computer or a printer. She wondered if Stella looked the part. Or for that matter, did she? Hannah glanced at her image in the window as she walked out. A sign in the corner read, "Equal Opportunity Employer." Yes, give a person clothes, education, a computer, and a printer, and we will consider you eligible. The whole idea of *equal* seemed erroneous.

As she walked, her ideas on rhythm and equality gelled. Listening to the variety of dance music at the studio, it had struck Hannah that each form was beautiful. None were equal or better. Just different. When she first started dancing with Luis, he had tried to explain the various rhythms of salsa, mambo, rumba, conga, and Afro-Uruguayan music. Something about the clave pattern. He had made her laugh when he had told her about alignment and direction.

"Think of it as if you were walking to Vancouver, B.C., from Sedro Woolley. You're walking north. And if you are walking from Vancouver to Sedro Woolley, you're walking south. But if you put your left shoe on your right foot, *cruzado*, no matter which direction you walked, it would be awkward. When you move from side to side, you have to be aligned."

They had tried dancing with their shoes crossed and fell into one another. Hannah blushed thinking about what had happened afterward. Luis's answer had been to dance barefooted and without clothes. She realized how aligned they were. Not the same, not equal. The Equal Opportunity sign at the Food Co-Op was misaligned.

Back outside, Hannah hurried through the last of her errands. If she wasn't careful, she'd miss her bus. By the time she had walked to the bus stop, she had only five minutes to spare. She spotted Vladimir and Yuri again, running down an alleyway. An older man dressed in black pants and a black t-shirt was in hot pursuit. A few minutes later, Miguel surfaced from the same alleyway. He waved to her as if it were the most natural of occurrences. As she boarded the bus, the boys reappeared, doubled over in pain. Miguel hustled them into a midnight-blue pickup. Her father was at the wheel.

# CHAPTER 20: *Bent Out of Shape*

Luis remembered each day as a blur, up before the sun rose, down after it set. But he couldn't recall when he had last rested. Although he bedded down at the cabin at night, he barely slept. Joseph failed to appear when he was there. At first, he dismissed his absence due to conflicting work schedules, but now he felt Joseph's presence everywhere, as if he were hidden in plain view.

He rolled out of bed, threw on his jeans, a t-shirt, and grabbed a bowl of cereal. A large bowl of blueberries sat in the middle of the table. As he tossed them on top of his cereal, he realized they were freshly picked. He looked for more traces of Joseph. He found a book about silk lying open by Joseph's reading chair.

Even the birds still slept as he walked to the shop. When he opened the door, a flood of light blinded him. In Joseph's clean area, where his stone sculptures remained covered, Miguel had cordoned off a section where he carved small pieces of driftwood. Every day since they had met at the beach, Luis had found him in the shop. Today his head hovered over a miniature scene that reminded Luis of the village where he had been born. Unlike topographic maps, where the mountains and trees lie on top of a flat area, Miguel carved a *worldscape* out of the driftwood's knots and cavities. Embossed, the people resembled animals, and the fields rolled as if the wind had come through and confused the land with the ocean. A fisherman's boat rode the waves of produce. A fish flew out of a picker's hands. All the people's faces mirrored two or three ethnicities. Eyes, lips, cheekbones, all combined so that one face became a multitude of faces.

Stepping quietly so as not to disturb Miguel's steady hand, Luis whispered his greeting: "Good morning. Looks like you've been here all night. Can I get you something to eat?"

Miguel looked up. His eyes flickered his hello. "I'll get something to eat after I finish. I lose my appetite when I concentrate. Best natural diet there is."

"You haven't seen Joseph by chance?"

"No, not today."

"I'm worried. Something is going on. We've gone days without connecting. Usually Joseph leaves me notes, or we catch up at dinner. I have this eerie sense that he's around but hiding. Why would he do that?"

Miguel put down his chipping knife and turned toward Luis. "I don't know, but he might just be taking a low profile. The break-in was a minor annoyance. Joseph took too many risks lately. He forgot about history."

Luis stepped back as if he'd been punched. "Are you talking about me?"

Miquel shook his head. "Why would you jump to that conclusion? If anything was amiss with you, Joseph wouldn't disappear. He defends others."

"You haven't answered any of my questions. Do you know where he is?"

Miguel walked to the other side of the shop where Joseph worked on his latest project, a lightweight wing. Luis followed. Where there had been a loom with woven silk threads and sets of blueprints for a wing and a hybrid plane, now stood a clear space, swept clean. Luis remembered Joseph's annoyance and the first of his many tales, almost lectures, of his past. Luis cringed thinking back on the talk about Russia and the pogroms. How he had erroneously compared his parent's deportation to the Jewish plight.

"Miguel, where did Joseph's wing prototype go, his experiment with using the silk weave?"

"Calm down, Luis. He took them. Said that he didn't want another invention to get in the wrong hands and fail."

Luis exhaled slowly, but the hairs on his arms rose. Hannah had mentioned the end to Joseph's mushroom experiments and how disappointed Shelly had been at the cancellation of Robin's trials. Something had changed Joseph's life and work. "He must have been here during the night. Where did he go?"

"I'm just a visitor here. I brought him bad news, a warning. But I'm not really in his confidence. He trusts me only as a friend of Rosie. Even Rosie keeps secrets from me. I doubt she knows where he went. Sometimes it is safer not to know."

"You said that if this was about me, Joseph would defend me." Frustrated, Luis continued, "Shouldn't we try to help Joseph? Who would want to harm a man who only thinks of helping others?"

"That is a very naïve question coming from someone who was beaten for no apparent reason except for perhaps your ethnicity, or color, or that you were just there. Joseph came to this country a long time ago. Those who know him, value him. The problem isn't who he helps, it is what he represents, what he won't do. You left the fields, not because you didn't like the work but because your parents were deported and you hated the infighting."

Luis paced as he half listened. He wasn't as naïve as Miguel thought. He had been living with Joseph for half a year. He knew that if there was a problem, friends like Frank would help. Joseph lived away from people for a reason. Luis knew that Joseph had been more visible because he was there and because of Hannah. If Joseph had taken a risk that endangered his life, Luis blamed himself.

"I need to talk with Joseph. I'm living under his roof with all his support. His problems are my problems. You can't share a space and not care. Just so you know, living as an immigrant, you don't know who to trust. I never had that problem with Joseph."

Miguel nodded. "Do what you have to do, but remember that Joseph isn't on any particular side. He doesn't represent good or bad. He only tries to make life better. Joseph sets his bar high, but his ideals aren't protected by laws."

Luis looked over again at the vacant area where the silk wing had been. He remembered the book about silk sitting by Joseph's chair. That had to be a clue. Either Joseph was messing with him, or he really wanted Luis to understand something. "I forgot something up at the cabin. Will you be here long, or should I meet you at the beach? Hannah will be there this afternoon to help. Oh, I forgot. She said she saw you and her father pick up Vladimir and Yuri the other day. Is this another incident that I should keep to myself?"

Miguel turned away and went back to his workbench. "The boys got into trouble. Mr. Henderson and I were lucky to be there. They are okay. I'll see you later."

Realizing he wouldn't get any more information, Luis ran back to the cabin. He was sure about one thing: Joseph had been progressively teaching him his trades. First the mechanics of motors, gardening, and gradually, he showed him the mushroom experiments and then his ideas on creating a lighter airplane wing using silk. It wasn't easy to think like Joseph. He made weird connections in his brain. Luis slowed down when he got to the stone pathway.

On his first visit to Joseph's cabin, Joseph had explained the significance of the pathway: *I don't have an address where people send me letters. I don't have a phone. But this pathway is a message board, for me, the community, for the world. Nothing gets erased.* Luis kneeled closer to the stones. He noted the embedded swastika placed there a few weeks ago. Joseph chose to leave it, even with its negative energy. Someone had painted flowers around the edges of the sharp angular black lines so that the symbol appeared as steps moving upward. Like an art piece of a never-ending staircase.

As Luis approached the entrance, his foot caught on the lip of the doorway, dislodging one of the ornamental stones. He looked down at the hole and saw a stream of light filtering upward. Puzzled, he walked around the perimeter of the cabin. He didn't see a foundation or any indication of a basement. Back inside he walked the various ramps that connected bedroom to kitchen and kitchen to living room. He listened to the floor for a change in density, a creak to indicate a loose board.

Luis felt a cool breeze. Excited at the prospect of finding a hidden trap door, he turned to instead see the front door open. A man and woman stood in the threshold carrying a basket of bread and fresh vegetables. Startled, Luis jumped.

"You must be Luis, Joseph's best apprentice. We're your neighbors down the way."

Extending his hand, he covered his disappointment with politeness. "You're correct, I'm Luis." He shrugged. "As far as I know I'm the only apprentice, but I'll still accept the compliment. Joseph isn't here right now. Was he expecting you?"

"No, Joseph was at our house, and now he is off again. I'm Ralph, and this is my wife, Sharon. I guess he hasn't talked that much to you about us?"

Relief washed over Luis. Joseph was safe. "Oh no, I'm mean, yes, I just didn't put it together. You're the friends he's helping with the contaminated soil and working with Sharon because of some illness. But if you knew Joseph wasn't here, why come?"

"Joseph told us to bring you some food. He said you'd be so busy that you might forget to eat or sleep. He didn't want you to worry."

"So he isn't coming back?" Luis stared at the floor, the ramps. He walked over to the doorway and peered down the space where he had seen the stream of light. Darkness. Whatever relief he had momentarily felt, vanished.

Sharon walked past Luis and set the basket on the kitchen table.

"Come back inside. You won't find Joseph in that hole. Just cover it up. After I fix you something solid to eat, Ralph will update you on Joseph."

Ralph moved closer to Luis. "According to Joseph, life isn't just what is in front of you. As farmers we know stuff about nature's ways, but Joseph reads nature differently. Take his miracle use of mushrooms for example. Those of us who live this far upriver know the woods, but he has sensors for the pathways, roots, stumps, and the living holes. Joseph is never far."

Luis looked at his watch. He had to leave for work. "Sorry, but I can't stay long. I have to get out to the airport for my day job. But I'll take some of that bread for my lunch."

Ralph shook his head. "No need to worry about the gardens. Frank will see that they get watered and weeded. He'll even mow."

"I don't want to sound ungrateful, but I'm used to paying my way . . ."

Sharon handed him a sandwich made from her bread, tomato, and homemade goat cheese. Their silence puzzled Luis, as did the cool air that continued to flow through the room. He'd forgotten why he had come back to the cabin, he'd forgotten about Joseph's book on silk, the missing airplane wing, and even his own circumstances. He watched through the kitchen window as Miguel loaded Joseph's truck with tools. Luis finally turned back to Ralph. "Sorry, I didn't understand. You're here to tell me that nothing is the same anymore. Today isn't work as usual."

The smile across Ralph's face and the twinkle in Sharon's eyes seemed odd. They nodded, and Ralph went to the kitchen table. "Take a look at this." Ralph rolled out a hand-sketched map of the woods. "Joseph said you were a fast learner but an innocent who looked too linearly at the world. Since we've known Joseph—and that's longer than you twice over—he's found solutions to problems we didn't know existed. He's plain spoken. His mind focuses narrowly, but the results echo into all aspects of our life. Don't worry about getting paid for your work. Wages only buy what is sold in stores. For the most part up here in the hills, we find ways to exchange goods and services."

"The only part of what you just said that didn't make sense to me was that Joseph speaks plainly. Even though I'm fluent in English, I have to think on each and every word he says. Maybe I'll understand eventually."

Luis took a bite of his sandwich and bent over the map.

## CHAPTER 21: *Silo—If you don't know me, I'm still hidden.*

With the hatch propped open with a pole used by apple pickers, a tiny stream of light shone down on the makeshift workbench. Joseph hummed to himself as he embedded strands of silk through pin-sized holes on the wing frame. The success of his DNA alterations changed the filament size and strength. Now each thread was the equivalent of over three thousand filaments, spun so tightly that the strength would double that of the Kevlar composite that would cover it.

Holed up in the concrete silo, Joseph dealt with the tensions of life just as he always had. A low profile kept him safe. Years ago, when the cement factory left the area, he discovered the empty silos. It hadn't taken much to convert it into a workshop and safe house. Ventilation had been a problem, but the dry space and even temperature made the area perfect for living as well as his experiments.

The metal-framed staircase zigzagged through the silo, so he could access three stories. The lower two were used for living, and without windows, the only direct light came from the top hatch, where he made room for his work. A door midway up the silo provided the lone entrance. The ladder to the door hooked onto the inside curve, and unless someone knew to look for it, the door blended into the sandy color of the silo and the *R* of the word *Concrete* painted on the outside.

Hiding had never been Joseph's intention, but no matter how much he believed in change, history repeated itself. It had been over ten years since he had used the silo. Even as he hummed, he worried that he would run out of time. Not that it mattered to him how long he lived, but he needed time to fulfill his great-grandfather's promise. The consequences of pogroms, his great-grandfather's flight to freedom, weighed heavy on his heart, as Joseph had no heirs, no one who felt the pull as he did, to do good.

He marveled at the silk's strength and flexibility. Even as he worked with the tensile, modifying the worms' DNA ever so slightly so that the silk strains resisted stresses, his thoughts were on medical uses for the silk. With each new idea for invention, he felt an internal tug-of-war between furthering the overall health and wellness of those around him and the tightening pulls from outside controls. He wanted nothing to do with those who used money and judgment as their measure of importance. As if profit had become a religion.

His father had once showed him a string puppet. How each pull on the string moved the puppet up or down, and that the puppet couldn't move without the puppeteer. It was the puppeteer's motives that created the show. It struck him as odd that as long as he was invisible his projects would succeed. But the meeting with the university proved that his involvement impeded his mushroom research. He had disappointed Rosie. He had disappointed the patients in the cancer trial. But he wouldn't be pulled by someone else's motives. He couldn't change who he was any more than create paperwork to validate his existence. So much for progress. So much for strings.

After he tied that last silk thread, he stowed the miniature wing in an envelope and sealed it. Joseph heard footsteps on the metal staircase, a prewarning of sorts. Minutes later the door opened, and Frank walked in.

"No need to ask me if anyone saw me coming. I parked my rig over on the other side of the highway and walked. You doing okay?"

Joseph smiled. He could depend on Frank to bring him back from his lofty thoughts. Frank understood his compulsion to right wrongs. Frank's sister's actions still haunted the town, yet Frank walked with his head level with everyone. No hiding for him.

"*Okay* is as good a word as any. I'm keeping busy. Will you have any problem getting the wing over to the composite factory?"

"I still have my connections over there. No one faults me anymore for dumping the waste." Frank shrugged. "They now see me as a vigilante, looking out for their property. Besides, it isn't like I'm taking anything from them. Just dropping something off. I'm the delivery boy."

Joseph liked Frank's simplicity. "Yes, but you don't go in through the front door." Before he continued, Joseph turned the envelope over, placed another swath of packing tape around the edges. He fidgeted with the scissors and tape, a battle of sticky wills. "I'm letting them use my research, but I don't want anything to do with it."

Frank stared up at the hatch and then walked over to Joseph's bench. "You aren't okay, are you? You're talking like you're afraid. I've never seen you like this. What's got you so shaken?"

"Could be lots of things. I just decided that it's safer to work without ties. Less problems for the people I care about."

"You can get away with those thoughts with everyone else, but you and I know that you're worried about Luis and Hannah. You can't protect them from the world. Besides, they can take care of themselves. What besides the mushroom project has set you off?"

Joseph sat down on the workbench. He held his head between his hands, elbows on his knees. When he looked back at Frank, he wiped a tear from the corner of his good eye and made an effort to smile. "Just a moment of remembering and being tired. Don't worry."

Frank walked around Joseph as if he were on display and finally answered, "My life's pretty good now, compared to when my sister's bullying ruled me. I have fewer things and more friends. I can't just let you fret on your own. Seems to me you don't mind my past, but you mind yours. What are you going to do about it?"

"That's the million-dollar question." Joseph tucked away the paper design of the silk wing. "I thought my ingenuity would cure the world of problems. Just invent solutions and life would improve. I forgot about human hubris."

Frank nodded. "If by hubris, you mean greed, I know about that. Molly was worse than a dictator."

"Ah, but that's where it gets sticky, Frank. It isn't the dictators I'm worried about. Everyday common folk don't see that they've devised rules and barriers to exclude and hurt. Sure, I'm angry about the switch in funding from the university to the government for the cancer research. But I don't want my work to get into the wrong hands."

Joseph stood up. A stream of sunlight came through the hatch and fell across his gnarled knuckles. He turned his hands over so that his calloused palms curved upward.

Frank shifted his weight from one leg to the other. "You're a worker, with the physical pains to prove it."

"I don't know. When I read the news, I question all our efforts. Look at what's happening in Syria now, all those displaced people running from one border to the next. Dying because they've taken a chance with smugglers and no country will take them in. It isn't just our southern border that has an immigrant problem. The Middle East, Central America, and Europe, just switch it around. My great-grandfather was lucky. He escaped by running along the train routes, slipped out before borders were shut. He wasn't shipped off to a concentration camp. You're right. I am afraid. Afraid that even here in the United States, we reject people based on economic need. That's just a lazy way of saying some people aren't worth saving. Seems like rules change based on the colors of someone's skin or their beliefs. We seem to have a convenient case of amnesia."

"Dang it, that's ancient history. What does it have to do with you hiding out today?"

Joseph shook his head. "I seem to be running from the Russians and my own government. The break-ins all come back to me. They're my fault. I wish I could . . ." Joseph trailed off midthought. He stood up and handed Frank the sealed envelope with the wing. "Enough of my self-pity. I voiced my opinion, but it's a dead end. I get stuck on a closed idea sometimes. My father always kept the good thoughts close at hand and quickly let go of the negative ones. Something about not wasting energy on what you don't like."

Frank took the envelope. "Where do you want me to deliver this?"

"Same place as always. The new research lab. There's a young guy there, Rex, with red hair and freckles. He reminds me that we really can't figure out nature. Ever since he was a kid, he has studied pigment and the genetics of redheads. He can trace skin variations all the way back to the migration from Africa. I'll put my faith in him. One day he'll change the world."

"I didn't know freckles were a problem in the world."

Joseph laughed. "They aren't. But Africa doesn't have enough sanitation or water. My redheaded friend is one of the engineers who designed a waste-filtering system that gets clean water from composting toilets. Fixing a problem for something we all have in common."

Frank turned to leave. "You have to admire a guy who makes shit look good. Don't fret about this human hubris part. They have mirrors for that. I'll make the delivery and get back with you. Will you be here or some other spot?"

"I'll let Ralph know. I sent him over to talk with Luis and reassure him that I'm okay."

Frank nodded. "I didn't see Luis at the airport, so I guess he got the message from Ralph that I'd be helping out. The boy doesn't take kindly to shirking responsibilities. His parents taught him well."

Joseph felt a twinge of sadness. "I had hoped to have more time to show him stuff."

Frank shook his head. "You're not making sense. Time remains the same. That is, unless you are planning on disappearing permanently. I know Luis won't be going anywhere."

"Oh, Frank, it's not what I plan that worries me." Joseph made his decision. "No more hiding."

Joseph listened to Frank's fading steps echo through the silo. He hummed as he packed his tools in a satchel. His idyllic life would not return. First, he had to find Rosie and make sure that she would be able to continue Robin's clinical trials. Only Rosie could find a loophole in the medical protocol. Next, he had to protect Yuri and Vladimir from breaking the law and getting ahead of themselves. Word on the street was that they'd been beaten for not following orders. Miguel had cautioned him that the gangs wouldn't take their defection lightly.

As he plotted out his route downriver, he mentally went through a checklist of who to visit. Although Joseph believed more in the laws of nature than any form of government or religion, he knew that the only way for people to get along was to have a set of basic rules that everyone understood. The promise of his father to his grandfather and his own promise to "do good" in the world was a stepping-off place, but not enough.

Joseph knew of only a few individuals who could master the written word, give an idea form, and disrupt engrained biases. Oddly enough they were never visible. The whole idea of visibility made him laugh. Frank had been right about mirrors.

By the time Joseph had sealed up the silo, the sun beat straight down on the highway, creating heat waves. Most of the cars slowed down as the mirages played with their vision. No one focused on a guy making his way along the side of the road. He crossed over near the airport and dipped down a path that lead nowhere. The dead end stopped at a mound of debris, which hid a small river kayak. Joseph lowered himself in with his satchel. He hugged the shoreline and let the Skagit River sweep him along.

He made three stops at each of the small towns: Birdsview, Hamilton, and Lyman. One at the local bar, one at the post office, and one at the daycare center. In Mount Vernon, he stowed the kayak at Edgewater Park, behind the dumpsters. Joseph shadow-played with cars and buildings until he made his way over to the Food Co-Op. He found a table in the back of the restaurant, sat down, and waited.

Most of the tables near the doorway were crowded with either mothers chatting with friends, young professionals sitting with open laptops and discussing business, and those there just to feed an empty belly. Laughter from the ice cream counter filtered toward Joseph. He noticed that all the young kids looked the same. Their heavy backpacks, their holey jeans, and caps worn backward created a sense of oneness. Power in anonymity. The real shopping for groceries was behind the restaurant. Signs declared in large print: Sustainable, Free Range, Organic, Home Grown, Local, and Natural. Displayed in smaller print, the various prices reflected a complicated formula that increased the appearance of value. Joseph wondered if he was similarly valued.

Without a wristwatch to confer, Joseph people-watched for what seemed like a half hour. Anxious to get his ideas moving, he kept his eye on the door. A blur of wild black curls and a swirl of pastel greens, blues, and violet announced Rosie's arrival. Her dress reflected the tropics, muted by a white sweater and a leather shoulder bag. She walked with authority toward Joseph. Miguel ambled in behind her, more subdued in his stained khaki pants and black t-shirt. His eyes shifted as his body idled forward. As he pulled out chairs, Miguel had already cased the room. Joseph appreciated that he wasn't the only person scrutinizing his safety.

Joseph reached over to each of them and squeezed their hands. "Glad you could both come. I need to apologize for disappearing. Call it a moment's lapse in thinking, but when issues become complicated and I get confused, I've learned to pause. An old habit that has served me well since I was a kid. Besides, anger and frustration seemed all my brain could handle. At least now, I'm not fretting, as Frank has so aptly put it."

Rosie pushed a stack of papers forward. "I've been working on the grant papers. The university is bound by their original contract, at least for this trial. Your name isn't mentioned, only the description of the research. I will hold them to their commitment. I won't let Robin and Shelly down."

Joseph smiled. "I knew you'd read between the lines and find a way to make this work with insurances and liability. Their professors can take the credit, as it seems I wouldn't have gotten it anyway. I've come to realize, with the help of Frank's prodding, something mothers have always known: once a child is born, you must set it free. Once I launch a project, I can't control the world and how it uses my work. I'll do my best to educate and guide."

Miguel interrupted, "You're not out of the woods yet. You've raised some eyebrows in the government on your citizenship, and Yuri and Vladimir are now considered outlaws by the local police and the gangs. They can't help you without getting beat up, and if they retaliate, the real law will put them in jail. I'm waiting to hear how you will educate us out of this conundrum."

Joseph took a deep breath. He looked at Miguel and Rosie with his good eye, a smug smile on his face. "I'm working on it. Rosie, you remember Russell, don't you, from the Concrete Fly-In? He knows everyone in the county. I bet he can still muster some hidden support along the river. Ralph visits him often now that he can't get around. I've just talked with the most influential people in the towns along the way—a teacher, a bartender, and the postmaster. I'm not sure the community will be ready for their basic premise on decency and humanity. They have a philosophy of life that goes beyond basic education to wisdom."

Before Rosie could answer, Hannah's mother walked into the restaurant. Joseph waited to see if she noticed them. She seemed nervous, fidgeted with her handwoven grocery bag, and kept her head bent. Joseph knew something was amiss—it set off alarms for such a well-known member of the community to display the classic signs of fear. He and Rosie both stood up, and she called out, "Mrs. Henderson, when you're done shopping, come join us for a cup of coffee."

# CHAPTER 22: *Change the Dialogue*

Frank left the composite factory without a hitch. No one had paid any attention to his entrance. Each of the workers, intent on their projects, oblivious to their surroundings, kept their focus. Frank had to hand it to Joseph—his keen sense of duty and ability to ingratiate himself to the strangest of companions made odd sense. Rex, the freckled lad, had been expecting him. With a nod and a handshake, he accepted the package and handed Frank a note that read, "Shit happens. Stay away from the fumes."

A funny note that Frank took seriously. He couldn't tell if it was a warning, but Joseph would accept the words as such. Frank shook his head, knowing that everything counted, even sarcasm. His encounter with Mrs. Henderson puzzled him even more than the message. He had found her wandering the streets of Burlington in a daze. Worried, he had parked his car and followed her into a tavern. The tavern was on the seedier side of town and he decided that it wasn't a drink she was after; for that she could have gone to a fancy restaurant.

Frank put his talent of eavesdropping to use. As Mrs. Henderson made her way to a dark booth in the back, he shadowed her and sat at the table adjacent to the booth. Just after she sat down, the postmaster from the town of Hamilton entered and took a place next to Mrs. Henderson. Frank crossed his fingers that this wasn't a lovers' meeting. He didn't want to know anyone's personal business, only the information that would help or hinder his friends. As Joseph's neighbor and Hannah's mother, Mrs. Henderson's actions mattered.

There was nothing to hear as Mrs. Henderson sat stiffly, rearranging the paper napkin, wiping her hands on her pants and avoiding touching the table. It wasn't until the tavern owner from Birdsview and the head teacher at the daycare center in Lyman arrived that any noise came from the booth. The head teacher took the lead: "I guess we all come from upriver and know each other by sight, but it would be good if we introduced ourselves. You can call me Marmalade. That's what the kids at the center call me." Frank noted that the teacher looked as sweet as her name.

The tavern owner spoke next. "This isn't where I usually hang out, but I guess all taverns have some similarities. You can call me Bill."

The postmaster took longer to speak. "If I seem nervous, I am. I should be at an AA meeting right now, but Joseph convinced me that this was more important. My coworkers call me John."

Mrs. Henderson was the last to speak. She spoke so softly that Frank strained to hear her. "My name is Connie. I don't recall meeting any of you, but here we are. Joseph assured me that I could be of help. Do any of you know why we are here?"

Frank watched everyone lean in to the table. Their voices lowered to a whisper. Frank moved his chair to face the group so that he could read their lips just in case he missed hearing a word. The whispers quickly changed into a buzz as each person talked at once. Finally, Marmalade put her hand up. "We won't get anywhere if we continue like this. Why don't we each describe how we can help Joseph?"

Even though Mrs. Henderson appeared not to know the purpose of the meeting, she had come prepared. With a notebook in hand, she took notes. After a few minutes, she cleared her throat. "Okay, I think I've summarized Joseph's intention. He believes that our community is stuck in a place that is hurtful to those living on the fringes. He wants us to show everyone the value of the hidden people. Each of us has been chosen because . . . Excuse me, but this is where I get lost. I can't imagine why I'm here. I'm one of the people who is biased, or at least that's how I'm often perceived."

A silence fell on the group. Frank shuddered at Mrs. Henderson's self-analysis. Most of the town saw her as stuck-up, wealthy, and privileged. Everyone knew she lost a child to cancer. Her good deeds were accepted, but her need for recognition made her acts seem more self-serving than generous. No one had ever seen her heart.

Marmalade took Mrs. Henderson's hand. "You can take notes later. I think we're all missing the point. Joseph called us together to tease out the best in all of us. For some reason, he has placed value on our abilities. I see kids from an early age when they are pliable. I see them struggle to find themselves. My job is to treat them as individuals, to pull out their best and show them how to share, interact, and create with others who are not the same. Connie, this isn't about you. It's about Joseph and the problems he's facing. Joseph is in trouble. Trouble that is brewing in our communities."

Frank almost jumped up from his table when he saw Mrs. Henderson's tears. This woman might be spoiled, but she had feelings, and she had brains. To see her so vulnerable and out of character left a sour taste in his mouth.

"I'm sorry. I was thinking of myself. Joseph is my neighbor. We have a large cabin next to his place. I hated when my daughter Hannah would go over there. She seemed to prefer Joseph's company to mine. I forbade her, but she went anyway. Now I let Hannah go there. I don't know why, but I do."

John took a drink of water. "None of us are angels. Joseph knows that we get second chances. It's a test for me to even be in a tavern. I agree with Marmalade. The post office is the hub of a small town. Most people have a post office box, either because they don't have a mailbox or don't want anyone to know where they live. Fewer money orders go out to families who live outside our borders. More money comes and goes through overseas banks now. Legally I have to track amounts and places for the government. So far, all seems legal, but I have a sense that some of the money is dirty. When people send or receive the money orders, there are no smiles, no chit-chat of how they are going to spend it or how happy their families will be to receive it."

Bill looked around at the tavern's crowd. "Don't you get it, Joseph knows we see the raw stuff of the community. We're the observers, and we solve problems. My tavern is busier than this one. More people drinking their sadness away. I have a system of honor at my bar. A glass pickle jar sits on the counter filled with cash. It isn't the tip jar. On the outside of the pickle jar, it says, 'If you're in a pickle, ask for help. If you need some cash, it is yours. Place an IOU and return the money for someone else to use.' The jar has money in it that my customers donate. Sometimes customers sleep in the back of the tavern. You'd be surprised at the variety of skin colors, languages, and jobs they have. It isn't always the poor or the migrants who need help. Sometimes money isn't the issue. You can't legislate compassion, or decency, or tolerance, or accountability."

Frank put a dollar on the table and headed to the door. Just as he was on his way out, Mrs. Henderson lit up as if a bulb had flashed on in her head. Smiled at the group. "Joseph is a sly one. He knows my talent is to raise money and get attention."

Outside of the tavern, an inebriated old lady stumbled along with a grocery cart filled with aluminum cans. Her eyes held Frank's. Normally Frank would walk on, but this time he smiled. Her face lit up, and she pulled her shoulders back and waved. He thought of his mean sister, Molly, who had made it her life's mission to make others invisible. He had almost disappeared within his sister's grasp. It didn't take much to give presence. His simple acknowledgement of the old lady somehow transformed her.

Frank hadn't wanted to leave the tavern meeting, but Mrs. Henderson didn't seem to need his protection, and she wasn't on his errand list. He had two more stops to make for Joseph: the courthouse to pick up an application for citizenship and the hospital to check on Robin's condition. Joseph had a plan, but Frank wasn't even sure what problem he was trying to solve.

A protest outside of the courthouse blocked the sidewalk and entrance. Frank circled around the group and went in by the back door. Silence filled the hallways. His steps echoed off closed doors as he walked through the lobby. Frank looked on the shelf racks along the wall for citizenship forms. Where they should have been, a handwritten sign stated that you could download them from a website or request them from a clerk inside. Frank recognized the sign for what it was: one more barrier, a way to keep people out. Any extra step was a deterrent for those challenged by literacy, economics, or fear.

Frank had no such handicaps and walked up to the counter. "Nice to see you, Sheila. Looks like you're having a quiet day. Doesn't anyone need the government's help?"

Sheila looked up, startled, until recognition hit. "My, my, you clean up well, Frank. It's been a while. Sorry to hear about your mother. I'd like to say the same about your sister, but I'm glad you're free of her—nothing bad intended. What brings you in here?"

"I do miss my mother. She was kinder than most people I know. Anyhow, I'm looking for the papers to file for citizenship. The rack outside is empty. But you do have the forms, don't you?"

Somewhat flustered, Sheila bent her head down. "My boss says I have to ask some questions first."

Sheila had known Frank since high school. With all the articles in the newspaper about his life, he figured there wasn't much she didn't know. "What do you need?"

"Are you a natural-born citizen?"

Frank smiled, lowered his voice. "You know I am."

"Then what do you need the form for?"

"I just need twenty booklets, Sheila."

Silence. "I might have to get my supervisor. You know they're picketing outside for equal pay on the farms. Everyone feels like foreigners are taking our jobs. Why look for trouble?" Frank sighed and looked at Sheila with a furrowed brow. "We have enough issues with citizens, why bring in . . ." She paused mid-sentence.

"I don't mean to cause a problem for you. We should get together for coffee sometime. My mother always said there wasn't a reason in the world not to be nice."

Sheila broke into a smile. "Forget my supervisor. Coffee sometime would be nice."

Frank mimed tipping his hat, and then he took the twenty booklets and walked out. "I'll look forward to it."

Drained, Frank hoped that the last stop at the hospital would be less contentious. With Joseph in hiding, he was forced to do his good work, but Frank preferred living his quiet life at the airfield in Concrete.

. . . . .

He found Robin in her hospital bed; her door open. Three other beds had drapes surrounding them. There was an eerie feeling to the quiet. Joseph had told him that Rosie would be there with Robin, but the room was empty except for the small girl staring out in space. "Hi, Robin, I'm a friend of Rosie's. How are you?"

"Rosie had to leave. Some emergency at the research lab. I wish she was here. They removed all my friends. I was only home for one day, but Rosie came to our house to get me. She said it would be okay. Even better since my mom had to go to work. I'm worried."

Frank closed his eyes. He could walk into any room, be invisible, deliver messages, and get any job done that worked with his hands, but kids weren't his specialty. "Do you need to talk with the nurses? I could go get one. I saw them milling around the snack room. They don't know I'm here because I waited for them to take a break."

"No, the nurses can't fix what bothers me. I'm worried about the other kids that used to be in the room. No one is looking out for them. They don't have money. I can tell. Two of them speak Spanish, and the other one's mother came once, but she was kicked out. It isn't fair, you know? I'm no more special than they are."

"Do you know their names? I could ask around."

"Rosie promised to find out. She was so upset when she found out that everyone wasn't being treated the same. Something about citizenship. I think that is why she left. Either she didn't think I should have special treatment, or she was going to get help for them. If I live—and I want to—I'll have so much to do. I think my mom needs help. She wants to fix the world."

Frank just nodded. The goodness of Joseph, Rosie, and Luis. Even Mrs. Henderson and the people at the bar had softened him. "I have a gift for you. Nothing special, just a stone. I keep it in my pocket, and my thumb has made an indentation in it. The smooth part is for wishing, and the back part is rougher. I call it my wishing and working stone."

"What will you use, if you need to make a wish or work on a problem?"

"I'll find me another one. Take care, and don't worry. Wishes are good."

# CHAPTER 23: *The Love of Power*

Luis unfolded Joseph's handmade map and laid it out on the truck seat. He'd been following the list for the entire week. Now, he could barely read the markings near the worn-out creases. Lost on the logging roads, he banged on his cell phone and held it up in the air, watching the bars of signal rise and recede. So much for the new reception tower built near the airport. Three messages from Hannah, and he had no way of contacting her. Even texting failed.

It wouldn't matter anyway. All of Joseph's friends lived off the grid by choice. According to the map Ralph had shown him, only Russell had a normal house visible from the logging road. He saw the house atop the hill and drove up the gravel driveway.

Luis found Russell splayed on the ground, his body a twisted blob with one hand holding fast to the porch rail. Alarmed, Luis prayed that he could find a sweet spot where his cell phone worked. His prayer was answered, and his call went through to 911. It seemed to take forever until he heard the sirens of the first responders.

Russell mistook Luis for someone else. As Luis approached, Russell called out even as he struggled for breath, "Someone's garbling the radio transmissions. Better spread the word that we have bootleggers bootlegging more than booze."

Luis wondered if Russell had lost his mind or if the shock had disoriented him. "Joseph sent me. My name is Luis. Keep still so you can breathe."

Russell nodded, struggled for breath, and continued, "Tell him we'll protect him, keep him safe. But the woods aren't ours now."

Before Luis could answer, the ambulance arrived. Two EMTs ignored Luis and rushed to the stairs with a stretcher.

"Russell, we need you to keep quiet. Dispatch says your breathing is labored. That's the third time this week, so we're taking you to the hospital."

Luis backed away, but Russell waved him in closer. "Listen to me. It's the installers of the new cell tower, they did something. Look near the church."

The EMTs put Russell on the stretcher and placed an oxygen mask over his mouth. "Sorry to break up your conversation, but we have a hard enough time getting up this hill in the daytime, and we don't want to come back in the dark. You can follow us to the hospital if you want."

"No, I just happened to drive up."

"Good that you did. Russell is one of our most stubborn patients. He insists on living alone."

Luis watched the EMTs load the stretcher into the ambulance and drive off with gravel flying in all directions. Soon after came the steady crunch of another car. An elderly woman was at the wheel. She didn't get out but rolled down her window. "You must be *the* Luis, Joseph has been talking about. I'm JoAnne, his neighbor. Russell must be bad off for the ambulance to peel down the road like that. I'd get out to talk with you, but I don't want to bother with my wheelchair."

Luis judged that JoAnne, with her gray strains of hair pulled back in a bun, was in her late seventies. "I'm sorry, but you seem to know more than I do. I take it you are friends with Joseph too?"

JoAnne smiled. "You could say that. It wouldn't be false. Everyone knows everyone here, like it or not. Russell has been so upset since Joseph's gone into hiding. He has never disappeared for more that a few days. It's been two weeks, and Russell *is* counting. He remembers too much from the past. Whatever Russell said to you is important. Don't let his age and appearance fool you. He keeps on top of everything that goes on in the area with his radio control buddies. If he said anything at all, tell Joseph. Got to go. I'm heading to the hospital."

Luis stood still for just enough time to make sure the driveway was clear before he took the winding road out. He drove higher into the hills. The snakier the road became, the more he remembered his visits to his parent's home in Ecuador. He felt his parent's presence everywhere. Their home in Ecuador sat on a knoll, a mere stucco hut, with no amenities, no trees to provide shade. The white walls outside reflected the sun, making it too bright to see hope. The darkness inside kept the heat at bay and depressed their will. In Joseph's world, the neighbors had their backs. He wondered who looked out for his parents in their world of drugs and gangs. Trust didn't exist. His mother clung to the church, believing that her faith would make the world right. He had never talked to Joseph about religion and faith. Why had Russell mentioned the church?

His cell phone vibrated, Hannah again. Annoyed by the intermittent pings, he stuffed the cell phone in his pocket while he studied the hand-drawn map and searched for a dirt road that wound around a stump. He privately cursed Joseph with his instructions. Looking for a stump in a logged area was like looking for a pearl on a rocky beach. Frustrated, he pulled off in a dimpled space by the side of the road. And there it was—not the dirt road, but an old church with a brand-new wooden steeple that towered above the area. Even Luis knew that it appeared out of place. His phone pinged incessantly.

Russell's warning put Luis on edge. He locked the truck, soft-stepped his way through the brush and peaked into the structure. It was a shell covering a cell tower. Afraid that his phone would signal someone, he turned it to vibrate only. Luis shrank himself down into a squat, supporting his back with a tree, and waited.

Within the first half hour of his vigil, six cars pulled into the driveway. Like a choreographed dance, they'd park, pop open the trunk, two men would carry out boxes from the church, fill the trunk, and the drivers would hand off an envelope for another envelope. Luis timed each exchange, which took less than five minutes. The precision set off alarms. Russell wasn't kidding about the cell phones or the bootlegging.

To avoid detection, Luis needed to leave between exchanges. He circled back to his car without incident. He sat inside and locked the doors. Staring at nothing, he waited for his thoughts to catch up with his observations. When they didn't, he backed up onto the road. His phone vibrated in his pocket, an insistent buzzing along his leg.

He'd forgotten about Hannah. Scrambling, he drove with one hand while he pulled the phone out. "Hello, Hannah, I can barely hear you. I'm up in the hills. Are you okay?"

Static, pings, more static and then her voice. He couldn't even make out every other word. " . . . Problem . . . hospital . . . agents . . . farm."

Behind the static, he heard other voices from another connection. The wires seemed crossed. And then it hit him. The cell phone tower wasn't just interfering with his call; the pings were a type of hacking. "I've got to go, Hannah." He pressed the off button and put the phone in the glove compartment. With both hands on the wheel, he focused on the road. The slightest movements in the brush caused him to swerve and turn his head.

The old man's warning about garbling radio transmissions hadn't made sense. But now Luis suspected more than just a scam. He resisted the urge to toss his phone out the car window. Instead, he pulled over to the side of the road and scrummaged through his tool kit. He found an old magnet that he used to pick up nails. Inserting his knife in the back of his phone, he opened it and took the battery out. He didn't know enough about cell phone technology, but he knew that a magnet would mess up the signal. He taped them together and placed both pieces back in the glove compartment.

Joseph's quiet life had been intentional before Luis had arrived. Luis feared that he had exposed Joseph yet again, just by being up here hiding. The only phone call he had made was to 911 for Russell. If his suspicions were valid, the hackers could connect Luis now to an old dying man, to Joseph, and to Hannah and her father. He didn't even know what that meant, but Hannah had voiced concern. Something was amiss. He worried that while he couldn't make out all the words, the hackers could.

Abruptly, Luis turned the truck around, spewing dust mixed with loose gravel, and headed back into town. Luis had been trying so hard to think like Joseph, he had forgotten to think on his own. Of course it was connected. It went back to Yuri and Vladimir. They might be innocent, caught in the crossfire, but Luis didn't want to take any chances. Whatever good Mr. Henderson wanted to come out of his artistic experiment, he clearly had bigger problems than just a boycott of his fields, since Hannah had connected the hospital, agents, and farm together in her call.

By the time Luis curved his way back to Highway 20, his gas gauge read empty. He pulled into the first gas station he spotted. Bad choice. He recognized at least three of the drivers from the church. He could hear his mother's voice in his head say, *Todo lo que pasa, pasa por una razón*—everything that passes, passes for reason.

Luis filled his gas tank and went inside to pay. The boxes he had seen loaded into their trunks sat by the cooler. Each had a fancy label plastered on the outside, a picture of a vineyard and words written in Italian. He didn't need to translate *vino*. Russell's suspected bootleg was wine, not distilled liquor.

The employees seemed to ignore the boxes, and the wine cases sat in the middle of the aisle. The cashier greeted the guy in front of Luis. "Spencer, good to see you. You haven't been in for a while. Things okay with you and your lady friend, the pilot?"

Spencer smiled. "You'd know if it wasn't. Everyone knows my business. So tell me, what's with importing Italian wine? That's a first for this gas station. My vineyard is just a mile from here, and your boss turned his nose up at my offer to set up a section in the cooler. He said it would crowd out the beer."

The cashier shrugged. "Who knows? Each week the cases appear and then disappear. We never open them."

Spencer took his change and asked, "Do they appear on the same day each week?"

"My schedule changes, so I couldn't tell you. But I could ask?"

"Don't worry about it, I was just curious."

Luis rushed to pay his bill and followed the man named Spencer out the door. "Excuse me, sir, I couldn't help overhear your conversation with the cashier. I saw the boxes being loaded upriver, from a church." As soon as the words were out of his mouth, Luis wished he could swallow them. Joseph wanted him to be discreet, and here he was talking to strangers in public.

"Holy wine, is it? You say you saw them at a church upriver. I live upriver, and I don't think that is the church's normal practice."

Worried that he'd said too much, Luis put his "I don't understand English" look on his face, and stepped toward his truck. "I could be wrong. Never mind, I've got to go."

Luis heard a tap on his window. Spencer motioned to Luis to roll down his window. "Sorry, I was being cocky. I didn't ask your name. You caught me off guard. Please accept my apology. I'd offer you a bottle of my wine, but you're underage. Gauging by the worried look on your face, you don't want trouble. I'm Spencer."

It took Luis a few seconds to respond. He looked down at the map Joseph had prepared and saw a circle with the words *Spencer's vineyard* inside. Relief washed over him. "You've got that right. There is enough trouble brewing all around me. I'm Luis."

"Oh, you're the one who called 911 for Russell. He has had me worried sick. I usually get up to see him a few times a week, bring him food, make sure all is okay. Work at the vineyard has me busy preparing for an early harvest of a new strain of grapes."

Luis didn't like the coincidence, didn't' like that everyone knew his whereabouts. He couldn't discern if it was just the norm of small towns or if he was being followed. He started rolling his window back up.

Spencer put his hand on the lip of the window. "Luis, what's got you so skittish?"

"How did you hear about me calling for help?"

"JoAnne, Russell's neighbor, stopped at my house on her way to the hospital. Anything else you want to know?"

"Do you have a cell phone? Russell warned me that something strange was going on with the signals. Lots of pinging, and well, I think someone is spying on my conversations."

"Russell doesn't own a cell phone. He must be worried about his radio transmissions. Do people have a reason to spy on you?"

"No, but JoAnne told me to listen to Russell. I guess it made me feel paranoid. Do you know a man named Joseph?"

Spencer shook his head no. "Can't say that I've made his acquaintance, but Russell considers him a friend. Why? Is Joseph in trouble?"

Luis pointed to his map. "Apparently you are one of the people I'm supposed to contact. Joseph didn't tell me what to say or how to find the people on the map, but he'd like everyone to gather."

Before Spencer answered, Luis heard a series of high-pitched pings. He stared at the glove compartment where he had vanquished his cell phone, but the pings came from outside. He'd forgotten to watch the men from the church leave the gas station. A rhythmic concert of ringtones echoed around the three drivers as they hopped into their separate vehicles. As if on cue, motors started, and they lined up at the driveway exit to Highway 20. One driver left, the next waited a few minutes, the last one followed toward Sedro Woolley, each with three cars between them. Luis noticed the pattern of pings coincided with cars, tracking the tracker. He turned his attention back to Spencer. "Check out the wine. I've got to go."

Luis pulled onto the highway, keeping the last of the trucks in sight. He rolled down his window and stuck out his hand to pass. His speedometer hovered just over fifty-five, close enough to the speed limit to avoid a ticket but fast enough to see where the convoy of trucks headed.

# CHAPTER 24: *Hate*

Hannah swallowed the last bite of Abuelita's rice and beans and made her way over to the sink to wash her dishes. "I should do this more often. Do you cook lunch every day?"

"'Everyone has to eat. Why, are you planning on visiting more?"

"Since I can't work in the fields, my father offered me a job in the office. With the boycott, he is out scrambling for new places to sell the berries. He doesn't have enough time to be in the office. It shows. His paperwork is a mess."

Hannah washed the pans, and Abuelita dried. Hannah's thoughts drifted until she heard sirens. Abuelita pushed her aside and said, "Go into the other room. Quick."

Abuelita's tone of voice moved Hannah's feet quicker than she could respond with any objection. Two cars had pulled up to the house. Hannah peered out from behind a curtain. Her father stepped out of his car and stared at the house—a silent warning. The second car jerked to a halt, almost knocking her father down. She didn't recognize the second car. Yuri and Vladimir sat in the back seat. Her father moved forward to open the back door when two plain-clothed men hopped out of the front with their guns pointed at the house.

Abuelita came out running from the house wielding a cast-iron pan in one hand and a wooden spoon in the other. She yelled an expletive in Spanish and held the heavy pan in front of her body. Hannah ran from the house toward her father. The two men turned their guns on her. Fearing the worst, Hannah held her hands over her ears. She changed course when they flashed badges and put their guns back in their hidden holsters. Why did her father just stand there?

"Hannah, don't move. Do as I say."

She froze as the two men handcuffed her father and bent his head to fit in the back seat. Yuri and Vladimir slipped out the other side and ran off. Abuelita remained poised to defend. As the car drove off, Hannah broke out in tears. "Where are they taking my father? What just happened. He promised me he wouldn't break any laws."

Abuelita stood with her arms by her side, still holding on to her kitchen weapons. "*Mi hija*, you must find your mother. I've seen those men before. One came here as a telephone repairman, the other snooped through our garbage. Today they flashed their badges, FBI and CIA. This is big trouble, not our kind."

Hannah called home, then her mother's cell phone. Nothing. Frantic, she called the beauty parlor, the bank, and the yarn shop. Everyone denied seeing her, but someone heard that she was drinking at the Burlington Railroad Tavern. Hannah ignored that information as too bizarre to be believable. Finally, she got ahold of her neighbor. "Oh yes, I saw your mom with a small man with a funny eye, a lady with curly hair, and some outsider at the Food Co-Op. They were huddled together at a table whispering. I'm sure it was your mother as she had that purse she always carries."

Each call made her feel more desperate. As a last resort, she called the old contact list that had been set up for emergencies when her sister had cancer. After about seven calls, her mother finally texted her: *Come to the hospital as quickly as you can. Robin and Rosie need us.*

Hannah's entire body shook. Was this déjà vu? She texted back, *I'm on my way. Dad is in trouble. They arrested him.* Hannah waited for a reply, but after a few minutes she panicked. "Abuelita, what should I do?"

"Take you father's car. Go to the hospital. Your mom needs to know."

. . . . .

Hannah circled the hospital looking for a spot to park. Four loops and nothing. Even the emergency lot had a Do Not Enter sign posted. She pulled into a driveway of an old friend's house and walked three blocks to the main entrance. Her mother's text shook her more than seeing her father handcuffed and taken away. None of it made sense. Nervous, she called Luis. Too much static, her words dropped as if he was on the other side of the world. Her mother must have been with Joseph, Rosie, and Miguel. What did that mean?

Hannah marched through the main entrance to the hospital. She pushed the revolving door with such force that an elderly lady, one turn ahead of her, stumbled. Hannah rushed to the woman's aid.

"You young folk are always in such a hurry. Don't you have some respect? I nearly fell."

The charged words of indignation snapped Hannah out of her panic, but the tone triggered her stutter. "I-I'm so sorry. I g-got a message from my mother. I wasn't paying attention. Are you okay?"

"Yes, I am. Now get on with it, if you're in such a hurry."

Hannah noticed the crowded reception area. Standing room only. "The least I can do is find you a seat."

"I'm here to help, not sit. Didn't you hear? The bridge on I-5 collapsed. Some truck nicked the top, and the post gave way. A few cars fell into the Skagit River. Everyone is here looking for family members."

"E-excuse me, then, I'll leave you to help."

With all the elevators busy, Hannah made for the stairway up to the cancer ward. She texted Luis again. No response. She feared that Luis might be on that route. At least she knew where her father and mother were.

The seven flights up left Hannah winded. She opened the staircase door to an unusual clatter. In the center of the floor, in front of the nurses station, her mother and Rosie had set up camp. Robin was seated in a wheelchair and a white mask covered her mouth and nose. Alarmed, Hannah made her way through a lineup of other children to Robin's side. "Mom, what's going on? I got your message. Why is everyone out in the hallway?"

Her mother pointed over to Robin. "Seems that your little friend has refused care. She told Rosie, that if the other patients on the floor had to go home, then she wouldn't take the trial treatment. We had no choice."

Hannah opened her mouth and then shut it. The hair on her arms rose, and a ripple of strangeness ran up and down her spine. She recognized her mother's tone of voice. Stern, persuasive, no nonsense, the tone that she had used when Jenna had refused care. "Robin, are you too sick to continue? I don't understand."

"I don't know why I'm special. I don't want my friends to die. My mom says you have to stand up for what you believe, otherwise you're not living."

Tears filled Hannah's eyes. She stared at Rosie and her mom. "So what's the plan?"

Hannah's mother glanced around the room. "These children must have an opportunity to thrive and give back, but first we have to raise the money. I've asked each one to give us their first name and three thoughts. We'll take a picture to help tell their story."

Exasperated Hannah looked at Rosie. "And then what?"

"Your mom can be very persuasive in seeking financial support. Take her lead." Rosie turned her attention toward Robin and took her hand. "You are my most tenacious patient. Already you have given me wisdom. Let's get moving, as I promised your mother you'd rest." Hannah picked up a camera from the table and snapped Rosie and Robin's picture. She wrote down, "*R* & *R*, crazy ideas. Stubborn, fearless, seers." Swept up in the moment, she had forgotten her father. She hugged Robin and went over to her mother.

"Mom, d-did you get my text that they arrested Dad. Abuelita said you'd kn-know what to do."

Her mom's eyebrow rose in a question mark. "They, who? Not the local police?"

"Abuelita said it was big trouble, not our own. I thought it had to do with illegal migrant workers, but we don't hire people without paperwork. You're right it wasn't our local police. It was the FBI and the CIA."

Her mother's resigned reaction unsettled her. The floor seemed to shift. Hannah reached for the table to steady herself and said, "Tell me th-that Dad isn't doing anything illegal."

Hannah felt her mother's warm breath, an elongated sigh, brush her cheek. This was as close to a kiss as she had gotten since before Jenna had become ill. Her mom whispered, "We didn't want to alarm you. Your father discovered some odd activity on the farm, not with our workers. This was before Luis left and his parents were deported. But the odd deposits and withdrawals into the bank continue."

Ugly distrust swirled inside her stomach. A wave of nausea caused her to gag. The very mention of Luis and his family in association with odd activity felt like an assault.

Hannah recoiled. "You know Dad is working with Luis. He asked for his help. Have you put Luis in danger?"

Rosie returned just in time to hear Hannah's exchange with her mother. She stepped forward. "No more danger than befriending a neighbor. It's Joseph who is in danger. Hate has a long memory and takes all in its wake. If we let it blind us, we all lose.

Hannah's jaw dropped. "What does Joseph's safety have to do with my father and the farm?" She glared at Rosie. "You asked for my help." Hannah shuddered as she remembered her first encounter with Yuri and Vladimir. She wondered if this was all her fault.

Hannah's mother made an awkward attempt at hugging Hannah. Her words were still stern. "Enough, Hannah. This isn't about your friendship with Luis. That's a matter of your heart. I have to make a phone call to our lawyer and get your father out of jail. Abuelita was right. She has been our eyes and ears all this time. I've been the blind one. Come on, go help Robin and these kids."

Hannah stood next to Robin, who had already snapped the children's photos. Next to each name, Hannah wrote their words. Amrit, the young Somalian, posed with his older sister, who wore their traditional burka, and said, "Bull's-eye. You can only see dark circles of pain. No tears." Sara, with blue eyes and the remnants of red eyebrows, had her picture taken with her head wrapped in a red, white, and blue scarf. Her words were more hopeful: "Red is for kisses, white is my hope, blue sky for peace."

When Hannah came to Jorge, she had to stifle her tears. He was by far the youngest in the group and his father held him in his arms, as he was too weak to sit. His father had shaved his own head to match the shine from his son's. The two wore matching wire-rimmed glasses and huge smiles. Thomas held up his fingers on his right hand. *"Cinco años. Cuéntalos. Si puede, Dios me da mas."* Hannah translated his words: "Five years. Count them. If god is willing, he will give more."

Hannah heard above the background noise an announcement over the loudspeaker. "Attention: All available medical personnel, please head to the emergency room for mass incoming trauma." Rosie wheeled Robin back to her room. The rest of the children were escorted out of the hallway and into a waiting room for cancer patients

The announcement meant that there were more casualties. Hannah tried calling Luis. No answer. She gathered the camera, pens and paper, and the rest of the children's thoughts. As she headed out, she flipped their words like shuffling a deck of cards. Flashes: *Make my mom smile again, soft touch, I will be brave for you, I see a light behind the stars, tend the garden, did I do something wrong?*

If only the answers were simple. If you did something wrong, there was always the hope you could fix it.

## CHAPTER 25: *The Dot on the Line*

Joseph was on his way home, just seconds after he crossed the bridge in Burlington, when he heard the crunch of metal and felt the shake of the earth. Even before the bridge shook, he noticed a truck speeding the other way. Odds weren't in its favor for making it across in time. Joseph held his breath, cranking his head backward to see the result. What he saw scared him more. For some crazy reason, Luis followed the speeding truck in hot pursuit. Joseph pulled off and parked by the side of the road. Luis's truck teetered on the edge of the collapsed bridge. Two vehicles had already fallen into the Skagit River. Joseph rushed back to help.

Riverboats, drift boats, fishermen, horns honking, and bystanders appeared out of nowhere. Joseph zigzagged through the menagerie of helpers. He witnessed Luis contort his lean body through the sliding rear window. Joseph needn't have worried about counterweight. Luis, with his dancer's sense of balance, kept the truck stable while two bystanders leaned into the truck, slipped a rope through the back bumper, and hooked it to their vehicle. Joseph's eyes locked with Luis's for just a second. He followed at a distance. Luis hurled himself off the bridge and into the water. He surfaced by the vehicles where frantic drivers struggled to escape.

The look in Luis's eyes stayed with Joseph. A flash of trouble, resolve, and determination. It was a warning to Joseph to stay his distance, one Luis would understand, would be impossible. Joseph used his size to his advantage. He slipped in behind the crowds, listening to the boatman as he observed. "Get the guy out of the water.

Crazy stunt. He's in our way."

Joseph held his breath as Luis dove under the truck with a heavy screwdriver, found a branch in the shallow water, and then pried the truck door open. A burly guy fell on top of Luis. He flailed as Luis struggled to get in position behind him. Keeping the man's hands in front and out of the way, Luis reached around the man's neck, held tight, and swam. Another raft pulled up beside Luis and lifted the guy on board. By then the Coast Guard had arrived, and its crew turned to the other vehicle as Luis waved them on. At first it seemed he was headed back to shore, but with everyone's attention on the survivors, Luis swam back to the truck and rifled through the front seat.

To create a distraction, Joseph yelled out from the banks of the river, "There's another guy in the water. He came through the opened window." The boat swerved. One of the crew motioned an "okay" sign with his fingers and doubled back. Joseph caught up with Luis as he dragged himself out of the water. Before Joseph could question him, Luis handed him a wallet, a soggy notebook, and a cell phone. Reporters circled around Luis as Joseph slipped away.

. . . . .

The summer sun had already set when Joseph arrived back at his cabin. A long day, extended by light, made its way into the night, but not quite dark enough to obscure the stone pathway to his door. The newest addition made him smile. He suspected that Miguel had left him a gift of encouragement. He needed it. No matter how simple he wanted life to be, twists in fate complicated outcomes.

If the collapse of the I-5 bridge wasn't enough, Joseph heard that Jeff Henderson had been arrested earlier in the day. The farmworkers had sounded the alarm. News traveled with embellishments, worry, and judgment. The night would be a long one. Joseph knew that when events collided the idea of coincidence seemed farfetched. Two stones thrown from different directions hit the same target only because the target was there.

Joseph opened his cabin door and slumped into a chair. Enjoyment of Miguel's artistic gift would have to wait. Starved, he eyed the loaf of fresh bread and bowl of fruit left behind by Ralph and Sharon. His brain was as tired as his body. Both needed nourishment. His father always said that too many people languished because they didn't have the food to feed their minds. Too young to understand, he had mimicked his father's habits of eating as often as possible, small bits, offered in payment of work. Then, he thought his father had meant the brain needed information. He wondered how many geniuses were never discovered because they just weren't getting the proper nourishment.

He spread out the contents of the wet wallet Luis had given him and the notebook. Built a small fire in the woodstove and hoped that the heat would dry out the pages more quickly. He figured the cell phone was destroyed by the dip in the river, but just in case, he stored it in a canister of rice. Luis must have thought these important, otherwise he wouldn't have risked his life.

Deep in thought, Joseph ignored the knock at his door. The third series of knocks drew him out. "No need to make so much noise, Miguel. My light is on, so come in."

Miguel walked in and didn't waste time with a greeting. "I assume you heard about Jeff's arrest. You need to be careful. You might still be a target."

Joseph nodded as he walked around the table where the truck driver's personal effects lay. He stared at the photo identification. "Come look at this. I'm just one of many targets. Seems like they are coming out of the woods. Luis chased one of the truck drivers from upriver all the way off the collapsed bridge. This is his stuff. What do you make of it?"

"I recognize the guy's face. He is one of the thugs who got ahold of Yuri and Vladimir. He has felt the other end of my knuckles."

Joseph looked up. His good eye widened. "We don't cure anything with violence. I prefer your other talents. Art at least expresses emotion without doling out pain."

"Sometimes violence is justified. My other talent, my art, was my way of exposing corruption without getting kicked in jail. Living on the island we knew that corruption existed everywhere. The trick was finding a line of intolerance that tipped the table."

"So is that why you used your knuckles here. What table did you tip?"

Miguel ripped a piece a bread off the loaf and ate some of the berries. "Yours."

"You think I'm too passive, too complacent."

"Are you?"

Joseph dismissed the thought with a wave of his hand. He stared at the curled paper from the notebook. "Two things work better than violence: brains and a heart."

Miguel shrugged. "You've tried that for years. It might have worked when no one knew who you were or what you did. But not now. Seems like you're the prey."

Joseph thought back on the afternoon, Luis's heroics, the Good Samaritan. "You should have seen what Luis did. He jumped to save the drivers and risked his life. So many people rushed to help. I may be the target, but I fight with my head, not my hands. I won't change who I am, even if I'm killed."

"Bingo. Nothing changes if you die. The status quo remains."

Joseph smiled. "Your nudge is well taken. No violence on my part or yours. Exposure is worse."

Miguel chuckled. "You would like my friend Jesus from the island. Rosie did say you reminded her of him. Just an older version."

"When we have some social time, I'll ask Rosie about her personal life, but right now we have to figure out what all of this means. I wouldn't rule out my research as another line of inquiry. Seems like the government is casting a wide net. I'm not at all certain they know what they're fishing for."

"Do you really believe that the government arrested Henderson for undocumented workers at his farm?"

"Either that or something more grievous. Luis didn't know about Henderson's arrest. He was upriver because I sent him to visit Russell and some other friends. Yet he chased the drivers. There must be a connection here, or Luis wouldn't have had to risk his life. I have no idea what he intended to do."

"Maybe too much of a connection. What else do you know about the driver Luis saved?"

"Look at this notebook. It's got GPS coordinates."

"Salmon? They swim upstream before laying their eggs. Maybe these men were poachers."

Joseph pulled out a map of the Skagit River and circled the dams along the way. "Miguel, you may have something there. I don't think the feds were fishing for salmon. These dams generate electricity. They're part of the backbone of the area. Ross, Diablo, and Gorge Dams all are part of the Skagit River Hydroelectric Project. The GPS coordinates follow the fish but also the new cell phone towers. The spill of water crosses into Canada. Maybe something else is running through the northern borders?"

Miguel took a piece of paper and doodled a series of waves, added vertical lines, shaded them into posts, which snaked along the curve of the Skagit River until it hit the Canadian border. "What moves in waves, has no borders, and isn't a river or an ocean?"

"Digitized sound, electrical waves. They're trafficking in stolen identities and credit cards, maybe eavesdropping." Joseph took the pencil from Miguel and added a treble clef sign on the lines. He smiled as if he had just found a prize in his cereal box. "I have an idea, but first we need to find out what else Henderson was protecting. Yuri and Vladimir seem to be the connection between me and the farm."

## CHAPTER 26: *If It Isn't One thing, It's the Other*

Frank had almost made it out of the hospital without succumbing to what he called "the shakes of memory." He pinched his right arm to make sure he wasn't dreaming or having a flashback. Giving Robin his wish stone didn't free him from the past, just lightened his heart.

Frank was just ten feet from the exit when he spotted Russell atop a gurney, emerging from the imaging department. Frank couldn't leave, not when one of his staunch supporters was ill.

JoAnne sat in the waiting room, glasses midway down her nose, with a magazine on flight in her lap. Frank's heart skipped a beat.

He smiled and offered his hand. "I knew I'd find you here. Russell has his dedicated entourage. I guess I'm a fan too. What's going on?"

JoAnne folded the corner of the page she was reading and sighed, then answered, "Russell went and had another stroke. I'd say he was lucky that a young guy was up there to call the EMTs. It's touch and go. He's been in a tizzy since he noticed something amiss with the radio signals."

"Did he mention any theories?"

"Frank, you do get to the point. I haven't been down to the hangar much lately. But some things don't change, do they? You're still mister know-it-all, passing along information. It's good seeing you doing so well."

"I'm sober, if that is what you mean. They let me live at the hangar and have hired me to keep an eye on things. I suspect you and Russell had something to do with that. So what's going on? Who was the guy who found Russell?"

"Someone said it was the lad who lives with Joseph. But you knew that, didn't you? I'd be more concerned about Russell's heart than the lad who found him."

"I am worried about his health, and his mind."

"Frank, you know his mind is sound. If you're fishing for answers about problems upriver, find out for yourself. You know how they gossip. The small talk bounces from one home to another, but if you want the truth, you'll just have to talk with Russell."

Frank let the conversation drift off, still embarrassed by his old infatuation with JoAnne. He excused himself and went over to the nurses station to find out Russell's situation. In the past no one had noticed him, and if they had, they would have called security. The nurse looked up with a smile. "What can I do for you, sir?"

"I was wondering when I could talk with Russell, the gentleman that was wheeled into room 352."

"Are you a relative?"

Before he could answer her, Frank felt an arm slip into the crook of his elbow. "Don't worry, Mr. McCain can come in with me. I was just going in to visit and make sure Russell felt comfortable."

Frank accepted Rosie's arm. As they walked down the hallway, Rosie put her finger to her lips and said, "You're to sit next to Russell and keep quiet. Let him speak, and do not say a word. Do you understand?"

He smiled. "Yes, keeping quiet and not saying a word. Got it. Thanks for the easy entrance. What brings you here?"

"Shh—don't ask me questions either. I figured you'd find a way to visit Russell no matter what, so it might as well be with me. If you remember, Russell and I are also old friends. Besides I'm the one with hospital privileges."

They entered a darkened room with one bed, an overstuffed chair from another era, and the smell of bathroom freshener. Rosie pulled the curtain aside and opened the windows. Russell lay under the covers, eyes closed, arms crisscrossed over his chest.

Frank swallowed a few times, taking extra breaths as he watched Russell struggle for air. He pushed his pointer finger deep into the bend of his arm, felt his blood pulsating—anything to distract him from his fears. The stillness crept along his skin, raising the hairs. Death seemed to hover.

With the windows open, a breeze rushed in carrying the aroma of honeysuckles.

Rosie took Russell's hand and held it, checked his pulse, and waited. With each waft of honeysuckles, Russell's face softened until a thin smile appeared with a hushed plea. "Emma, is that you? I've been missing you."

Rosie whispered, "Russell, your sweet wife, Emma, is long gone. You'll have to bide your time with me."

Russell raised the lid of his right eye. His words were labored, resigned. "*Hmpf*, I'm still of this world. If you aren't my Emma, you must be Rosie."

"This is serious. I don't like the déjà vu. Last time I saw you at the Concrete Fly-In, you were so upset that your heart missed a beat or two. What's got you so riled up now?"

Russell tried to raise his head, but he collapsed back on the pillow. He offered a grimace for his answer. Frank kept his promise of silence but pulled a pad of paper and a pen out from his pocket and handed it to Russell. Without warning the pen and paper flew across the room as Russell showed his frustration.

Rosie gave Frank a stern look. Russell mumbled a series of garbled words: *impostors, bootleg, airwaves, reverse.*

Frank slipped off his assigned seat and picked up the pad of paper and pen. Seated again, he wrote the words down, knowing he'd forget. Frank listened for more, but Russell had already closed his eyes. All that was left was his labored breathing. Frank hadn't felt this sad since his mother had passed. He stood up to leave, but Rosie shook her head back and forth, and Frank returned to his chair.

"Russell, I know how tired you must feel. I'm tired too. Your work is almost done. I'll let you rest. Tell me what you need."

A breathless word was his answer: "Home."

Frank had never seen Rosie upset. Rosie's spirit seemed to wither as she held Russell's hand. Frank felt like a voyeur, spying on an intimacy that didn't belong to him.

Rosie nudged Frank's knee and motioned for him to head out. He exited to the hallway with Rosie at his heels. "Rosie, we can't just leave him here to die."

Finally, Rosie looked up. Her eyes had lost their sparkle. "We need someone with the power of attorney to get him released. He can't be left alone. He'll die no matter what we do, but I agree he needs his own surroundings. Can you alert JoAnne and Spencer and the others? Home holds the comforts of memories and, in Russell's case, a place to cross over."

Frank broke his promise. "I know I said I would keep quiet, but you're not doing good either. What do you need?"

"It's enough that you noticed. I'm just weary, too many urgencies, and I too would like to go home. I'll head back to the Puerto Rico when I can."

"Okay, but if you need anything, you know where to find me."

Frank left Russell and Rosie and returned to the waiting room to find JoAnne. She sat in her wheelchair and stared out the window. As he approached, she turned and said, "You saw Russell. I checked with the nurses, and they said you were in his room."

His words caught in his throat. "Do you have power of attorney? He's got to get out of here. They'll keep him if we can't find a way to get him home."

An eternity passed before JoAnne answered. Her face appeared as that of an angel, eyes moist with remembrances. "Yes, I share the power of attorney with Spencer. Russell didn't want either of us to carry the burden of decisions alone. I'll make the calls."

Frank waited a minute, until JoAnne had wiped her tears and her composure returned, before he said, "I don't want to bother you, but Russell mumbled some stuff about why he was upset. Thought he might have said something to you that might solve the mystery."

## CHAPTER 27: *Tight Rope*

Hannah fidgeted. She slid down in the seat of the wooden chair. She felt the grooves on the side arms, imagined the fingernails that had carved initials and pleas for help. Other families waited, but only her mother sat with her back straight, head facing the police officer.

Hannah looked around. "Sir, how l-long will it be? My f-father should be out now." The police officer ignored her, and no one else had heard her question. Maybe she had just imagined that her voice spoke. She heard her old familiar stutter, yet her mother hadn't interrupted, taken over. Hannah placed her fingers along her lips. Closed, sealed. The words must have been her whispers of fear.

Background static moved to the foreground as the radio newscaster broke with a special interview with one of the heroes at the collapsed bridge site. "Luis, tell us how it feels to be a double hero. First your truck barely escaped falling off the I-5 bridge when it collapsed, and then you dove into the Skagit River to rescue a stranger."

Adrenaline zipped through her heart. Hannah jumped up. "Sir, can you turn that up?"

"Miss, the radio isn't for your enjoyment."

From the corner of her eye, Hannah saw her mother rise and approach the counter. "It's okay, Mom, I've got this." Reading the officer's name tag, Hannah continued, "Officer Morales, please. I think they're talking with my boyfriend, Luis."

Hannah noticed Officer Morales's face change. His jaw dropped, and his eyes widened with a sympathetic look. He held his tongue, nodded, and turned the volume slightly louder.

Luis spoke with precision, soft but intent. " . . . all, really. I just did what needed to be done. I'd rather not talk."

"Did you know the gentleman?"

"Please, I have to go. I'm late for work."

Hannah squeezed her mother's hand. She could hear the tension in Luis's voice, how he was treading a thin line.

The reporter pressed harder. "I'm sure your employer will understand. Where do you work?"

Voices, horns honking—the chaotic scene vibrated through the radio. "And there you have it; the heroic Luis has left us. We'll see if we can get a follow-up interview later."

Hannah's mother bent over and whispered in her ear, "He'll hide, you know. He doesn't want to bring attention to himself, the farm, or you."

The two sat back down and waited. Hannah hadn't even known to be fearful for Luis. Layers of worry rattled her insides. Her foot twitched on its own, and she sat on her hands, not sure how to control her anxiety and anger. Almost anything could make her snap.

Another half hour passed before the door from the hall connecting to the jail opened. Her father, the great Mr. Henderson, walked out with his head held high, but the slight roll of his shoulders revealed a different man. He stared at Hannah and her mother while a gentleman, suited and carrying a briefcase, guided him over to the counter. Hannah's mother stood, and Hannah followed.

While her father signed papers, her mother talked with the gentleman. This had to be the lawyer, the special person her mom had contacted, someone outside of the community, someone with more authority to deal with serious matters.

Finally, he spoke to her in a hushed voice: "You must be Hannah. I'm Allen Ferguson, your father's lawyer. When we leave here, I want you to hold your father's hand, and your mother will hold his other hand. The press is outside and will try to engage you. Later, people will try to contact you. Do not use your cell phone. Do not talk to anyone but your mother, your father, or me. You needn't worry—your father is in good hands."

If ever Hannah had wanted a voice, now was the time. "Mr. Ferguson, I won't question your skills, but you don't know this community. You don't know what I know. My mother and I will support my father without question. We aren't ignorant just because we're from a small town. Whatever this arrest is about, it isn't about my father."

The lawyer doubled down with his stern response. "Young lady, lower your voice. Do as I say, as lives depend on it."

Hannah felt her mother's hand slip into hers and a squeeze as she whispered, "Calm down. Dad will be okay."

Her father turned toward them, and their charade began. The minute they walked out onto the sidewalk, the press advanced. Not just the local newspaper, but reporters and TV stations from Seattle.

Hannah and her parents walked slowly, aligned together in a Henderson formation. The last time they had walked like this was at her sister's funeral. Instead of averting their eyes, each one stood taller, mouths closed, focused but looking directly at the cameras.

Camera lights flashed. Hannah tried to block out the voices and questions hurled at her father and mother:

"Mr. Henderson tell us why you were arrested. Have you been harboring illegal aliens?"

"Mrs. Henderson, do you have migrants working in your home?"

"Is it true that your daughter gets paid more than the hired workers?"

One question seemed to come from left field, but Hannah heard a thread of truth in it: "You've been spotted along the coast at odd hours. What brings you to the secluded beaches along Chuckanut Drive? Are you smuggling contraband or laborers?"

Her father stumbled slightly at the accusation. Hannah readjusted her hand so that she held on to the crook of his elbow. She realized that their life was on display. Even she wondered at her father's odd habits. The journalist would have a field day if he had found her father's discarded sweatshirt smelling of paint and turpentine. She just didn't know what was real anymore.

Across the street and standing behind a car, Hannah thought she caught a glimpse of Luis. Even with a stocking hat and coveralls, Luis couldn't hide from her. Miguel popped up farther down the road. The gang rallied, but she and her family remained isolated.

A black sedan pulled up to the curb. Mr. Ferguson opened the door and they all got in the back seat. Hannah stared out the window and waved toward where Luis had been. Both Miguel and Luis had vanished. Hannah closed her eyes to all the visions—the violent arrest of her father, Robin's protest at the hospital, Luis's sudden appearance in the limelight. Hannah had never meant to rock the boat. She thought about her first dance with Luis, Joseph's kindness, Shelly in the hospital that day she had witnessed Yuri and Vladimir steal her mother's purse. She tried to get beyond her anger to understand. Her father held the key, but to which door? She wasn't sure she wanted to find out. Mr. Ferguson's words stuck in her head: *Lives depend on it.*

Once on the road, Hannah expected her father to say something. Still holding on to each of their hands, he kept his focus on the road. Mr. Ferguson conferred with the driver, who Hannah suspected was anything but a chauffeur. With his shaved head, dark suit, and almost invisible earpiece, Hannah sensed he was their silent bodyguard. They headed east on Highway 20 away from town. Mr. Ferguson rolled up the windows, and music filtered through the speakers. Her father said, "I'm so sorry, Hannah, for all that you witnessed. I've kept so much from you. You're all your mom and I have. I only wanted to protect you. Can you forgive me?"

"I don't understand. What have you done that needs forgiveness? Why all the secrets? I already know about the odd deposits at the farm. I know that you're working with the laborers on the farm. What else are you keeping from me?"

Mr. Ferguson interrupted, "Your father and your whole family are in danger because of what is going on at the farm. The investigation is ongoing. It's easier if your father appears guilty."

Hannah unbuckled her seatbelt and scooted toward Mr. Ferguson in the front seat. She choked out the words. "G-guilty of what?"

"Hannah, calm down. I can be guilty of anything. That's the irony of being a wealthy farmer. It doesn't matter to the public. Our government is investigating issues of national security. My helping the farmworkers gives them an out. Sometimes we can only help by getting out of the way."

"Mom, what isn't Dad saying?"

Ignoring Mr. Ferguson's signals to refrain from talking, Hannah's mother reached over and took her hand. "You know how Robin had to protest unfair treatment of others at the hospital, and your father is trying to make life better at the farm? Well, sometimes the source is bad. Your dad is helping dig out the rotten roots."

The anger Hannah had been keeping in abeyance ignited. "How long have you been keeping the 'rotten' story going. First it was Luis's family, and now who is it? Joseph, is he rotten, too, or have you decided that these people are okay? Whose lives are at stake—ours or Abuelita's, Robin's, or who? Tell me who I have to protect and why!"

Her father turned. "That's enough, Hannah. Mr. Ferguson will make sure no one is hurt. I assure you that you will understand. Right now, we have to keep up the show. Abuelita will keep everyone safe at the farm. We just have a few more things to figure out. It's best we go upriver to our cabin. We'll be safer there."

# CHAPTER 28: *Gridless*

Luis had been driving all day and into the evening hours, through the flats of the county, looking at the farm fields. Cornstalks, cabbages, the shifting acres of produce. He looked for signs, any signs that life was normal. But the fields were empty of workers, a still painting of an idyllic life not realized.

Nothing in Luis's life resembled the typical comings and goings of his friends. He couldn't remove the image of Hannah and her family escorted away from the courthouse. His every muscle ached. His arms hollered. He hadn't realized the strength needed to pull someone out of the water. Adrenaline masked the pain. The muscle that hurt worse was his heart.

Luis's truck sputtered—a sympathy choke for the truck that had fallen off the bridge. Luis rolled down the windows as he curved along Chuckanut Drive. He listened for the rhythmic swoosh of the tide, but the trees and distance made that impossible. He heard the wind's ripple. The sun hung along the horizon, a fanning of color and sparkle. Exhausted, he ignored the hope and the beauty—jewels too precious to squander with his tainted mood. He fought against his desire for solitude and drove past his favorite spot where the rocks danced with the tides.

The inclination to hide made Luis feel weak. Instead he turned and headed up Bow Hill Road, past the Rhody, to Highway 20, and on to the only home he had known since his parents had left. Luis found himself back at Joseph's cabin. He parked his truck behind the shop, covered it with a tarp, and made his way toward the front door.

Luis paused along the pathway, not sure if he heard movement or just the rustling of leaves. No shadows, just a slight breeze of cool air. The solidness of the stone path assured him that something had remained true. It was too dark to see if there had been any new additions, but as Joseph constantly reinforced, each stone mattered, told a story, and wouldn't be erased. Joseph would have felt the changes, the messages, with his bare feet, but Luis needed the visual. Too tired to check, he sought refuge in the cabin.

The room was almost dark except for the faint light of the kerosene lamp and the silent concentration of someone solving a problem. Joseph sat at the kitchen table with a map, a ruler, and a notepad. The flickering light made the wrinkles on his forehead waiver, and with his bad eye, Joseph appeared dwarflike, but with the presence of a giant.

Luis leaned his tired body against the kitchen counter and waited for Joseph's gesture, a wave, or a whisper to break the quiet. When none came, he turned and headed to his bedroom.

Joseph whispered, "Shh, be quiet. Hannah's asleep on the couch. She's been crying her eyes out. I told her you'd turn up, but she was impatient. You gave her a scare."

Luis turned back, now wide awake with alarm. "Oh no. When I heard that Mr. Henderson had been arrested, I went to the jail and saw her and her family get into a black car. I panicked, hid from the cameras and reporters. How long has she been here?"

"A few hours."

Luis lifted his hands, exasperated. "I wasn't even sure you'd be here. I expected you'd still be hiding out in the silos."

Joseph waved him on. "Go and be with Hannah. We can talk later. I told her you'd come back. Go—now isn't the time for your questions."

Hannah lay curled in a ball on Joseph's overstuffed couch. Luis stared, taken aback at her beauty and innocence. Her breath was a purr that murmured inside his heart. His first inclination was to turn and leave, but instead he lay down beside her, spooned inside the curve of her back and legs.

Afraid he'd wake her, Luis slowed his breath to match hers. The even pace lulled him into a hypnotic peace. Slowly Hannah unfurled, arms reaching upward, her back arching as her legs straightened. Each held the other, their arms a tangled knot of brown and white. Hannah was the first to speak.

"I thought I'd never see you again."

Luis pushed he short curls away from her forehead. "I thought the same. Seeing you drive away at the police station confused me. I wondered what had happened and if I had caused a problem for you."

Hannah pulled herself up and wrapped her arms around her knees. "My mom said you'd try to protect me and go into hiding. Whatever my father is involved in, I know you aren't the problem. I just don't know what is."

Luis scooted over on the couch, giving Hannah space. He studied her eyes, the almond curve that drooped in sadness, her eyebrows framing her concern. He felt older since the last time he had seen her. As if the world had hurled him backward in time and way into the future. She, however, had remained firmly in her world. Maybe it was better that way.

"Joseph said you'd been here for a while waiting for me. Won't your family be worried? Will you get into trouble?"

Hannah smiled, and Luis recognized her strength and determination. She had the devilish look that pierced his core. "I snuck out. Took the old way here, like I used to do when I was a kid. My parents didn't miss me then. I doubt they'd notice now. Besides, Mr. Ferguson, my dad's lawyer, is there. I pretended I needed to sleep."

Luis fidgeted with a blanket on the couch. First he folded the corners down, and then he pulled them out and flattened them. His loyalties to Joseph and Hannah seemed divided. He couldn't wrap his brain around the facts. "Hannah, your parents notice more than you think. If you've been gone as long as Joseph said, someone will come looking for you. Joseph is still in trouble. He's been in hiding for so long. He lives off the grid for a reason. This could make things worse for him."

"I hadn't thought of that. I was worried about you." Hannah got up and refolded the blanket, draping it over the top of the sofa. "What happened when you dove off the bridge? I'm proud of you, but that was crazy. What were you thinking?"

"It was crazy, but I had been chasing the other truck. The man I saved has something to do with all the drama in Joseph's life and, I think, in your father's business. I'm not much of a hero. Just loyal."

Hannah blushed. "Your loyalty could have killed you. Was it worth it?"

"It all depends. I've got to talk with Joseph, fill him in on what I know. He's in the kitchen, poring over maps."

As Luis walked the short distance from the living room to the kitchen, Hannah grabbed his hand. "I'm not going to stay on the sidelines and not know what is going on."

"I didn't ask you to. Wondering is too confusing for me too."

. . . . .

Joseph was at the sink. "Dinner is almost done. I'm sure you'd like something to eat. I've made a garden soup. Leftovers."

Luis pulled out a chair for Hannah and sat next to her. There were four place settings. "Thanks, you read my mind. I'm starved. Are you expecting someone else for dinner?"

Joseph ladled the soup into their bowls. "I'm hoping that Frank will appear, but you never know. It's a superstition of sorts from my past. The extra setting is for someone gone, a stranger, or a friend. It's a reminder of sorts. No matter. Help yourself to the bread."

Just sitting at the kitchen table restored Luis's sense of familiarity. His eyes welled up as he looked at Joseph and Hannah through the steam of the soup. Somehow Joseph had created a sense of home with bare necessities. Even the cement floor with its varying ramps leveled heights in such a way that Luis hardly noticed the difference between the floor by the sink and that of the dining area. The cabin became an equalizer. Luis ate quickly, while Joseph talked, and Hannah pushed her soup around. When his bowl was empty, Luis said, "I didn't realize how hungry I was. Now I can at least think. Were you able to make sense out of the notebook?"

Joseph chuckled. "Good thing I made lots of food. I figured your dip into the river would give you an appetite." He passed Luis some cheese and more bread. "To answer your question, the notebook took a while to dry out and decipher. I've got some theories, but I'm waiting for more information. My decision to hide in the silos took me out of the loop. It was a bad decision."

Luis knew the feeling. "That's why I came back. Besides, I'm not even sure who the bad guys are. I don't want to be invisible."

"No chance of that." Joseph smiled. "You're the talk of the town. Your stunt diving into the water made you a celebrity. Your refusal to talk made you a mystery. I'm not sure that was what you were going for."

Luis closed his eyes and took a deep breath. "I'm not sure either. I just figured that I should speak out when something is wrong. If I hide, then I look suspicious. I become part of the problem. I'm not like you. Even though you stay hidden, Joseph, you solve problems."

"Hmm—I'm not so sure." Joseph pushed his chair away from the table. "My past seems to have followed me. We know that much. So my desire for privacy backfired. Not entirely, but it could make things worse for others. I suspect that if I had been out in the community more, I would have been aware of, as you put it, the 'bad guys.' Maybe Hannah can help out with her observations."

Midspoonful, Hannah choked, and her pale skin turned red, as if she'd been caught doing something wrong. After coughing and clearing her throat, she said, "Sorry, I was thinking about Luis's diving into the river. I was listening, but you shouldn't ask me, I'm the least informed. My father and mother seem to be hiding information about the goings-on at the farm—their attempt to protect me. I'm not even sure what the charges were against my father. But Mr. Ferguson says it's a ruse. I don't know who is fooling who. I don't know about any notebook. Luis didn't mention it."

Joseph shook his head. "I'm not talking about what we see, what the town sees, or what the newspapers print. What have you observed that has changed, that seems odd?"

Hannah pulled a piece of the bread off the loaf and dipped it into her soup. Luis noticed that her leg was jittery and that another blush appeared on her face. "Everything is different. I'm not sure how much is normal. I just turned sixteen, and the world isn't how I thought it was."

Luis placed his hand on Hannah's thigh, coaxing it to relax. "I don't think Joseph wants that perspective, even if it coincides with us meeting. What do you remember at the farm that changed or even at the ceremony for your sister?"

Luis's question hit a nerve. Hannah stood up and took her bowl to the sink, though she hadn't finished her soup. He collected his dishes and cleared the table. Joseph busied himself and wrapped the cheese and bread. Luis washed the dishes. Hannah dried them. As the last of the dishes were put away, Luis wiped the counter.

Hannah finally spoke. "Sometimes I don't want to remember things. Especially if they make me feel bad. After the ceremony, I watched Yuri and Vladimir outside of the hospital with another stolen handbag. I didn't know who they were, and I envied them. I mean, they seemed so free."

A tear fell from Hannah's eye. She looked at Joseph and Luis. "Why would they be around the hospital? Don't think bad of me. But what I really remember is that my parents have been different, not kind, uptight. It's because I remind them that Jenna died. I want to be free of that. I wish my parents weren't so guarded."

Luis realized that Hannah's rambles were just like his own—making up reasons for things based on half facts and insecurities. "Hannah, don't think bad of me, but before my parents were deported, there were rumors at the farm. Some said that your father was going to sell it. Others said that he was acting odd. He'd disappear for hours and come back annoyed. He was never unkind, just distracted. My parents thought the farm had financial stresses. They would have chosen to continue working for almost nothing if they could have stayed."

Joseph sat by the window in an overstuffed brown chair. He cleared his throat. "Even though I haven't been in the loop, I still have my messengers. Some of these things aren't connected. Your parents' deportation came from federal laws. That tragedy has to be fixed, but it's separate from what's going on now. I'm puzzled by the bootlegging and the credit card scam and what I believe the notebook Luis found shows—a new way of hacking. Even I, in my isolation, understand about secrets and leaking information."

Luis picked up on the tremor in Joseph's voice. Something more sinister was at work. "Are you saying that it's all a coincidence? That our association with you is why Mr. Henderson is in trouble? Would that explain why I was beat up on the beach? I don't buy it."

Pained, Joseph closed his eyes and took a deep breath. "I didn't mean to belittle your lives or make mine more important. Like I just said, your parents' deportation is part of a larger issue. I'm the same as your parents—undocumented—only no one knew. You're a target because of who you are, where you go, who you see, and because like me, you remain isolated. I'm trying to give you the bigger picture.

Immigration, deportation, unionization of undocumented workers—none of this is new. What is new is our association. I've been involved with Hannah since she was a child climbing up the tree outside of my cabin. You're here in my home. I think of you as a son. Yuri and Vladimir suddenly appear here, too—mischief or an intentional message to threaten the ones I care about?"

Luis found the notebook he had given Joseph on a shelf with a map. The notebook's pages curled on the sides, and the ink blurred. He flipped through it and then handed it back to Joseph. The markings meant nothing to him, but he knew the notebook mattered. "I met Spencer in the gas station where the drivers delivered boxes with fancy wine labels. He thought it odd that good wine would be left in the aisles of the gas station and then disappear."

With this information, Joseph's eyes lit up. "No wonder Spencer was out of sorts. I met him on my way back from the silos. I wasn't in the mood to talk either. He didn't mention the gas station but told me about you saving Russell. Heard you were a hero there as well. I guess it's a good thing we aren't hiding anymore. If the newspapers find out that you saved Russell's life, the press will come knocking."

Luis busied himself checking the pocket of his pants. He was no hero and he didn't want the attention. He found his cell phone and placed it on the table. Hannah gave him an admiring look that made him feel uncomfortable but pleased. Luis tried to focus. He had forgotten the older man. "How is Russell? He's the one who warned me about the pings, that something was funny with his ham radio signals and that I should check my cell phone. Russell wasn't exactly coherent. But I understood his garbled words—*bootleggers bootlegging more than booze*. I'm sure he meant the wine, but with pings of the cell phone I got the feeling that we should be paranoid. He thought we were being robbed of our privacy."

"We should be paranoid." Joseph's voice lowered. "This has me worried. The connection runs deeper than I thought. Trafficking in wine, hacking at the cell tower, stealing credit cards—these seem like distractions. But if you add them up, it's a way to launder money. Perhaps another cover?"

Two taps on the door. Luis looked up expecting Frank. Instead, a tall gentleman dressed in a dark suit walked in.

Hannah broke loose from Luis's side. "Mr. Ferguson, how did you find me?"

"Miss Henderson, your path is well worn. I suggest you come back home and that your friends keep a low profile. We might need to speak with them later."

Luis reached for Hannah's hand. He gave it a squeeze, and then her fingers slipped through his and she was gone. Silence hung in the room. Luis stared at the door in disbelief. He turned to Joseph. "Is that it? That man can do that? I hope Hannah can trust him."

## CHAPTER 29:
## *Innocence—She was fishing, but I didn't take the bait*

Frank stared out at the dark sky from the edge of his hangar. He sat on an old wooden stool, legs propped up on an empty barrel. Without lights, the stars popped. This was the third electrical outage in the week, and he'd taken to keeping a flashlight and battery-operated radio by his side.

As the guard and keeper of the Concrete Airport, Frank appreciated the extra solitude the lightless night presented, but his gut told him that something was amiss. He had walked the property each hour, starting at eight- to ten-minute intervals, just in case someone knew his routine. He even cut through the middle of the runway and circled around the hangars, stood in the garden beds that still needed attention. His mistrust magnified when he got word that the composite factory had been broken into. The only physical item taken was the wing model he had secretly delivered for Joseph. While the electricity was down, the factory's computer system had been breached as well. Laptops with their battery backups offered the hackers an easy entrance.

Tired and chilled, Frank buttoned his denim jacket and thought about Russell. Frank couldn't remember a time without Russell meddling in the town's business. Russell didn't care about gossip—that was for the judgmental folk. No, Russell had always been fair with Frank, even when Frank's sister had poisoned the river and farmland. He could look Russell in the eye, and Russell would look back.

A man of few words, if Russell spoke at all, the town listened. Frank stared at the stars, wondering which one would shine on Russell as he lay dying. And there it was—a shooting star, a bright arch and a poof.

A shiver ran up his arm. He stood as an unfamiliar car drove parallel to the tarmac and straight toward his hangar. Frank waited until the driver turned off the headlights to see who was inside. He shook his head in disbelief, made sure his shirt was tucked inside his pants, and patted his hair back. Frank opened the car door and said, "Sheila, this is a surprise. What brings you out to the airport on a night when the electricity is off? Don't tell me you have more forms for me. I could have stopped by the courthouse."

Sheila took her time answering. She looked directly at Frank, the make-do table setup, and through to the tidy living conditions of the hangar. "They said I'd find you here. It's business of sorts. You know me, I can't let a thought go."

Frank didn't like the way her eyes inspected him. "What business would that be? Some trouble at the court?"

Sheila sat down on his stool. "Can I have that cup of coffee we talked about? We could've talked in town, but you don't come in much. You forgot to give me your phone number when you were at the courthouse. I'm sure it's just a misunderstanding that we can clear up. My supervisor found some interesting citizenship forms filled out. I thought you might know something about them."

Frank headed inside and called out from the sink, "Whatever I can do to be helpful." He took a deep breath and wondered what he could say. He feared he might reveal Joseph's status as an undocumented immigrant and thwart Joseph's plans if he said anything. Whatever he discussed, he promised himself that he wouldn't lie. "You are in luck. I have a propane camping stove, so I can make us both a cup."

He carried out another stool and a plate of bread and cheese.

By the time the coffee had brewed, Sheila had already eaten a slice. He placed the cups on the barrel. "Got the coffee here to wash that down. Ralph and Sharon always leave me homemade bread and cheese each week. Payment for handyman work."

To fill the awkward silence, Frank took a slice of cheese and began describing the constellations. "The stars tell me stories. Over there is Cassiopeia, named after a queen in Greek mythology. She boasted a lot about her looks. I guess she couldn't see herself too well. No one liked her."

Sheila tilted her head up and stared out. "I never could make out the patterns. Can you show me another one?"

Frank moved closer and pointed. "Follow my finger. That's the bottom of a ladle. See the seven stars. You know that, don't you? Little Dipper with the tip Polaris, the North Star?" Sheila held on to his arm and offered a few appreciative comments, but Frank ran out of steam. He stepped back. "I guess you've looked at the stars enough in your life. You don't need me as an expert."

Sheila held on to the coffee mug; the steam rose to meet her lips. Frank held his breath, waiting for her to speak. Finally, she said, "Seems odd that you'd request twenty applications, and in the same week thirty people applied for citizenship. We don't get that many in a year. Figured you'd know something."

Frank knew lots of things, but none he wanted to share. "Is there a problem with the applications? I mean there are rules, and if someone wants to be part of this great country, that's a good thing isn't it?"

Sheila gave Frank a slow smile that started with her eyes and ended with parted lips. "At first I suspected that you were looking for a wife. But I didn't see a foreign bride application with your name. Seems like teachers, store owners, and even the farmers are adopting kids, trying to get green cards. You wouldn't know anything about that, would you? I mean, I can understand a single guy looking for love. But this is different."

Frank didn't like the way Sheila's voice slithered in and out—accusatory and provocative at the same time—sweet talk that was anything but. It reminded him of Molly. Not the sexy part, but the toying with his emotions. Already he felt hives rising on his arms. He couldn't tell if the trigger was because he was holding back the truth or if Sheila was making fun. As he searched for a distraction, the lights flicked on. "I can't speak to that, Sheila, but I can say that our town has a problem with the power grid." He stood, happy to have an excuse to leave. "I've got to do my rounds and make sure the airport is okay. I'm sure you have somewhere you have to be."

"No, not really, Frank. My nights are lonely, but I'll leave. Just thought I'd give you fair warning. My boss isn't as nice as I am. I can be persuasive if needed."

Frank wondered if this was a threat or an invitation. "You best be going Sheila. I've got work to do." He gathered up the bread and cheese.

Sheila walked into the hangar with the coffee mugs. "You know, Frank, you're my friend. I just wondered if all your friends were adopting immigrants seeking citizenship. I mean, even Ralph and Sharon have applied."

Frank felt the pull, the line reeling him in slowly. He turned on the water to block out the sound of her voice. He counted to ten, then twenty, and started again. By the time he was at twenty for the third time, he answered, "If you were really a friend, Sheila, you'd know that some things are private. You have no right to be meddling in other people's affairs. I think it's illegal, given your position in the courthouse. Like I said, you best be going."

"Suit yourself." Sheila made a show of removing her jacket as she settled into her car. "At least I know how you live now. Better than I thought. You don't need to be a stranger. Keep the airport safe. Maybe you could do that for the hospital. There was a break-in yesterday. Probably one of those migrants looking for drugs."

Frank waved her off and headed back into the safety of his hangar. The stars seemed less bright after she left. Now he knew that his inclination had been correct. The electrical outages and burglaries weren't coincidences. He didn't think migrants wanted drugs. Why target a guarded facility?

# CHAPTER 30: *Heebie-Jeebies*

Hannah's hands shook. Even when she placed them under her armpits, her feet took over. No taps, no snaps, just the stifled rhythmic seesaw of toes and heels stuck in place. She glanced over at her mother to see if she noticed. The two of them had escaped Mr. Ferguson's watch with the excuse of volunteer work.

Her mom's delicate hands gripped the steering wheel. She held on with the appearance of control, but her hunched posture and scrunched neck told Hannah otherwise. The stress exposed a hole in her strength, a crack in her normal demeanor. Hannah didn't want to admit to herself how the fear had slipped in.

Joseph's warning held fast: *We should be paranoid.* What did that even mean? Yet here she and her mom were in the car with anxiety running the show. First the news of a break-in at the hospital and then Robin's frightened voice on the answering machine. Hannah waited until they stopped at a light to ask, "Mom, tell me again what Robin said. I can't believe this nightmare."

"She was crying. I couldn't make out her exact words. She was scared. Her mom and Rosie hadn't appeared. I mean, Shelly and Rosie disappeared. I don't know what to say Hannah."

Hannah pictured Robin's brave protest at the hospital just a few days past. She had made a stand for all the other kids. "This is too weird. It can't be coincidental. I don't think any of your financial connections can fix this." As soon as those words were out, Hannah felt horrible. Her mom didn't deserve the blame. The silence that followed felt worse than if her mom had protested or yelled. Hannah understood their old spats, but neither she nor her mom knew how to behave now. Hannah whispered, "I think we should stop by Robin's house or her mother's dance studio. Maybe that will tell us something. I know there is a connection somehow. It might be linked to Rosie's cancer study."

Silence. Hannah thought her mother hadn't heard her, but slowly the car turned, and they pulled up in front of Dance for Delight. Hannah jumped out, and her mother went to park.

The door to the studio stood ajar. The last time Hannah had been there, the floors shone, buffed so the dancers could glide, and the mirrors twinkled back clear images. Hannah felt a twinge of guilt because she still had the CDs she'd taken from the studio that day. Today's chaos frightened her. Shoeprints lined the floor. The mirrors were smeared with dirt. The outside was inside. She held her hand out to block her mother's entrance. "Wait, Mom. Shelly would never leave the studio with this mess."

The two walked inside holding hands. Strewn across the floor, Hannah found sheet music, notes from Shelly's desk, and a trail of water mixed with dirt. Her mother bent down and collected the papers. "Mom, don't do that. We shouldn't be here. Leave it." The faintest of noises caused Hannah to pause. She put her finger to her lips. "Shush, listen, don't you hear the tapping? There's a pattern. Five taps like a pulse: one, one-uh, two-and, three-and, four."

All she got from her mother was an incredulous look. With Hannah in the lead, they followed the taps, which coincided with the drips of water and dirt, to a backroom closet. They found Shelly on the floor of the closet, huddled over a tray of mushrooms. Tears streaked Shelly's cheeks. Her eyes held fast to Hannah, who kneeled in front of her. Shelly whispered, "I waited till they were gone. I figured it would be a student who heard me. They'd recognize music. I'd be safe then."

Although Hannah smiled, she wasn't sure of the logic. Anyone would hear the taps and search. She noticed that Shelly made no effort to stand or let go of the mushroom tray. Hannah's mother tried to retrieve it, but Shelly tugged it back. "Shelly, are you hurt? What happened?"

"It was Rosie's idea. She was worried that with the robbery at the hospital, Robin wouldn't be able to get her mushroom treatment. Rosie said the treatment was still in the research stage, and she had to protect it from outside interference. Someone followed us. Rosie was in the front of the studio. She argued with two men. They forced her to leave with them. I hid."

Hannah's mother appeared pale and unsettled. "Mom, sit down. You look like you're going to faint. I can't take care of the two of you." But it was Hannah who felt dizzy with fear. The world seemed to be spinning out of orbit. To what universe, she didn't know.

The three of them sat quietly on the floor—Hannah and her mom, just outside of the closet. Shelly clung to the mushrooms, but at least let them rest on her knees. It was Hannah's mother who broke the silence. "Okay. Shelly, you have to go back to Robin, or at least get your husband there. We have to find Rosie and make sure that Joseph knows about the mushrooms."

Relieved, Hannah let her mother step in. But something still felt wrong. "Mom, it feels like we're missing something. Do you trust Mr. Ferguson? I mean, why would he make me come home and then let you and me leave? Why would he let Dad take the blame for things he didn't do? Mr. Ferguson must know about Joseph's research and the break-ins. He knows everything else. Who is he protecting? Maybe he followed us here? I don't think he cares about anyone." Once she stated her thoughts out loud, Hannah couldn't shake the paranoia.

Shelly handed the mushroom tray to Hannah and stood up. Still shaken, Shelly made her way from the back room into the studio. Hannah and her mother followed as Shelly surveyed the piles of paper, the floors, and the windows. Methodically she walked around the room. She paused in front of the mirrors to examine her face. "I'm none the worse from the scare. If Robin can fight her cancer and help others, I've got to do my part. I won't let these bullies, whoever they are, take ahold of our lives. Help me clean up. I'll call my husband at work and send him over to be with Robin. We are going to act like nothing happened. I'll teach my class this afternoon. I suggest, Mrs. Henderson, that you call this Mr. Ferguson fellow and let him know what's happening."

It took Hannah a few minutes to understand, but her mother followed Shelly's reasoning. "So if Mr. Ferguson isn't to be trusted, he already knows about the mushrooms. If he is truly looking out for my husband and us, then he should be informed. I'll make the call."

Shelly and her mother's calmness unnerved Hannah. When Hannah had first met Shelly at the cancer center's dedication, she almost envied Robin. Not that Robin had cancer like her sister, but that Robin's mother, Shelly, had been positive and energetic. She would have done anything to switch mothers. Hannah approached Shelly. "Are you sure you're okay? I can clean this up. I know you must be scared for Robin."

Shelly's eyes still held a speck of her old spark. She opened her hands as if she had been holding something precious. "Sometimes mothers just *do*. And if we do enough, we get through. I need to expend some energy, get rid of the bad vibes. Music and dance cleanses."

Music filled the studio room, and the three of them cleaned to the rhythms of the mamba. While Shelly picked the debris off the floor and mopped, Hannah and her mother sprayed and washed the mirrors. Occasionally Hannah would glance at herself only to see her mother's face and that of her sister, Jenna. The triple reflection blurred around the edges until Hannah moved in closer and the lines disappeared.

By the time the mirrors glistened again, Shelly had the floor polished. She opened the window curtains and turned the sign to open. Hannah looked out to see her father and Mr. Ferguson parked outside. She wondered how long they had been waiting. Shelly waved to Hannah's father. Her mother straightened her skirt, and her demeanor. Hannah looked back into the mirror. A woman's eyes reflected back from within a teenager's body.

Hannah's head ached. Her eyes itched. She hugged Shelly. "I'll stop by to see Robin. Don't worry. I'll find Rosie. I know she'll turn up."

Shelly returned the hug and held Hannah at arm's length. "Even with all this craziness, I'm so glad I bumped into you at the hospital. Things happen for a reason. Robin loves you like a sister."

Hannah mumbled in response and faked a smile. She walked out of the studio. Her first inclination was to run, but her body felt heftier, weighted by an inner stillness that didn't correspond to her thoughts. She stretched her arms out and peered at her hands. Rock solid. Everything shook inside, but no one could see.

Her father stepped out of the vehicle with Mr. Ferguson. Hannah's mother reached out to her father. The two stood embracing in the middle of the road. Hannah couldn't remember the last time she'd seen such a display of affection. The roadway was still quiet. Pedestrians crossed to the other side of the road and gawked.

Without thinking, Hannah inched away. She walked to the end of the block and turned—a test of sorts to see if she was free to leave. Mr. Ferguson watched her every move yet didn't call out to her or follow. Who was she trying to fool? Hannah didn't know what to do or where to find Rosie. She had meant to tell Shelly about the dance routine she had worked out. Trivial stuff compared to these threats and break-ins.

Hannah peered down the street and saw a shadow pass between buildings. Miguel's shape imprinted inside of her eyes. Drawn by an invisible pull, Hannah ran after him. The ease in which she anticipated his next move surprised her. She slowed her pace and circled back to a brown doorway that melded with the front façade.

He waited with his hands inside his pants' pockets as if their meeting had been preplanned. "Are you following me?" he asked.

Startled by Miguel's question, Hannah stepped into the doorway alongside of him. Her shoulder nudged his shoulder slightly. A push of ideas clamored in her brain. She had been following him without knowing it. She nodded. "Not exactly. I had this sense you'd appear. This might sound funny to you, but I've been tasked to find Rosie. Just as I stood out on the sidewalk, I saw your shadow."

"Rosie has that effect on people. She gets inside of you. Kind of scary."

Hannah moved off the doorstep and back onto the sidewalk. She conjured up Luis in her mind and remembered how much he liked Miguel. "Is that a warning? I thought Rosie was your friend. I saw you two together at the Rhody. Don't you care that she might be in danger?"

Miguel's eyes held steady, and his voice remained calm. "If she is in danger, she'll guide us to her. I think she is working her voodoo powers already. I'm not here because of Rosie, though we are friends from Puerto Rico. On the island, they call her a healer. Here she has a more official name with a PhD at the end of it."

"I don't care what they call her, we need to find her! Robin's life depends on Rosie's mushroom experiment, and Rosie fought with some people who followed her to Shelly's studio."

Miguel dropped his eyes, and his presence flickered between brute strength and an inner peace. His voice was shy of a whisper. "You have to calm down. Rosie chose you to help. Listen, breathe, let go. Your boyfriend, Luis, would understand. Some things have no explanation. If you want to help Robin, I need you to focus."

Since Jenna's passing, Hannah had found solace in sensing others' needs. Her stutter gave her time to evaluate situations and people. This sensation differed. Hannah focused, but she battled the chatter in her brain. The more she tried to make sense of her life, the less she understood. She closed her eyes and focused on Rosie, Robin, Luis, Joseph. Even with this concentration, her mind drifted from thoughts of money, the farm, cancer, foreigners, love, family, fraud. With a jolt, an idea pushed through—wouldn't let go. "Rosie is with a family. Not her own. She's the negotiator of a deal. She's okay, but tired." Drained from the intense concentration, Hannah crumbled onto the sidewalk. "Miguel, you figure out what that means. There isn't a family I know of that would put anyone through this. To tell you the truth, I'm tired, and this freaks me out."

Miguel helped Hannah back to her feet and turned to leave. "Thanks, that helps."

"You can't just walk away. I don't even know what I said to you. You're impossible."

Miguel bowed slightly at the waist and took off.

Hannah wrapped her arms in a self-embrace. The words *family that is not her own* stuck in her brain. She thought about Joseph—how he had given her a sense of belonging over the years, and how he had done the same for Luis. She thought of her father and how he loved his workers; some thought of him as family. And then she realized that family might mean something bad, not a family that loves and gives, but one that takes—a gang. She conjured up Yuri and Vladimir, and immediately Abuelita came to mind.

Propelled by an inner force, Hannah ran.

## CHAPTER 31:
## *Farm, Famine, Family*

Joseph rose before the sun, before the birds, and even before the wind woke the leaves. In the solitude of his workshop, his brain strained with connections that followed history but twisted into the future. He knew that the only way to rest his mind was to sculpt.

It had been weeks since his hands had felt the raw stone, the curves and lines of a story not yet told. When Luis had innocently asked him to unveil his work, Joseph had resisted. Even now, after three years, he wondered if he was ready to finish the vision. Joseph paused. He flexed his hands; each gnarled knuckle was a reminder of troubles and his arduous efforts to manage life.

Joseph took his time surveying the top portion of the stone. He had chosen Fraser River jade for its soft properties and solidness. He needed something harder than soapstone but not as rigid as marble. If he was to carve his way inward, he wanted to feel each turn of the drawknife, the shift of movement as the chisel and files pulled the best out.

To reach the upper section, he set a ten-foot ladder alongside the stone. Dressed in a black apron, safety glasses, and flexible garden gloves, he mounted the ladder and took his first cut. In deep concentration, he subtracted material that didn't belong. He closed his eyes, felt the stone, envisioned the smell of fear, the woods, the ocean, the wind. He felt fire run through his fingers, the flames of hope. Time traveled through the stone—ancestral journeys.

The statue mirrored a more hopeful time when another sculptor from France had a vision of liberty. Joseph modeled it after the gift given to the United States even before his great-grandfather had left Russia. The hope of a life filled with freedoms and possibilities had withered as the symbolism of the Statue of Liberty faltered after many wars and as people forgot their history. For this reason, Joseph had changed the base. Skirted within the body of the goddess of liberty were carved faces of indigenous people—laborers, farmers, businessmen, and children.

Joseph continued the lines left from his last session, the arms reaching toward the sky that merged into one hand. Each arm muscled with twists, paths taken by immigrants from around the world. The ligaments entwined, tinseled with horror, hate, the agony of expulsion. Yet as Joseph painstakingly blended the seven arms, he etched within them a pulse from all the continents. The power of the heartbeat rose through the arms to the one hand. The hand reached past the crowned head and extended upward with a lighted torch.

Hours passed as Joseph lent himself to the stone. Drained, he covered his work and cleaned his space. His only thought was of perseverance. He, like so many, might be without a nationality, but he belonged to a larger family. The stone spoke of a deeper energy that preceded his existence.

Joseph pulled the shop door open to a day of sunshine. The rays adorned the leaves with dew bows. Here was the hope he still needed. Still early, he felt compelled to check on Luis. He tried to convince himself that Luis didn't need to be watched. It was true, but a fatherly instinct had been triggered. First with Hannah, now with Luis. Just as he suspected, Luis had already left. His cereal bowl was washed and turned upside down.

Relieved on all accounts, Joseph focused on what his father had referred to as the lure. With so much secrecy and differing agendas, Joseph had to draw out the villains. Luis had unwittingly exposed the Russian drivers as part of a hacking credit card scam and wine bootlegging scheme. But Joseph knew the reach went further. The two most recent break-ins—first at the composite factory and then at the hospital—put technology at the center. Both robberies stole Joseph's work.

Only a select few knew that Joseph's research sat in the middle. He made the perfect target. An old vendetta would be the explanation. Untraceable, a fact of life, regrettable. *If you bait a fish, what happens if you reel in a whale?*

Joseph noted that his father's witticisms still made sense, even though the world seemed to have advanced. His father had always kept to his goals. Even after the death of Joseph's mother, their migration from Costa Rica to United States to work on the silk trains, the loss of work at the railroad—nothing stood in the way of family. His father never met a man who wasn't his friend, and with time the friendships were their family. His father's death left him orphaned before he had even grown a beard. He was used to going it alone, so Joseph wasn't dissuaded by the distractions. He thought of his family of friends—the postman, the tavern owner, the teacher, and Mrs. Henderson. Let them do their magic, and he would do his.

Joseph took the worn path between his cabin and the Hendersons'. Over a decade of Hannah's small feet plodding across the leaves had left her imprint. Unlike Joseph's pathway to his home, where even strangers left stones, this route held life impressions of only one child growing into womanhood. Joseph never had the desire or need to venture across the divide. People change. Some friendships start slowly. Families extend.

The pathway opened into a clearing. The shade of the trees disappeared, and a house with solar panels stood in the center, absorbing every ray of light. Joseph admired the curved flower beds and walled-in garden space, but the two-story house with its wraparound deck looked naked. The covers had been pulled back, and all the natural flora had been taken and replaced. Joseph sighed at the paradox of paradise. The Henderson home and his cabin stood as testimony to the difference in visions between farmers and woodsmen. Joseph followed the voices to the back deck and called out, "Good morning, it's me, Joseph, from next door."

Mr. Henderson and Mr. Ferguson sat on the deck. Even though they faced a spectacular view of Sauk Mountain, their attention was directed on files that lay strewn on a glass table. Mr. Henderson jumped up to greet Joseph. "My, my—what a surprise. Is everything okay? I mean, you've never come here to visit before."

Joseph ignored the awkwardness. He climbed the stairs and reached out to shake Mr. Henderson's hand. "I thought it would be easier if I came to you, as Mr. Ferguson seems to have staked out your domains and mine. We both know that nothing is okay. You've been framed for some criminal infraction, your farm is at risk, and I'm supposed to hide from the world because of an old vendetta and my dubious legal status in the United States. I figured with all the electrical outages, robberies, and accusations, we should put our heads together."

The reaction wasn't what Joseph expected. Mr. Ferguson stood and gathered all the paperwork from the table and stuffed it in a briefcase. Mr. Henderson's eyes dropped, and his handshake went limp. Even though he towered over Joseph, he seemed to shrink inward. Joseph felt the territorial riff, the pissing on corners, the wall that closes communication. Joseph glared at Mr. Ferguson. "What's going on here, Mr. Ferguson? Are you part of the problem?"

The words had fallen out of Joseph's mouth before he could catch them. Joseph had come with pure intentions, but the secretive atmosphere pushed a button. Now with his clandestine antennae up, he took stock of his setting and the men in front of him.

Mr. Ferguson's face went placid. A mask of no tells. Eyes almost vacant, lips between a smile and a frown. Joseph read the signs as exactly the opposite. His words should have provoked the man. Joseph took a chance and sat down at the table. The two men now had the advantage. They stood above him. Joseph just waited.

Silence leveled the advantage. By the time the hummingbirds had fed on all five feeders, and a Steller's jay won its place on the birdfeeder, the battle of wills ended. The two men stood down and sat on either side of Joseph. Mr. Ferguson cleared his throat. "Yes, in a way I am the problem. I'd tell you I was just Mr. Henderson's lawyer, but you know I'm not. I am here to protect him and his family. You are free to talk and engage with us, but frankly I can't. We may be on opposite sides at some point. You are here illegally. It's better that I don't know you."

Joseph stared at Mr. Henderson, the pillar of the farming community, the man everyone in the community respected, the philanthropist, the father of Hannah. His neighbor, a citizen of this great country—he needed protection. Joseph tried to tamp down his rising feeling of injustice. "Tell me, Mr. Ferguson, who else is worthy of this kind of protection?"

Mr. Henderson's voice returned. "Joseph, don't blame Mr. Ferguson, and please, call me Jeff. I don't deserve a title. No formalities, please. It's complicated. I'm trying to fix things, but my answer to injustice isn't the same as others'. You have to understand that I'm caught between laws, regulations, and none seem to work. Even now I've had to hide things from Connie and Hannah. They're off trying to help others—upset about stolen mushrooms and a woman who is missing. I couldn't stop them, even if I wanted to. I'm bound by reputation. You are freer than I am."

A knot formed at the bottom of Joseph's stomach and rose to his throat. His damaged eye throbbed. Unwittingly Jeff had put his two loved ones in harm's way. "Perhaps you're correct, if you mean by freedom, the ability to live off the grid. To be hidden from society. But if you believe that because I am a bachelor, living without a wife or child, that I don't have a family to protect, you are wrong. If you only protect what's yours, you're more vulnerable than I thought."

Mr. Ferguson busied himself with his phone, kept looking at his watch, until Joseph made a point of including him in the discussion. "Even Mr. Ferguson must realize that the moment you sell freedom, define it based on one set of beliefs, everything is lost. Your family is in more danger than you."

"What do you mean? What do you know? My wife is resting upstairs, and I thought Hannah was with you and Luis."

"Jeff, I know nothing more than what I've already said. Only that whatever you believe Mr. Ferguson is doing for you, isn't for you. I'm here to share information. That is what makes me free. I never separate myself from the present or the past. I believe that all the good I have done to help others is being jeopardized. Mushrooms may not seem important, but cancer hits us all. Rosie is my partner in the research. If she is missing, it proves that more is at stake for the community. This isn't just about me, but what harm the mushrooms might do in the wrong hands. I believe that your vision of a farm that produces food with happy workers is at risk. I believe that while we squabble over small things, there is a bigger threat. I may be undocumented, but that isn't the point. You have rights, the same rights we all have. Don't lose sight of yourself. Distractions win. Now, what do you want?"

Mr. Henderson shrank back, defeated. "To find Hannah."

"I'm sure Mr. Ferguson can help with that."

Joseph left them, the way he came. He walked slowly away, wondering who was the fish, who was the whale, and who was reeling in the catch.

## CHAPTER 32:
## *Within the Crack Lies Another Truth*

Out of breath, Hannah felt dizzy. It had been silly to take off on foot. Without her mother's car, she had to rely on a bus and her thumb to get out to the farm. As small as Skagit County was in terms of gossip and privacy, the physical area extended miles beyond the town streets. She had promised Luis not to use her cell phone because of the hacking. Luckily, she had caught a ride with some of Joseph's friends, a couple delivering fresh corn from their fields to various stands along the freeway.

Hannah walked slowly along the road to the back entrance of the Henderson Farm, where prying eyes would be unaware of her approach. The late afternoon lull of activity had set in. All the workers had gone home, but even so, Hannah sensed tension in the silence. The air felt taut and reminded her of when she had played hide-and-seek with her sister. Whenever Hannah hid and Jenna got close, she had felt that same tense vibration.

As she neared Abuelita's home, Hannah knew it was too quiet. She peered into the kitchen window. Rosie sat at the table with her hands tied in front of her. Two men sat on either side of Rosie with their backs to the window. Abuelita washed dishes and tended a pot on the stove. By all appearances, she was cooking dinner, making everyone feel comfortable. Stunned, Hannah didn't know what to think.

She backed away from the window, alarmed at Rosie's appearance. Rosie held her head sideways with a vacant look in her eye—almost as if she had been drugged. Getting Rosie's attention, even this close, seemed impossible.

She wondered if these two men were the ones Luis had seen at the gas station. If so, the peaceful scene made even less sense. Why bring Rosie here? Hannah remembered her conversation with Miguel: *Rosie is with a family. . .She's the negotiator of a deal.* All Hannah could think about was making a deal with the devil. The devil shifted sides so easily.

On Hannah's last visit to the farm, she had taken a tour with Abuelita and Rubio to see all the changes and modernizations. The blueberry fields aligned with the road. To arrive at the office area, where the workers picked up their checks, a new gravel road wiggled back a quarter mile. Just past that stood Abuelita's house. All the other migrant workers lived past a small field and a row of trees. None of the workers could see Abuelita's house. Hannah took one more look inside before she headed toward the other cabins.

A gust of hot air moved through the trees, brushed across her face. Hannah shivered with the sensation of evil spirits. With the breeze came the smell of fire. Hannah followed the wafting smoke to a set of trees, beyond the line of migrant cabins. Yuri and Vladimir sat huddled together, eyes glazed over. Hannah stood off to the side, and then she realized that what appeared as a campfire was a brush fire. The boys were so out of it that they didn't seem to notice her or the heat from the fire.

Hannah nudged Yuri, then Vladimir. When they didn't respond, she puffed herself up to the size of a mother bear and yelled, "Hey, you've got to move." Then she slapped each one across their face.

The response was instant. Yuri snapped awake and looked at her in disbelief. "You stupid girl, what did you do that for?"

Hannah pointed to the brush fire.

Vladimir stumbled and fell backward. Hannah tugged at his body and asked, "Why is Vladimir so stoned? Yuri, help me move him. We have to beat back the fire."

Hannah and Yuri pulled Vladimir off the grass and behind the trash cans. Vladimir slumped over and leaned against a rubber water barrel. The two filled buckets and doused the fire. The flames smoldered. Afraid that another gust of wind would bring the fire back to life, Hannah shoveled dirt into the bucket and threw it on the burnt grass.

Spent, she tripped and almost fell on top of Vladimir. Yuri caught her. He whispered, "Thanks, that was a close one. Must have been the weed and the wine those guys gave us." Yuri shrugged as if this was the explanation for the brush fire, the reason that Rosie was held up in Abuelita's house.

Hannah counted the wine bottles that lay by the trash cans. "Yuri, that's too many bottles of wine for you and Vladimir to drink alone. What's with the matches and turpentine? What's going on?"

Yuri looked toward Abuelita's house and around the property. His voice dipped an octave lower. "You should just keep out of the way. It doesn't matter what you and your friends think. Joseph is in big trouble. He's made somebody mad. Not just angry but the kind of mad that might get him killed. Or maybe worse. We don't want to get in the way."

Hannah watched Yuri's attention fade in and out. She had to find out more. "Yuri, where is everybody else on the farm? I don't see any activity in the other cabins. If these guys are so bad, why are you still here?"

Yuri mumbled, "Lucky, I guess. They need us to do more dirty work."

"Like setting the field on fire, or were you just playing with matches?"

Yuri raised his hand and made the peace sign. He closed his eyes and ignored the rest of her questions. Hannah knew she hadn't gotten through to him. So much for Joseph's and Abuelita's beliefs in second chances and befriending your enemy. Yuri and Vladimir were still trouble. But if that were true, why did Yuri tell her anything?

Hannah placed her hands over her ears. She could still hear Miguel yelling at her to focus on finding Rosie. She heard the voice of Luis telling her not to live someone else's life. Her mother's chant that she needed to be strong. Her brain shook with opinions. The two voices she didn't hear were that of her father and Joseph. For some reason, her father's voice had been silenced. But Joseph, even in his quiet way, always saw the path to understand. He listened. Hannah knelt to touch the ground and listened with her ears, hands, and feet.

From the distance, she heard trucks on the gravel road. She felt the rumble of tires leading to the migrant cabins. A click of the door from the back porch of Abuelita's house. Movement on the farm signaled Hannah wasn't here alone. Her mother believed that Abuelita would keep everyone safe on the farm. If this were true, why had Rosie's hands been tied?

Hannah glanced back at Yuri and Vladimir. Still in their stupor, their snores made another statement: *Obliterate any chance of rebellion, and there would be no need to silence people.* Hannah listened to her heart. *No one would silence Abuelita.* Abuelita drew out the best in everyone. She worked her charms even on the vilest.

Hannah took a chance and left Yuri and Vladimir. She walked to the farthest cabin, where her father insisted the supervisor live. His philosophy was that no matter what your status was on the farm, you lived the same. The only difference in cabins usually was the garden surrounding the building. Rubio's garden fed his family and most of his neighbors. She crossed her fingers that Rubio would be home.

Without hesitation, she knocked on the door. From the corner of her eye, she noticed a slight movement of the window curtain. When there was no answer, she knocked again. This time, Rubio opened the door and motioned her inside. No words, no emotion, no surprise, just the slight turn of his hand and the door shut.

It took her a moment to adjust to the dark room. Rubio guided her to a chair. At least ten of the workers were crowded in the front room.

Some sat on the floor, others on the sofa. Hannah wondered what she had interrupted. "I'm sorry to disturb your meeting," Hannah said, "but you should know that there is a problem on the farm."

Rubio and the men's blank stares struck her as odd. Either Rubio and the crew knew something was amiss, or they were afraid. Hannah waited for a smile, some snide remark in Spanish, some signal from Rubio. Finally, he squeezed her shoulder. "*Mi hija*, you shouldn't be here." He looked at the workers. They nodded.

No, of course, she shouldn't be. Hannah wanted to scream. Fear mixed with her anger. "You may not care about me or my father, but I think Abuelita is in trouble. Unless you know the two men who are holding a woman named Rosie hostage in Abuelita's cottage, then she is in danger. Don't you understand, Abuelita is protecting the farm." Hannah gasped for breath as tears and uncontrollable sobs washed over her.

Rubio squeezed her shoulder again. "*Mi hija*, you misunderstood me. We have meetings here each week. They are hidden from some of the workers, but your father knows about them. Tonight, the rest of the crew was persuaded to leave by the two men you talked about. They offered the crew money and wine. When I said you shouldn't be here, I meant because we have seen those men before. They're bad."

A thin line of light filtered through the window blinds. Hannah looked closer at the men's eyes. She noticed the wide pupils, the flicker of fear. Each seemed to be holding their breath. "What about Abuelita? She needs you."

Rubio shook his head, defeated. "She is a citizen with rights. Most of the crew has only their green card. They can't get into trouble for fear of deportation."

Hannah for the first time truly understood the catch: To gain citizenship, they had to ignore what was right, for fear of being found in the wrong. "Well, that isn't my excuse. I'll take the risk." She turned and walked out the front door, while twenty eyes stared at her back in terror.

# CHAPTER 33: *Wings Take Flight*

Frank knew better than to put worry into an equation. The result always added up to disaster. After Sheila's nighttime visit to his hangar, he pondered the break-ins at the composite factory and the hospital. Joseph had sought safety for his wing design. Frank had prided himself on the delivery, the ease of slipping in and out, handing off the prototype.

Worry came when Frank bumped into the freckled engineer, Joseph's contact, at the Food Co-Op. Rex confirmed that Joseph's wing prototype had been stolen. Plainclothes men had swarmed the facility. The breach triggered an investigation from the CIA, as their computer server had also been hacked. Somehow, the factory's system connected to the national security system. Frank remembered the boy's warning at the factory: *Shit happens, stay away from the fumes.*

After shopping, Frank headed over to the Mount Vernon Library to meet with Joseph. He walked past the courthouse and past the jail. He glanced up at the windows, thinking he might catch a glimpse of Sheila. He knew this was an impossibility as her office was deep in the bowels of the federal courthouse. Her adventure out to his hangar stuck with him. She'd soon find another stack of citizenship applications on her desk. Frank crossed his fingers that Sheila would keep her silence about his involvement and deal with her boss's questions.

He turned on Second Street and slowed his pace, trying to clear his head. Frank also knew about investigations. It didn't matter what side of the issue you were on—heads rolled, and blame would be doled out. Worry seeped in. Despite Joseph's attempt to provide a safe place for the prototype, the invention had been confiscated and was in, as Joseph had put it, *the wrong hands*. Frank wasn't sure whose hands it should be in, but he suspected it was part of a new defense system that used lightweight drones.

The library bustled with activity. Summer and winter were the library's most active times. Frank knew because that's where he used to hide out as a kid. He imagined that he looked just like the skinny boy who walked up to the counter with books stacked to his chin. The boy's grin soothed Frank's apprehension.

He searched for Joseph among the reference books. Usually Frank found him in the science section. After a walk down all the aisles, Frank checked his watch to make sure he was on time for their meeting. As he turned to leave, he recognized the postman, the bartender, and the teacher he had seen with Mrs. Henderson. They sat at a round table filling in the citizenship forms he had acquired. Each one had a stack of information by their side.

Frank pulled out a chair at the table. "Excuse me, I don't mean to bother you, but did either of you happen to see Joseph here? He told me to meet him at five o'clock."

The teacher looked up. "That's odd, he told us he'd be here to help fill out forms. We just thought he had met with Connie—I mean, Mrs. Henderson—beforehand and they were late. I'm Marmalade, and if I remember correctly, you're Frank. I knew your mother. Thanks for helping Joseph. He relies on you."

At the mention of his mother, Frank felt a deep sense of loss. Thankful that Marmalade hadn't mentioned the sordid affair with his sister, Frank waited as the bartender and postman nodded hello. He continued, "Looks like you've been at it for a while. When was Joseph supposed to be here?"

The bartender, Bill, shrugged. "Said he'd be here at three. I've got to get back to the tavern by six for the night shift. And this is John's late day too. He's got to go back to the post office to deal with new security training on the computers. Figured we could get some of the paperwork done before we left. We didn't think Joseph would mind."

Frank, still unclear on Joseph's plan, nodded but didn't feel at all confident he could even answer their questions. Who knew what Joseph had told them? "No, Joseph wouldn't mind. I'm not privy to everything he's doing. Where are all the migrants to go with these forms?"

Marmalade put her pen down and her hands over a stack of forms. "Some of them are at the church studying for the exam. Some are just kids and can't write, so we've started their forms. Don't worry, between Bill, John, and myself, we'll have all the documentation, the local families to sponsor or adopt the migrants, and the paperwork filled out correctly. We've got all the daycares organized, and the PTAs at the schools are involved. And of course, all the religious organizations. You'd be amazed at how you can network when it comes to issues of the heart."

Marmalade's assurance answered his question but didn't assuage his unrest. It wasn't like Joseph to miss an appointment or, for that matter, to have Mrs. Henderson not show up. The last time Frank had felt this unsettled, he had tried to make amends for his sister's actions. He wasn't worried about his own affairs now, but still his gut told him that something was amiss. "Well, if Joseph stops by, tell him I've gone to run some errands. I'll check back here before six."

He turned to go, when Bill tapped him on the shoulder. "I don't know if this would mean anything to you, but I have a police scanner in my car, and it seems that some of the workers from the Henderson Farm have showed up at the hospital. They're sick from drinking wine. Odd, as I've never known them to order that at my tavern."

Frank had assumed the bootleg Russell had warned about was the stuff made up in the hills, hard liquor peddled off as legal. But it could just as well have been wine. Frank added up the equation, and the sum equaled more worry. He thanked Bill for the information and headed out.

He stood on the sidewalk undecided. That was the trouble with worry, it held no logic or plan. An emotion with no direction. Frank felt his heart pound as he ran toward the parking lot. He turned his truck west and headed to the Henderson Farm.

## CHAPTER 34: *Dream Makers*

Luis tossed and turned most of the night. He heard Joseph slip out of the cabin while the stars held fast to the night sky. Despite his lack of sleep, Luis rose early with Hannah on his mind. Her abrupt departure with Mr. Ferguson caught him off guard. While working at the Henderson Farm, he had worried about his parents being taken away and the whole situation of green cards and deportation. He felt selfish that while staying with Joseph, his life remained hidden and secure. Thoughts of his friends and coworkers had seemed less significant. He missed his parents but not the in-your-face stress of politics. Hannah's departure challenged all this. If Mr. Henderson's life was up for grabs and Hannah's confined by some secret, then what laws protected any individual?

He rushed from Joseph's cabin with his eye on Hannah's home. The darkened house lights encouraged him. At least Mr. Ferguson, their official protector, slept and the Henderson family was safe. Luis figured he could drive up Highway 20 and be at the Concrete Airport before anyone had awakened, do his chores, and then seek out Hannah.

When he arrived at the airport, Poker's hangar door was locked. Luis missed the banter and needed to thank Poker for taking over his chores. He knocked a few times, but a hollow sound echoed back. Granted, Luis was earlier than usual, but Poker had always had a cup of coffee waiting for him. Within a couple of hours, Luis had mowed the field, weeded the garden beds, and watered. Still no sign of Poker. Disappointed, Luis cleaned up and headed back to Joseph's home.

Out of habit, he turned on the radio. Instead of playing Latino music and jazz, a broadcaster broke into the program: "This is a public announcement. Officials are warning residents to avoid buying or consuming wine brought into the area recently that does not have a barcode. Skagit Valley Hospital reports multiple cases of ill workers from the local Henderson farm who ingested this illegal wine. Notify the authorities if you know of anyone who has consumed this wine or know of its source."

Luis did know something. Visions of the gas station with bottles of wine in the aisles, the threatening men outside of the cell tower hidden within the church steeple, and the menacing truck drivers, left him shaking. His truck swerved, dodging imaginary foes. Was he complicit, an accessory to a crime? If he came forward, he could jeopardize Joseph's and the Hendersons' safety. He didn't trust himself with this responsibility. The only thing he knew for sure was that he was in the thick of it.

He fiddled with the dials, trying to block out the news with music. Music, he understood—the rhythms, the emphasis on a beat, the slow and then fast pace. Each radio station spouted the wine warning. Luis felt the words directed to his conscience. He turned the radio off. The truck sputtered along as if it, too, felt the pressure. He downshifted. The sputter turned to a shudder. Luis checked the gas gauge. Empty. With just less than a mile from the gas station, he coasted down the hill and pulled in.

Luis didn't believe in luck. In fact, his mother had always said luck was a curse that made you lazy. As he filled up his tank, he looked around at the parking lot. Unmarked police cars surrounded the gas station. Two at each exit, and more by the door. His heart raced. Without a credit card, he had to go inside to pay. The last place he wanted to be was amid a raid. A young lad sat at the register, face frozen in concentration. Luis paid and left.

As he pulled out, he looked in his mirror to see if any of the police had followed. Relieved, he felt less guilty. He figured the authorities had traced the wine to the gas station. Luis convinced himself that he didn't know the source—that his silence would not be detrimental to the investigation. He doubted that another wine delivery would be made to this gas station. He worried more about how the bad wine had gotten to the Henderson Farm and why. Why make bootleg wine to poison others?

Hannah had accused him of being a hero when he dove off the bridge to help the bootleg driver. His intentions had been selfish, not heroic. Now he felt like a coward. Who did his *silence* protect?

As Luis wound his way back on the narrow road to the cabin, a black sedan came out from the Henderson driveway, sped by, and pushed him off the road into a narrow shoulder. Mr. Ferguson drove with Mr. Henderson in the passenger seat. Instinct put Luis on high alert. He couldn't be sure, but he thought he'd seen Mr. Henderson signal him to turn around and follow. It was the signal used at the farm when it was time to head back in—a flick of the hand, pinkie finger lifted upward, sharp and to the point.

He revved the motor in reverse, made a three-point turn, and followed. By the time Luis hit Highway 20, the sedan was just a speck. Images of Hannah flashed in his mind. The only reason for Mr. Henderson to rush out would be his daughter. Luis kept just below the speed limit, a habit he still couldn't break. Apparently, Mr. Ferguson had law on his side.

Luis drove with myopic concentration. The truck nosed along the familiar route until Luis heard the clip of blades overhead. He snapped out of his narrow focus to see three unmarked black helicopters circling the skies. They hovered over the parking lot of the composite factory. He knew, like he knew his native tongue, that this was no coincidence. Joseph's notebook on silk and the wing prototype stuck in Luis's brain. He remembered searching for the research when Joseph went into hiding. He never doubted Joseph's reasons for going into seclusion. Now he wondered if Joseph's crazy inventions, mushroom cures and silk composite wings, were the problem, not the Russian vendetta. That didn't explain the bootleg wine or the hacking of cell phone towers.

Forced to slow down by the gawkers, Luis searched for the black sedan in the parking lot. The sea of vehicles included old trucks and old cars. The sedan had disappeared. Luis headed to the Henderson Farm. He might have abandoned farming, but not his feelings for old friends. His gut told him that Hannah would be there. He'd never abandon her.

. . . . .

Luis parked his truck along the side street that paralleled the long driveway to the Henderson Farm's office. An eerie quiet hung in the air. The blueberry fields shimmered with a blue haze as the sun and warm air hovered above the plants. He checked his watch. Not lunch time yet. He squinted against the sun and peered down the long rows, checking for movement. Just because he couldn't see the pickers didn't mean they weren't there.

As he turned the bend, he saw Frank's truck in front of Abuelita's house. Luis had no idea that Frank knew Mr. Henderson. He expected the black sedan with Mr. Ferguson and Mr. Henderson, but the car was nowhere to be seen. His heart skipped a beat at the thought of Abuelita, the mainstay of all the families on the farm, in need. He'd forgotten, in his short absence, her importance. A wave of shame shuddered through his shoulders. Abuelita had even counseled his parents, tried to help them with their paperwork.

Luis pushed his hand through his hair and tucked in his shirt. Usually Abuelita left her door wide open. Her only requirement for entry was to be clean and to come in with a smile. He knocked twice and waited for a reply. When none came, he walked inside. Abuelita sat stiffly at the kitchen table with her gaze fixed on the door, her lips pressed inward. Frank sat by her side. His hands encircled hers. Luis searched the room for a clue. Everything was in its place except for a heavy cast-iron skillet, which lay upside down on the table. "Abuelita, are you okay? Did someone hurt you?"

Abuelita emitted a sigh, her gaze still fixed on the door. "*Mijo, estoy bien.* I'm okay, thanks to Frank. I just need to rest."

Frank shrugged. "When I heard about the farmworkers being hospitalized due to the bad wine, I knew that it wasn't an accident. I've seen too many of the workers at the bars drinking cheap beer. I figured it was a ploy to cover up something bigger." Frank chuckled nervously. "They got more than they bargained for with Abuelita, but then Rosie and Hannah finished them off."

Luis's words rushed out. "Where's Hannah? Is she okay? What happened?"

Frank put his hand up, slowing Luis down.

Luis took a deep breath. "Abuelita, *digame*, tell me the truth."

"Luis, *mijo*, I did my best. Out of nowhere, two men came with a lady named Rosie, pushing their way into the house. I'd never seen them before, but they knew the layout of the farm. I'm so sorry, that I didn't know who they were. They got the workers drunk, so when I called for help, no one came. They tied her up and drugged her with some concoction. That's when Hannah came."

Abuelita's entire body shook as she talked. Luis went to her side and hugged her. "When Hannah saw you here, what did she do?"

"Hannah only saw us through the window. I ignored her, willed her away. She must have gone for help. But there was none. The crazy men wanted Rosie to tell them about her mushroom experiment. That lady played them. Hannah must have sensed something."

Beside himself, Luis paced around the kitchen table. Saw the rope on the floor, and then the blood. "Whose blood is that?"

Frank stood up and placed his hands on Luis's shoulders. "Look at me. It's okay. Hannah will be fine."

Before Luis or Frank spoke again, Abuelita pulled on Luis's arm, looked around the kitchen, and began again: "I'm telling you, Rosie somehow tapped into Hannah's thoughts. These men wanted to break Rosie down, find out secrets. Rosie went into a trance. It scared them. I played my part, as I always do. Made them comfortable with food and talk. The rest of the workers hid, afraid of the law."

"So everyone left you alone?" Luis tried to control his anger. "I should have been here, never should have left the farm."

Abuelita shook her head. "No, you have your own destiny to live. You're here now. Besides, the workers weren't cowards, they just needed a plan. When Hannah left them to save us, they lost their fear."

Frank interrupted, "They followed Hannah, surrounded the house. When she came in, she pretended to be here for a visit."

Luis listened, fearful of what happened next. "Tell me about the blood."

Abuelita broke eye contact with Luis. She folded her hands across her chest and took a breath. "Luis, can you get me a glass of water?" He handed her the water. Abuelita drank slowly, licked her lips. "Thanks. Like I was telling you, Hannah became the distraction. She talked to me in Spanish—or at least they thought she was. They were transfixed. Then Hannah acted like she barely understood English. She hovered around Rosie, patted her head with a cold cloth. Somehow Rosie signaled Hannah. Hannah spilled a bowl of beans, and Rosie went for the cast-iron skillet."

Frank added, "If you ask me, I think Rosie planned the whole escape in her trance. She wouldn't say anything to those guys about the mushroom research, but they brought the bootleg, knew where Joseph lived."

Luis stared at Frank. "I don't care about the trance, don't make light of the situation." Luis noticed a twitch by Frank's left eye. "What happened next, Frank?"

Frank closed his eyes. "I rushed in with my hunting rifle. The two guys ran outside. The farmworkers jumped out of the bushes and held them down with the nets they use to protect the blueberries."

Luis let the sequence of events settle in his brain. He looked at Abuelita and then back at Frank. "What have you left out? Both of you wouldn't be shaking and sitting here if this was over. Hannah, Rosie, the workers—where are they?"

Neither spoke. Luis watched them rise. They seemed to be moving in slow motion. Frank stood with his hands in his pockets. Abuelita held her arms out, embraced him, and said in a low voice, not even a whisper, "Hannah dove for the gun. A bullet grazed her leg. Just a nick. She is with her father. Mr. Henderson and that other man. They arrived just before you. Rosie cleaned the wound. She is okay."

Luis fell into a chair. Hunched over, he tried to breathe. "Did they take her to the hospital? I'd better go."

"Get ahold of yourself, Luis. I don't think they went there. It isn't safe for Rosie. Abuelita sent them with first aid supplies from the farm. Rosie knows what she is doing in terms of healing. You can trust her. And Mr. Henderson would never put Hannah in jeopardy."

Luis listened but didn't move. He stared at Frank and Abuelita as if they were from another planet. Couldn't they see how everyone was still in danger? Nothing had changed. Mr. Henderson had to hide, and so did Rosie. Hannah had risked her life. Her father *had* put her in danger.

Luis struggled to control his anger. Without Hannah, his dreams would be shattered. "Trust Rosie? I don't know her. I can't trust anyone when there is so much violence and corruption. I don't have faith in the system."

"Ah, *mijo*, you can't just dream. You can't wait for others to make the world just. You and I know this, because we aren't the *dreamers*. We expect nothing. My trust comes from the doers. Mr. Henderson, Rosie, Joseph, Frank, the farmworkers, Hannah—and you. I've had enough of our government and waiting for their promises, their dreams for the Deferred Action of Childhood Arrivals. We must all be *dream makers*."

Luis had no patience to debate Abuelita. Her words made odd sense, but if he was a doer, then he had to be a thinker as well. "Frank, something else is going on here. Why would those Russian thugs come here? Why is Mr. Henderson in trouble? All this secrecy has put Hannah in danger."

Frank looked out the window. He kept his back toward Luis. "I hate secrets. My sister made me keep her secrets. Her secrets put the whole valley in danger."

Abuelita wept silently, her head bent, her shoulders heaving with each breath. "Rubio and I were sworn to secrecy. We were only trying to protect Mr. Henderson. It was Rubio who found money discrepancies in the books. The bank account was off—sometimes with more money, way more money than he expected. Rubio couldn't explain it and feared he'd be blamed. Mr. Henderson went to the authorities when Rubio showed him. Some scheme with money laundering, extra payments in credit cards, and later large withdrawals. That's all I know. The last year has been so hard for Mr. Henderson with this and the protests. No one understood why he had to keep quiet. The authorities were always around. Mr. Henderson asked Rubio and me to watch everyone. Your parents were worried about me. I tried, I really did."

Luis hugged Abuelita, felt her tears on his cheeks. "Did Mr. Henderson say anything to you before he left? He nearly knocked me off the road on my way here. I thought he had signaled me to follow. I lost him on the way and just assumed he'd be here."

Abuelita answered, "Yes. It didn't make sense to me. He was in a rush. Something about Miguel and a project you're working on. But he was more anxious that you find Rubio."

"And where is Rubio?"

"Oh, he is out in the small buildings beyond the rickety old shed, where he teaches the workers how to farm. I think Vladimir and Yuri are there as well as our captors."

"Abuelita, where is the justice in this?"

"Luis, there's a saying, that truth and character guide until the laws can catch up."

"I think you made that up." Luis gave Abuelita another hug and walked out into the sun.

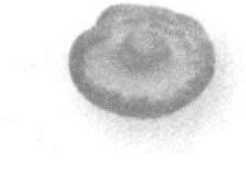

# CHAPTER 35: *Scrambles*

As Joseph drove up the hill and into Russell's driveway, he noted that Spencer and JoAnne had parked their vehicles backend in first. Not a good sign. He followed suit, feeling a sense of urgency, that maybe a quick exit would be needed. He left just enough space so as not to block anyone's path.

He didn't bother knocking. Instead he slipped in through the kitchen and followed the voices into the dining room. Set up by hospice, an adjustable bed took center stage, where Russell lay with his head propped up by pillows. Plastic tubing extended from an oxygen tank to his nose. Papers lay strewn on a tray. Spencer and JoAnne sat on either side of the bed. Joseph hid his concern. "Russ, if I'd known there was a party, I'd have brought something to eat."

Russell waved Joseph in and motioned him to take a chair. "Spencer will fill you in on the plan." He gasped for breath and sighed. "I'm short on energy—saving it for the grand finale."

Joseph nodded. "This is your gig. I don't know a lick about ham radios. I'm relying on your helpers. You were right about the jamming of the cell tower signals. Here I was worried about myself, but the Russians are sly. They target the vulnerable, create fear, and divert attention away from the real target. We have to make enough trouble to force the utilities and the government to take action."

JoAnne and Spencer watched Russell as Joseph spoke. JoAnne held Russell's hand and whispered, "Russ, let us know if this upsets you too much. You don't have to help."

Russell stared JoAnne down with his furrowed brow and pursed lips. "Damn it, I'd die if I didn't help. I'll die anyway. I won't have anyone scrambling my ham radios. Pun intended—even if I can't eat eggs with my ham anymore! Just take Joseph downstairs where I have everything set up. I wrote out instructions."

Joseph appreciated Russell's indignation. He was a fighter, always had been. Spencer led the way as they went through the basement and into Russell's ham radio sanctuary—hidden door and all. No room for extras, just two seats and a table with the radio equipment. Joseph sat next to Spencer and read the instructions on how to intercept calls from the new cell tower. Through the ham radio, they had to emit a signal stronger than the bogus cell tower. The sound would be emitted not just by Russel's radio but by every ham radio owner in the area, at the same time, on the same frequency.

"Spencer, are you sure this will work? It isn't just the newfangled cell tower that was built to look like a church spire that we have to block, but all the towers clear up to the Canadian border."

"I'm not Russell, but he knows his stuff."

A tense quiet filled the room, then the static of the airwaves crackled as Spencer turned various knobs. Using his call name, Spencer alerted the hams to be ready. Suddenly, voices bantered back and forth on timing and the use of proper frequencies.

"Russell said you had a list, a pattern of past interference. Can I have that?"

Joseph pulled the GPS coordinates from his pocket. "Here, it's a list of all the hydroelectric sites at the dams. Luis found it in the notebook of the Russian who fell off the Skagit River Bridge when it collapsed. Like I told Russell, I think the Russians are taking us for a ride. Hacking the cell phone towers to get credit card information, but way more. I think they want to hijack the electric grid here and in Canada. Even though we are a small town, the Russians must know that there are defense companies here. Utility reliability effects their work. Unless we force the issue, you know the electric companies will hide their vulnerability."

Spencer took the list of coordinates. "We have hams all the way up Highway 20 with their mobile radios and directional antennae. We'll broadcast on a GSM spectrum for ham radios, 900MHz—the same frequency used by GSM phones. Get ready. When everyone begins, the signals will spoof all the towers and the calls will be captured from AT&T and Verizon cell phones."

"Get ready for what?"

"All hell will break loose. The scrambling will confound the hackers but will also set up alarms to the cell phone providers and, if we're lucky, our government. Who knows what will happen? Joseph, you said you wanted to expose the scam. Why the sour face?"

Joseph's bad eye twitched. "Just realized that I'm placing people I don't even know in peril."

Spencer cocked his head toward Joseph. "I don't think it's yours to decide. We've got Russell upstairs trying to save the world. Just so happens you see a larger problem. Can't separate them, can we?"

"What'll happen to the hams?"

Spencer laughed. "Joseph, I've never seen you undecided. It's our turn to take a risk. You've been helping others, saving the world that denies your existence."

Joseph closed his eyes. The twitching stopped as he mentally thought of those he still needed to help. No one wanted to remain in the shadows. "Okay, then at least let me send out the first jamming signals. Any chance we could jam to the tune of "Que Sera, Sera"—whatever will be, will be? Seems appropriate."

Spencer placed headphones over his ears and gave the coordinated signal. "I'd give it less than five minutes before every cell phone carrier in the area will be at risk of having their data hijacked. Customers will call their phone company to report something wrong. Their switchboards will go down. Meanwhile the hijackers will get sandwiched in between."

Joseph stood. "That's it, you're done?"

As Spencer moved away from the radio, he pointed overhead. "It won't be long. Hear that? Down in the basement it's muffled. But I think helicopters are flying over Highway 20. I suggest we make a quick exit. Go, now!"

By the time Joseph had reached the basement stairwell, Spencer had locked the hidden door and rearranged the furniture to cover their path. Back upstairs, Joseph peered out the window. A swarm of black dots flew east, toward the dams. JoAnne ignored the hum of helicopters as she read a book. Russell feigned sleep. Joseph felt like he'd stepped back a lifetime, when his forefathers had hidden from the authorities. It didn't seem to matter how much time passed. He felt Spencer's nudge to leave. "JoAnne, I've brought you more problems. Sorry I can't stay. Take care of Russell."

JoAnne slowly placed her bookmark within the pages of an old copy of a primer on the United States Constitution. She looked up. "Go now, Joseph. I'm brushing up on ways to create a path to citizenship. But in the meantime, you must leave. Russell and I are old hands at standing our ground. We'll be fine."

Joseph paused to touch Russell's age-weathered hands. Russell raised his eyebrow and hissed, "Can't you let me sleep? I'm resting before either the feds or your Russian hackers arrive. Just do me a favor, and tell Rosie she needs to get back to Puerto Rico. Her research here is done. Let her go."

It was just like Russell to give him instructions that didn't make sense. Joseph had no control over Rosie. But maybe Russell had new powers as he neared death. Joseph felt a part of his heart chip off, knowing that yet another of his longtime friends and advisors would not be long for this world. Joseph walked out and closed the door. Spencer's truck was already down the driveway. He heard sirens over the hill. He doubted that the triangulation of the signals would target Russell's home so quickly. If the sirens came from the sheriff's vehicle,

Spencer would meet them on the road first.

Joseph decided to avoid the main driveway and turned down a dirt road that circled around Russell's property. He wound his way up to a hill that overlooked the valley and the highway. Flashing lights preceded a line of cars. He pulled out his binoculars to study the roads down to the highway and the surrounding area. To circumvent the stream of official vehicles headed his way, Joseph downshifted, edged off the dirt road, and crossed a newly plowed farm field to arrive at Ralph and Sharon's homestead.

Sharon stood on the porch, while Ralph lumbered down the driveway to greet him. "Joseph, I figured you'd find your way here once you heard the sirens." Ralph laughed. "It was Russell's idea to call an ambulance. Another diversion."

Joseph shook his head. "I'm not sure about any of this. Russell's too ill to be calling all the shots. But he sure has the valley swarming with activity."

Sharon called out, "Come inside. I won't have you two yammering out in the driveway. Not very hospitable, and besides one of those official cars might stop in for a visit. I made coffee and my bread for guests."

Resigned, Joseph accepted Ralph's handshake and a hug from Sharon's open arms. He sat facing the front door with his butt on the edge of the wooden stool. "I'll stay until it calms down." He drank the coffee and devoured the slice of buttered bread. As he wiped the crumbs from his face, he thanked Sharon. "Your bread always calms me. The yeasty smell reminds me of the mushrooms. Who knows what other healing properties yeast holds?"

Sharon smiled, and Ralph offered him another slice. "Take one more for the road. I know you're itching to go. Your feet keep tapping the floor, like a woodpecker hunting for insects."

"I'm the hunted one. At least the woodpecker has hunger as a driving force. I'm the prey of too many people. And yet, I'm nobody. My blood won't feed anyone."

"Joseph, even now you have science on your mind."

"Not really, my mind just works that way. Someone else can study yeast and insects. I've got to get back to the composite factory and the hospital. Rosie, Hannah, and the Hendersons are in danger because of my research and my past. I'm sorry about involving you in all of this."

Sharon already had the door open, waiting for Joseph. "Don't say another word. You've got a plan. We're here for you. I'm grateful that the mushrooms helped me."

Joseph bowed his head and then made his exit. Yes, he did have a plan, and his own welfare wasn't included in the outcome. He thought of all the stones that paved the way to his house. So many of them told stories. They endured. Whatever the outcome, he'd followed his grandfather's wishes to do good with his life. His penance for fleeing persecution and hiding his Jewish identity. He'd *step lightly . . . move with healing grace.* Joseph couldn't change the past, but at least he could influence the future.

He took the main driveway out to the dirt road. Fresh dust clouds lingered. As he approached Russell's entrance, he noted three vehicles—an ambulance, a sheriff's patrol car, and Spencer's truck. He drove past, pushing worry away. Russell's plan worked. Distraction with the truth was always best.

By the time Joseph turned onto Highway 20, both the east- and west-bound lanes were bumper to bumper with regular traffic and looky-loos. Horns honked as frustration mounted. Traffic jams weren't part of Skagit Valley's makeup. Joseph missed his cabin, his solitude, his privacy. For too long, he had used his isolation as a cover for lack of freedom. Now he needed to shout at the powers that be—not for his own rights, but to protect his friends and possibly the welfare of the entire country.

He pulled off onto the shoulder and drove illegally past the lineup of traffic. He almost wished a police car would pull him over.

## CHAPTER 36: *Wounded*

Hannah woke to the sound of gulls and the smells of fish and ocean spray. With summer daylight stretching until almost ten o'clock, she couldn't tell the hour. She recognized the salty breeze. Eyes still at half-mast, she tried to continue her dream of dancing along the sandstone boulders, the freedom of movement. The lazy roll of waves lulled her back to sleep, until the dream state vanished. She jolted up from her cot too quickly, and the pain in her leg forced her back down. "Ouch." Last thing she recalled was Frank's rifle and lunging at Rosie and Abuelita's captors. A gunshot, and then Rosie patching her leg. Appearing from nowhere, her father and Mr. Ferguson had arrived at the farm and insisted they all leave for a safer place. Now fully awake, she called out, "Anyone here? Dad, I'm up."

Hannah hobbled off the cot to get her bearings. So, this was the *safer place*—a shack on the beach. She noted the cot, the makeshift kitchen with a sink, and propane camp stove. One window that faced sculpted boulders, and a table with two chairs. Her heart dropped when she opened what she thought was the front door only to find a narrow but brightly lit art studio. Here was the window with the view of the waves and beach, but instead of the salty smell of the ocean, fumes of oil paint and turpentine filled the space.

Just as she approached a covered canvas, her father walked in. "Good, you're awake."

His matter-of-fact tone caused Hannah's throat to tighten. She swallowed her words, fearful she'd resort to stuttering. Her father stood with his arms at his side. Overwhelmed with emotions, she stumbled forward. They embraced.

It was her father who stuttered, “Oh, oh, my H-Hannah, I almost lost you. I couldn't bear losing another daughter.”

She'd only seen her father cry once before. Not at Jenna's funeral, but when the pain of her sister's cancer treatment made her so ill that Jenna begged the doctors to stop. Her mother and father had fought. He cried when he found Jenna in Hannah's arms sleeping.

“Dad, I'm okay. You aren't losing anyone. Just tell me what's going on. First off, where are we? Is this where you've been hiding?”

“This is my hideaway, what has kept me sane these last few years. It wasn't meant to be a secret, but it became one.” He shrugged. “Something like you and Luis.”

He had her there. Hannah suspected that her parents' lives ran parallel to each other and that they intersected only where she was concerned. “Not sharing with you about Luis wasn't meant to be a secret. Just that you and Mom were so protective of me and seemed to be so against anyone I liked. Joseph, Luis, even Shelly at the hospital. I just kept it to myself. But you and I both know that the events at the farm and hiding here in this shack go way beyond normal.”

“More complicated than I knew.” His shoulders slumped, but then he stood straight, adjusting his thoughts, and a slow grin formed. “You went and grew up. Now you're protecting everyone. You're worse than your mother and me combined. When you're passionate about something, watch out.”

Hannah wanted to laugh, but she could tell her father was deflecting. “Does this have something to do with your plan for the farm? You have Luis coming out to the beach to work on a project with that Miguel guy. Is this your idea of working around the system?”

“Not exactly.” His grin evaporated, and instead she saw the bags below his eyes, the thinness of his neck, the weight loss. Her father let his thoughts rush out: “I still believe that the only way to make a difference is to show the various stories. Regulations and opinions only solidify arguments about the rights of green-card holders, those seeking asylum. It divides us and forgets the human element."

Hannah wasn't convinced. "What does that have to do with me being shot, you put in jail, and this weird covert operation? What are you hiding?"

Her father's voice waivered. "You once told me about Joseph's path to his home. How he let visitors—anyone—put down markers in his pavers. Even if he didn't agree with the thought, he left them. I'm coming to that same conclusion." He shrugged, took a breath. "Everything changes, even my viewpoints. There isn't just one way, one right or wrong."

"Stop spouting philosophy to me—you sound like Joseph. Just tell me the truth and what we are going to do."

He opened the window and let in the salty breeze. "I'm trying, but my thoughts get jumbled. I wish I had Joseph's perspective. All I can explain is how I came to this point. Look at this room. This side faces the beach, the other side, the boulders. Two different views, depending on the outlook. That's why I paint, why I enlisted Miguel and Luis. I know I was naïve. I thought I was working with just prejudices and false accusations." He shivered. "But greed and politics entered. Our valley became a target. Me, Joseph, Rosie, and now you."

Hannah shut the window. "Don't let the bad guys win, Dad. I support you no matter what you did or why you were arrested."

Her father shook his head. "So much more is at stake. I'm not sure about the politics of this—most people won't understand. I thought I was targeted because someone thought I was doing something illegal on the beach. Then I thought it was the protesters who set me up. Later, I realized it was bigger, that the federal government was involved. I'm at a loss for how to answer your questions."

Hannah wondered when all this started. She faulted herself for being unaware, for taunting Yuri and Vladimir. She feared her relationship with Luis made it all worse. "I've made things worse, haven't I? I'm sorry. I wish I had paid more attention. Luis has become more paranoid since he found out about the Russians. He worried about his family before, and now he's frantic about Joseph. But Joseph isn't afraid. Neither is Robin, Shelly's daughter with cancer." Hannah's words rushed out. "She's younger than Jenna was when she was first diagnosed, and Robin set up a boycott, took on the system at the cancer ward." Winded from talking so much, Hannah hoped she sounded convincing. She touched her wounded leg, found a chair to sit.

Her father pulled up his painting stool and placed his hand on her shoulder. "You're tired. Rest now. No one will bother you."

A knock on the door told her to do otherwise. In walked Mr. Ferguson, her father's supposed lawyer. "Mr. Henderson, we have to leave now. All government departments have been put on an alert. Phones are down, and the electric grid all the way up to the border is unstable. I don't think you're safe here."

Hannah couldn't help herself. "No electricity here. Look around, it's pretty basic. Most likely, this is the safest place if you're worried about access by intruders. But you aren't really worried about our safety, are you?"

"Hannah, show some respect."

"Dad, retreating isn't doing anything. Your plan to tell this story through art is great. It's a lifelong project that will go nowhere. But you and I know the problem isn't about locals. There's a real threat to a trust in truth and decency."

"Your daughter has a point."

"Which point?" Hannah asked. "That you aren't worried about my family's safety?"

Mr. Ferguson listened to the microphone in his ear. Any semblance of concern vanished. "Your value in this situation has changed. You aren't the target. There are bigger fish to fry."

Hannah sprung out of her seat, ignoring the pain in her leg. "Great, we were all pawns. You used my father, didn't you? Mr. Ferguson, you got us into this. Here is your chance to prove me wrong. Give my father and me a ride to the hospital."

Mr. Ferguson walked to the door. "Why the hospital and not the farm?"

"You really don't get it. Even if I can't trust you, you'd find out. It's simple. Because Rosie isn't here, and you and I both know she isn't at the farm. I'm sure its chaotic there, but I trust Abuelita, Rubio, and Frank to take care of the two creeps at the farm. I'm worried about Robin. Besides, my intuition tells me you don't know what to do."

Before she walked out, Hannah pulled the cover off her father's canvas. Tears fell from her eyes, but she didn't say a word. Jenna stood atop a ridge overlooking the ocean. Her cheeks chiseled, her lips open, her eyes bright. Her arms were spread wide as if she were an angel ready for flight. In the corner, her father had painted each of them waving her off.

# CHAPTER 37: *An Education*

Immigration and Customs Enforcement pulled up with their van, spewing gravel as they slowed down. The farmworkers who remained after Hannah's injury and Rosie's capture scattered. Rubio ran after them shouting, "*Esta bien*, it's okay. This isn't a raid." As the farm manager, he expected them to obey. "*Mira*, look, they are here for the Russian criminals."

Even with Rubio's assurances, no one was willing to stay. Luis didn't blame them. They all remembered his parents' deportation. This time, however, ICE wore bulletproof vests and sported automatic rifles. Serious attire, for business more serious than a visa violation. The two Russian captors had gone passively, already subdued by the farmworkers, but Yuri and Vladimir, frightened and barely sober, fought. Luis tried to calm them, but the ICE officers pulled him away. "Be careful, son. Laws have changed, and even though you are a Dreamer, you don't want anything on your record. I'm trying to help you and your friends."

Luis recoiled, offended by the label, offended by the inference. He had only worried about his parents' status, not his own. He'd been stupid, lulled by Joseph's care and the kindness of others. What did he have in common with the Russians, or for that matter, why was his friend Joseph now a criminal?

He answered politely, "Yes, sir. No one wants to be on the wrong side of the law."

Luis wished he had said what he thought, but even so, one of the officers looked back at him as if he needed a scolding. The ICE officer rolled down his window to make his point. “We got who we were coming for. The two young boys were extra. They need a lesson. It’s for their own good. Who knows, if you get your citizenship, maybe you can work with us.”

Again, Luis played the part of a subdued migrant worker, standing with his arms crossed behind him, almost bowing as he lifted his hidden third finger in the air.

Rubio called out, “Luis, let it go. I need you. Seems the crew has disappeared. Can you load up the day’s pickings onto the truck?”

This was one of his old jobs when he worked at the farm. All four of the delivery trucks stood empty on the driveway. Luis knew the drill. Fresh blueberries had to be delivered on time and in perfect condition. He took the wheelbarrow and began. Luis’s arms strained as he carried the last of the filled blueberry crates onto the Hendersons’ trucks. Not what he expected after all the ruckus with the captors.

As he finished, Rubio approached. He shook Luis’s hand and embraced him. “We’ve missed you here. I don’t know if Mr. Henderson has told you that. He feels so guilty.”

Luis waited while Rubio looked over the fields, checked for inconsistencies and anyone lurking. Rubio’s welcoming smile transformed into a mask that hid his emotions.

“You stayed, Rubio. Even became Mr. Henderson’s confidant. Why?”

Again, Rubio surveyed the fields. He shrugged, and his smile returned. “I’m part owner of the farm. For the last few years, Mr. Henderson has developed a business model based on what he calls the six pillars of success: dedication, knowledge, skills, honor, development, and fairness.”

“Sounds like a formula, but not reality. He’s in trouble. He’s endangered Hannah and all of you.”

“Yes, and he’s saved all of us too. Don’t be so quick to judge.”

Here he was again, pushed into seeing more. Luis held back the flood of anger he felt surging inside. Tears slipped out. "What am I missing? Give me more to change my mind."

"Your parents would tell you to dig deeper. They'd tell you that injustice goes in all directions. They always believed in Mr. Henderson. Listen, evaluate, think. We need you."

Luis swallowed a snappy answer. "It's hard to trust the system."

Rubio nodded in agreement. "Same with faith. It's hard to hold on to what you can't see. Hannah sees more, feels more."

The mention of Hannah set off alarms. Joseph, Abuelita, and now Rubio seemed to mimic one another with their homegrown philosophies. Even Hannah pushed through all of the muck. Luis conjured up Hannah's smile, her independent streak. "I trust people and outcomes. I'm just not sure about blind faith or regulations."

"No one here is blind. Laws exist because of bad people. Open your eyes, Luis. I already know your heart is."

Luis felt like a ping-pong ball, batted back and forth by well-meaning friends. Rubio had reconciled his place in the chaos. Abuelita and Rubio balanced on a thin line—following laws, supporting the farmworkers and their culture, as well as establishing their own mark. Mr. Henderson created a new line, a new path. Luis imagined dancing along the boulders, the narrow edge where he teetered on the rocks above the beach, risking a fall but light and sure of his footing.

"Do you need any more help, Rubio? Otherwise I'm off. I've got to find Hannah."

"You haven't heard, have you? Cell phone lines are jammed, and there are blackouts all the way to Canada. Homeland Security is out in full force, with helicopters along Highway 2O and I-5. I suspect it has something to do with the business here at the farm. Just a feeling, but with Mr. Henderson's arrest and the Russians making the workers ill—these coincidences make me uncomfortable."

Luis mentally connected all the events of the last few weeks. He felt the weight of Rubio's words and said, "We've both been blinded. Mr. Henderson's problems at the farm were a distraction, done to catch us off guard. I've got to warn Hannah, and Joseph."

He heard Rubio call out to him, but Luis ran to his truck. He'd come here to protect Hannah but failed. She had a plan. Joseph had a plan. Now he had to figure out what to do. Dreams—that seemed like a distant luxury.

. . . . .

Luis sped out of the driveway, rolled down his window, and yelled Hannah's name. Of course, she didn't answer, but he kept on as if she were a lost dog. And between calls, he'd silently think, *Where are you?* He repeated the same phrase over and over until the chant channeled his energy into hers.

He reasoned that Hannah's wound was minor, otherwise Mr. Henderson would have ignored Rosie's reluctance to seek aid at the hospital. The only other place Mr. Henderson would have taken Hannah was his hideaway on the beach. But with ICE and DHS combing the area, her father wouldn't remain there. He'd already been falsely accused by DHS of smuggling drugs dropped by kayakers and the boys who beat him up. That would be the last place his supposed lawyer/bodyguard would want Mr. Henderson to stay. Mr. Henderson was supposed to be the agency's protective cover.

Confident that he knew Hannah's heart better than her mind, Luis figured she'd be worried about Joseph and her new friend Robin. He took the backroads into town to avoid traffic on the freeway. Overhead he heard the drone of a motor, the swish of blades coming in low—a helicopter searching.

Downtown Mount Vernon felt like a ghost town. The Food Co-Op parking lot, usually busy in the late afternoon, was empty. He drove at a snail's pace, searching for bystanders, anyone who might have seen Hannah. As he passed the dance studio, he noted a sign on the door that read, "Gone to the hospital." That made sense. Shelly would be worried about her daughter, and Hannah would go there.

What didn't make sense was that the antique store had the same sign. Further down the street, the kitchen store was closed as well. As he weaved along all the streets to the river, he noted five more storefronts that had the same sign posted. An unease crawled along Luis's skin. Even stranger was the absence of traffic. The only other vehicle on the road was Frank's. They both stopped in the middle of the block.

"Poker, why are you here? Have you seen Hannah?"

Frank turned down the radio and leaned over the steering wheel. "I've lost track of Joseph and Hannah. The only person I can find is Miguel, and he's worried about Rosie. Seems to me that everyone is chasing after their tails."

Luis pushed his hair back and drummed his fingers along the truck's window. "Don't go speaking in tongues. I get enough of that from Joseph. What happened? Why has the entire town gone to the hospital?"

"I'm trying to tell you. Wires are crossed. Create enough confusion and everyone scatters. I guess that's what Joseph wanted." Frank shook his head. "I can't keep it all straight. My friend from the composite factory told me that Joseph's silk wing design and formula was top secret. Our Department of Defense is scrambling to find Joseph."

"*Contra*, I don't care about that. What does any of it have to do with Hannah?" Luis banged on his horn. "I'm heading to the hospital."

"Why not? The whole town seems to be there." Frank squinted at Luis, a sidelong glare. "Don't do anything stupid. I remember when my sister tried to trick everyone. I followed like a puppy, not realizing I had the power to make a difference. Stay on the right side of the law."

Luis glared back at Frank. "I've never broken the law! Joseph's never broken the law. Neither has Hannah or Mr. Henderson. But we're all in trouble. I don't want to just follow the crowd, but something is happening at the hospital. Maybe I'm needed."

Luis waved goodbye. For some reason, Frank had a wide grin on his face.

## CHAPTER 38:
## *A Meal*

Frank slowed his pace to that of a hundred-year-old turtle. He had already waited a quarter of an hour in the Food Co-Op parking lot, and he tried to waste more time. Lunch meetings, not his style. Sheila's late-night trip out to the hangar had made him uncomfortable. Now she insisted on meeting him away from the courthouse. Her words had been straight to the point: "My boss doesn't want you around."

He found her seated alone at the back of the Food Co-Op's restaurant. With only a few customers, he missed the background chatter of patrons, the invisible shield of a crowd. Sheila stood out with her red hair, and he felt her stares as he walked across the room. She had already eaten half of her sandwich.

"Frank, how nice of you to finally arrive. Seems you've scared away most of the town."

He eased himself into the chair across from her and fiddled with the silverware. "What makes you say that?"

"Look around, the downtown is deserted, just like here. Usually it takes forever to get served. But it works if you're hungry. Are you going to order?"

"Nope, I'm not much for lunch. This was your idea."

Sheila took a bite of her sandwich, a drink of her juice. "Suit yourself. I just thought we should talk. It may be just rumors, but the local officials had a visit from the feds. Your friend Joseph's name came up. Seems he is undocumented. I did a search, and he doesn't exist—not a citizen of any country. How can you be best friends with someone your whole life who's living a lie?"

Frank wanted to ignore her question—too much prying. Instead he answered her directly: "Joseph has never lied. He never claimed to be anything but himself. Sometimes it's hard to pinpoint a problem. Easy to blame. Remember when you visited at the hangar how the lights flickered. When you left, I jiggled with the fuses—they worked. The light bulbs were all fine. But the electrical current was bad. Not my fault."

Sheila finished off her sandwich and made a show of licking her lips. "So you're saying this has nothing to do with you. That I've got my wires crossed."

"Something like that. Just that I never asked you where *you* came from. Never found the need to. Joseph knows who he is. And he is a good light bulb. Thanks for the warning." Frank waited. He knew there was more. "Is there something else I need to know, Sheila? Something that could help Joseph?"

Sheila yawned. "I thought you were more interesting, Frank. In case you haven't noticed, I don't have *faulty wiring*. I'm on your side. I do know that the local government has been put on high alert. Something strange for a small town like ours. What are you mixed up in?"

As much as Frank resisted, he felt his guard slip. He didn't quite trust her forwardness. He needed Sheila's insights, but he wasn't so sure about the personal attention. "I'm just helping a friend, following the orders of the court to help out at the Concrete Airport, to make myself useful. I can tell you that it's a good thing our government is on red alert. I'm just not sure they are focusing on the right people."

Sheila stood up. "I've got to go back to work. My lunch break is over. I'm worried about you. I'm worried about what's going on at the hospital. Half the town is up there for a protest. I don't get it, but somehow most of the protesters have filed citizenship forms. Please tell me that this doesn't have anything to do with the high alert."

Frank took Sheila's hand. Her soft palm fit exactly into his. He looked at her directly, willing himself to be strong. "I didn't know about the protest. My guess is that health issues sometimes get mixed up with immigration issues. But I can promise you that no one I know has committed a crime."

Sheila returned Frank's look and slowly removed her hand. "And the tension and high alert, that has nothing to do with you? You said it was warranted."

Frank moved back a step, avoided Sheila's probing eyes. "High alert—the government is protecting our country. You and I both know that we have manufacturing companies here that do exclusive work for the United States government. We're just fifty miles from the border. And vulnerable because we are a small town." In truth, Frank didn't know if Joseph and he were the reason for the alert. His stomach sank, his energy plummeted. "Promise me this, Sheila: if you do see Joseph, make sure he's safe. His research is more valuable than most work done by citizens."

"I can't promise, but I'll do my best." Sheila gathered her purse, gave Frank one last glance, and left.

A waitress gathered Sheila's plates and washed the table down. Frank remained seated staring out toward the street.

"Excuse me, sir, can I get you something?"

He gave the waitress a pained grin. "No thank you, ma'am, I've got enough to chew on. I can leave if you need the space for customers."

"Nah, we aren't busy. You take your time."

Frank appreciated the simple kindness. He wondered what would happen to Joseph now that he was on a marked list. The red alert, the protest—this wasn't in anyone's plan. The only thing for him to do was join the groups at the hospital. Maybe he could slip in again, unnoticed, and find out more.

. . . . .

The parking lot at Skagit Valley Hospital overflowed onto the streets. The entranceway was blocked by orange cones and local policemen situated in front. A group of young mothers, holding hands with their toddlers, picketed with signs saying, "Hippocratic Oath—A Hypocrisy," "Cancer knows no boundaries," and "Whose life is worth more?"

Frank circled the block looking for Joseph's vehicle, but he couldn't see beyond the sea of men and women surrounding the entrances. The signs were one thing, but to see owners of the local businesses holding hands and carrying the signs was another. He had a feeling that Mrs. Henderson had rallied more than Joseph's chosen helpers.

As he turned the corner and approached the intersection, the streetlights flickered, then went dark. Within moments, the road filled up with cars. Jammed with nowhere to go, the local policemen moved from the parking lot to direct traffic in the intersections.

Frank settled in for the wait. He thought of Sheila at the courthouse. She'd been right to be suspicious. Even though he had spoken the truth, wires had been crossed.

## CHAPTER 39: *When Old Becomes New*

By the time Joseph made his way past all the traffic on Highway 20 and onto Thirteenth Street, he realized that the scrambling of the phone lines and electrical grid had caused confusion in all of Skagit Valley, not just along the highway. Streetlights flashed, and police stood at each corner directing cars. Impatient drivers honked their horns, and tempers flared.

As he approached Skagit Valley Hospital, Joseph rolled down his window for a flagger, who said, "Sir, unless this is an emergency, no one can enter. The power failed, and the hospital is running on their main generator. We've been instructed to—"

"I have a large generator in the back of my truck," Joseph interrupted. "I'll need to get to the service entrance to bring it in."

Taken aback by the request, the flagger hesitated. "I haven't heard anything about generators. But my radio isn't working well. Who did you say you were with?"

Joseph felt sympathy for the young man. "I didn't say. I'm just a Good Samaritan. My name is Joseph. I think most of the local farmers will be here soon with their generators as well. Where can I park?"

Baffled, the flagger waved him in. "I don't even know if the electric doors are working. Just go in the back of the main building. I think there is a service door near the cafeteria and one by the new cancer wing. How many more people do you think are coming?"

Joseph shrugged. "Couldn't say for sure. Lots of the farmers have loved ones here. They're generous people. Good people help out."

With that he waved and rolled up his window. He drove straight to the back entrance of the new cancer wing. He hoped his story held up with those more informed at the hospital.

Joseph didn't worry who saw him. He had decided to use the confusion to his advantage. He pried the doors open, found an abandoned gurney, and then used it to roll his generator to the electrical room. Outside of the room, maintenance workers and a group of hospital officials huddled in conversation.

"Excuse me, sirs," Joseph said. "Thought you could use some auxiliary systems till the electrical grid is fixed."

His arrival startled them into silence and then smiles. "I don't think we'll need it. Our backup system is sound. The main generator can keep the patients comfortable."

Joseph nodded. "Should I leave it or take it back?"

Before the official could answer, lights flickered and then failed to return. A serious of pops followed.

Another official stepped forward. "Never mind. We'll take it just in case. How can we get ahold of you to pick it up?"

"No worries. I live way upriver. I'll come back when the electricity is on. But if you need me, you can send word with Rosie, who is a visiting partner in cancer research. Or you can get ahold of the Hendersons, who funded the new cancer wing."

As Joseph left, he turned to see bewildered faces from the hospital officials and then alarm. He slipped into a stairwell and watched through the door window as they passed by. Rosie would be on the floor for children, monitoring Robin. He'd climb the eight flights of stairs to wait for the show.

.....

Out of breath, Joseph hid in the stairwell until he felt his heart beat more normally and his lungs could catch up. No matter what happened next, he needed his sense of calm, his attention focused on those he cared about. It didn't take long to find Rosie and Robin. He spotted Rosie's wild hair and followed her into Robin's Room. He watched as Rosie tended to Robin and the other children in her room. Mrs. Henderson was huddled off to the side with the children's parents. He quietly made his way along the perimeter, reading the name tags on each bed. When he found Robin's bed, he stopped.

Robin opened one of her eyes. "My eyes are closed, but I'm not sleeping. Just resting like Rosie told me to. But I'll open both my eyes to see you. Rosie said a nice and really smart man would appear to talk with me. I think you must be him."

Joseph nodded. "Yes, Rosie thinks I'm nice and smart. My name is Joseph. I'm working with her on the mushroom experiment to help you feel better."

Robin sat up and smiled. "Come closer to me so I don't have to raise my voice. I'm supposed to whisper to keep everyone calm. Besides, after the stem cell transplant, my whole inside isn't too happy. They said they'd bring me ice to sooth my throat."

Joseph sat on Robin's bed. "Is your mom here? I'd like to talk with you both."

Robin reached for Joseph's hand. "I'm not afraid, if that is why you're here. I just want all the kids to get better. I'm the lucky one."

Joseph felt Robin's small hand in his own. He couldn't help but compare her hand to that of Hannah's years ago. He looked into Robin's eyes. "Miss Robin, you are a trusting soul. Where does all that come from?"

"Well, Mr. Joseph, dancing teaches you that. All those leaps. You have to have faith." Robin's voice drifted off as she touched her throat and scooted her back against the pillows. "What do you need to talk to me and my mom about? She should be here soon, but I guess lots of the parents are worried. My mom went to help with getting some food for everyone."

Joseph closed his eyes. The consequences of the failed electrical grid had already made its impact. He felt culpable for his part, but he had already rallied the troops to pitch in. Soon the government would pay attention. He held on to Robin's hand, willing her sense of faith to make his deeds and sacrifice worthwhile.

He felt a tap on his shoulder. "Oh, Rosie, it's you."

Rosie smiled at Robin and turned back to speak. "Joseph, don't look so worried. I anticipated all the children's needs. Already the hospital is running just fine on generators. Think of this as a practice exercise."

Joseph felt a squeeze of his hand and then heard Robin's voice. "Here she is, Mr. Joseph. My mom, Shelly."

Shelly bent down and kissed Robin. "Joseph, thank you for all your research and good wishes. I'm glad we got to meet. But I don't think you should stick around. I overheard some of the hospital officials looking for a small man that fit your description."

Joseph glanced down the hallways and at the exits. "Shelly, I'm not going anywhere. Whoever is looking for me will find me here. I'm more concerned about Robin and the children's health."

To block herself from the others in the room, Shelly sat at the bottom of Robin's bed closer to Joseph. She whispered, "No, really, I think you and Rosie are in jeopardy. You know that they captured Rosie at my dance studio. I had to hide the mushrooms from your experiment. Rosie almost lost her life. I have no idea why she came back to the hospital."

Anger rose slowly, pushing against gravity as it circled through his heart and up to his face. Ablaze with fury, he willed himself to envision his mentor. His grandfather who ran to escape the pogroms, escape the truth. The running had to stop. He glanced at Rosie. No one had told him.

Rosie turned her palms upward as if this explained her actions. She held his eyes to steady his resolve. "I'm okay, Joseph. We couldn't get ahold of you. Hannah was hurt in the scuffle, but she saved the day."

The air became stale, and he looked down at Robin and to her mother. Everyone was ready to stand their ground. Joseph wondered if he could take that leap of faith and protect the people he loved with action.

From the other side of the room, Mrs. Henderson hand signaled him—*okay*. Again, he looked down the hallway. He spotted Hannah, Mr. Henderson, Mr. Ferguson and the hospital officials advancing toward him. Relieved that Hannah was okay, he turned back to Rosie. "Well, we are both here. Protecting children, truth, research. It takes a village to do that."

As if on cue, the stairwell door opened. Joseph knew that this would be the last time he hid from any truth. Stepping into the hallways, he held his breath, and lights flashed as cameramen snapped the scene and reporters filed in. Breaking away from Hannah and Mr. Henderson, Mr. Ferguson approached Joseph. With a lowered voice he said, "I'm sorry, Joseph, but you must leave with me. Don't make a fuss."

Hannah gasped. "Mr. Ferguson! I kn-knew I couldn't trust you. W-why did I dare think you'd care?"

Robin pulled on her mother's arm. "Mom, do something."

Joseph kept his eyes fixed on Mrs. Henderson, Shelly, and Rosie. He felt waves of energy surround him as the three women crossed the room.

Mrs. Henderson said, "Excuse me, Mr. Ferguson, but why must Joseph leave?"

Joseph waited for Mr. Ferguson's version of the truth. Robin left her bed and walked over with her mother to Joseph's side. Rosie took Hannah's hand and followed. The women who had been talking with Mrs. Henderson came forward.

Mr. Ferguson placed his hand on Joseph's shoulder. "We need to talk with your friend. He seems to have information about the electrical failure, and other matters."

The words appeared benign, but Joseph felt Mr. Ferguson's fingers dig deep into his shoulder muscles. He adjusted his stance to ease the pressure as he listened to the sirens outside. Whatever Mr. Ferguson thought was happening inside the hospital, he had made the fatal error of looking linearly, failing to see how separate acts were associated.

"If anything," Mrs. Henderson said, "it seems that Joseph helped solve the electrical problem with his own generator. These children rely on him for his research. We all know that Joseph is a fixer. Last time you took someone away, my husband, you said it was to protect him. You used him. I ask you, who are you protecting now?"

Mr. Ferguson loosened his grip. Joseph felt the shift of power. He allowed a smile to enter his eyes as he faced the crowd that had gathered behind Mrs. Henderson. Rosie had been right in understanding Mrs. Henderson's passion and sense of dedication to the town.

But it was Robin who caught everyone off guard. Gripping Joseph's pant leg, she called out to Mr. Ferguson, "Joseph discovered a way to help all of us with his special mushroom treatments. He has been fighting to cure cancer. I don't think he should go with you. We need him." The other children's cries echoed Robin's words from their room.

The television reporters went wild, and cameras flashed. The hospital officials came forward. Mr. Ferguson moved Joseph off to the stairwell.

Joseph went peacefully. He took one last look back to see Rosie, Shelly, and Mr. and Mrs. Henderson with the other parents. The hospital officials, the journalists, and even Mr. Ferguson had no idea what was at stake. No matter what, he would not turn his back on those in need.

As the door shut, he heard Hannah tapping. She must have been in the stairwell waiting to see where they took him.

## CHAPTER 40:
## *My Turn*

Hannah focused on the sounds of Joseph's back foot dragging as he descended the stairwell. She kept calm by tapping her feet in response. A slow shuffle on her part and then a rapid tap to cover her advance down the steps. She hoped that Joseph recognized her taps within the noise of the officials' steps. At least he would know that she hadn't abandoned him.

Infuriated that Mr. Ferguson had tricked her, Hannah's brain strained to understand. She withered inside, felt older than Joseph. Her heart pounded against her chest, bursting with connections that couldn't be contained. She needed it to be elastic, to stretch past her years of silence. She'd tried for so long to control her emotions. Pain pounded with each heartbeat. She counted down the flights of stairs. A wave of dizziness hit, and Hannah grabbed the railing. She'd forgotten the bullet wound in her leg. A breeze in the stairwell told her that Joseph's entourage had arrived on the ground floor and was exiting. She hurried to catch up.

Sunshine blinded her as she opened the door to the back lot of the hospital. The press must have anticipated where they'd exit, as a crowd had formed at the door. Hannah held her hand over her brow as she scanned for a familiar face. She spotted Mr. Ferguson's car heading out of the parking lot with a police escort.

Her plan to stay close to Joseph had already failed. Another wave of dizziness hit her, but this time she felt a presence. With the sun in her eyes, she couldn't see straight. It looked like a sea of people coming her way, and then the flood of humans suddenly turned, pulled by a commotion of protesters. Hannah took a deep breath, tried to stay upright. Her leg throbbed, and she faltered by the door. And then came a familiar smell.

"Hannah, Hannah, wait."

It was if she had stepped out of her body. Hannah moved in slow motion, waiting for a smell. She closed her eyes and sank into the sweet aroma.

. . . . .

Luis held on to Hannah as she slumped into his arms. He moved out of the path of the crowd, walking awkwardly as her body leaned into him. He lifted her off the ground and found a corner in the shade, past the dumpsters, to rest. With his back against the wall, he sat with her on his lap and listened to her breathing—small hiccups of warm air expelled in fits.

Finally, Hannah opened her eyes. Her reactions tentative, one eye open then closed, opened again, and then awareness. "Oh, Luis what happened? How did you find me?"

"More like you found me. I had a feeling you couldn't stay away from Robin or Joseph. I followed your heart, not my own."

"You mean you didn't follow your heart?"

Luis sat up straighter. "You know I did, Hannah. This isn't a joke. You had me so worried. How could you take such a risk? *Ay Dios mio*, you got shot!"

Hannah blocked his protests out, closing her eyes, making him disappear. Tears slipped from her closed lids. Luis held her face, caught them in his hands, and gently said, "I didn't know you could cry in silence and tears could still fall with eyes shut. You're okay—that's what I care about."

A faint smile appeared on Hannah's face. "Okay, I mean, thanks. I can't have anyone angry at me. Least of all you. I'm worried about Joseph. We're over our heads in this, whatever this is. But I know for a fact that Joseph is in trouble. That Mr. Ferguson, whoever he is, just took him away. First my dad, now Joseph. I won't let anyone take more away from me."

Luis waited till Hannah finished her tirade. "It isn't about you, Hannah. You know that, don't you? The whole town is in an uproar. Look around at the protesters. That's your work with Robin and Rosie, even your mom. Organized—that is what you are, even in chaos."

Hannah's reaction wasn't what Luis expected. All he could think of was the acronym *LOL, laugh out loud*. But the noises coming from Hannah were hollow peals, haunted. He pushed her off his lap and stood. "What's going on?"

Hannah pointed to a throng of kids from her high school snapping pictures of them with their cell phones. And if that wasn't enough, Mrs. Henderson and Rosie advanced with another group of older women and men. Luis took Hannah's hand in his, gave it a squeeze. Together they walked toward the diverse ensemble of teenagers, mothers with children in tow, farmers, business owners, and elders.

Luis glanced over at Hannah. She looked like she had slept in her clothes and hadn't bathed in days. He wasn't exactly spotless, either: the grime of the farm was smeared across his pants, his fingers were stained blue, and he smelled like crushed blueberries. He had never met Mrs. Henderson, but he didn't hesitate. "Mrs. Henderson, I'm Luis. I don't know how you found us, but I'm glad you did. I was at the farm helping Rubio and then came looking for Hannah."

Still holding Luis's hand, Hannah interrupted, "Mom, we have to do something. You saw them take Joseph, and I couldn't keep up. Rosie, I let you down. You wanted me to watch out for him. I messed up."

Those gathered around them listened as if they were watching a television novella. Luis squeezed Hannah's hand again, hoping she'd realize they were in public. Not used to making a spectacle of himself, Luis gently guided Hannah so that they faced away from the crowd. He whispered in her ear, "Slow down. Remember who you are, who I am, where we are."

Luis's words were more for himself than Hannah. He knew she wasn't afraid to be in public, but there were risks with exposure. Hannah transformed. She stood taller, shoulders dropped away from her ears. He couldn't help but smile. She became a dancer, energized to take a leap. Without words she redirected his comments into the strength he needed. He followed her example, took a deep breath, and waited.

Mrs. Henderson moved closer, and instead of embracing Hannah, she gave Luis a hug only a mother could give. She held his face in her hands and then stepped back. "You two were easy to find. Rosie saw Hannah slip into the stairwell when they took Joseph. She anticipated the scene, even Hannah's pain. I knew you couldn't keep away. My husband told me of your dedication. But again, it was Rosie that sensed you'd be here. Trust me, Rosie is powerful."

Rosie was already by Hannah's side attending to her leg. As Luis and Mrs. Henderson gazed at her, she looked up. "No worries here. Her wound is throbbing, but not bleeding. Hannah, I need you to rest now. I'll need your mental energy to help with Robin and all that is going on with Joseph. You have insights that no one else has."

Hannah started to object, but Luis stepped forward and said, "I'll make sure she rests. How can I help Joseph and the town?" Luis waited for Rosie to respond. She faltered, looking at him, Hannah, and the crowd. She seemed distant, as if a premonition passed through her. He shivered. "Are you okay? Something is wrong, isn't it? Rosie, tell me. Joseph planned this, I know, but what's bothering you?"

Pale and shaking, Rosie took a deep breath. Her color returned, and she took Luis's hand. "*No te preocupe.* I'll be fine. Finally, I get to meet you."

Luis wasn't fooled. Her slip into Spanish surprised him. "*Que pasa?*"

Rosie looked at Hannah, Mrs. Henderson. She continued in Spanish as if what she said needed to be a secret: "Keep those two together and find Mr. Henderson. I'm drained. I think my energy left when the electricity went out. It happens."

"Where are you going?"

"Back upstairs to be with Robin. I'm worried about the kids, the mushroom research, and the townspeople. We can't forget the people. Then when they are okay, I'll go home."

Luis nodded, perplexed by the undercurrent. He felt the charged words *people, home.* He gathered Hannah and Mrs. Henderson. "I think it's time we find your husband and connect all the dots."

Mrs. Henderson didn't waste any time. She led the way. "I believe Joseph needs us to continue with his plans. He has the community to back him. I'll call my husband."

Hannah pulled Luis back. "I don't want to go."

Somehow her dancer body had gone limp again. Luis sensed her deflation. "Hannah, let your mother run her show. She's on a mission. So is Rosie. But Joseph trusted both you and me with helping. No one here is in control."

Hannah held on to his hand, squeezing his thumb and pinkie finger so tightly he gasped. "I can't face the crowds yet. I can't distinguish the notes. It's like I'm deaf to the music. I only hear static."

This Luis understood. The static of too many voices, too many tugs. Mrs. Henderson stood in the middle of the sidewalk, calling Mr. Henderson. As he scanned the parking lot, Hannah's classmates descended upon them.

. . . . .

Hannah held on to Luis's hand as if her life depended upon it. She placed her thumb over his wrist to feel his pulse. Infused with the steady throbs, she pulled Luis's energy inside, until her heart beat at the same pace. "Luis, I can talk now. Don't worry, just hold my hand."

One by one they came over, each smiling, clicking their selfie shots with Luis and Hannah in the center. Hannah felt like she was on display. None of the classmates really knew her, and she couldn't figure out why they'd be here. When she recognized one of the girls from her political science class, she asked, "Narissa, what's going on? Why is everyone here? Why are you all taking photos?"

"You haven't heard? Every newscast has your face on their screen. It was a live video of you and the children from the cancer ward. Then some old guy got arrested. You were livid. Some of the kids sent in their cell phone photos of you and Luis. The newsroom recognized him as the person who saved that guy who fell off the bridge? Wow, and you two are together!"

Hannah stared at her classmate. So much for rest and quiet. She decided to tune in to the chaos around her. She waved her classmates into a circle. The static receded as she said, "I need all of you to think for yourselves. Forget what you know, and find out what's been going in our community." She lowered her voice to a whisper, and the crowd moved in closer. Her words came out slowly as if she was telling a bedtime story. "I'm asking you to be brave. Hear my voice without the stutter. See Luis, my boyfriend, as part of your world."

Hannah expected her classmates to laugh and chatter, but the quieter she talked, the deeper the hush settled around her. She continued, "Stuff is going on under our noses. My dad was arrested, framed for drug dealing and hiding money. The farm problems aren't because of our workers. Don't just believe what you hear. I beg you all to protect the kids upstairs in the hospital. They're dying from cancer, and some are undocumented. That old man you saw the police taking away, well, he designed research to help them. Everyone is at risk of losing out."

Hannah suddenly stopped talking. Tears fell, and her breathing became labored. Luis stood behind her, hands on her shoulders for support. As Hannah looked out, Mr. Ferguson's car circled back. "Luis, move quickly." They disappeared into the crowd.

# CHAPTER 41: *Old Movements, New Actions*

Impatience got the best of him. Antsy from waiting for the police to direct the clogged traffic, Frank had dipped into an alley and headed back to town. He ditched his vehicle, and now, as a pedestrian, he felt more in control. He walked tentatively, glancing both ways as cars made traffic-light corners into four-way stops. Polite to a fault, the drivers seemed to be under some spell. No one noticed that the electricity worked again. The green light changed to yellow and then red, a full cycle, before the horns began to honk as everyone woke up to a frenzy.

A rush of flashing sirens and cars came barreling down from the Hospital Road. As he stepped off the curb, Frank was nearly run over by a black sedan with Joseph seated in the back. Though he figured that this must be part of Joseph's grand scheme, Frank had his doubts. Joseph made a scene alright, but from the direction the car was headed, they weren't going to the police station. Frank quickened his pace and arrived at the federal courthouse out of breath and sweating. The building looked deserted. Too early to be closing time. Frank walked in.

The x-ray machine stood idle. The two in-house guards appeared half-asleep with their hands behind their backs. They jumped to attention. Frank felt their guilt as his own and asked, "Did the electricity knock out your machines?"

The youngest guard nodded. "Just show us what's in your pockets. The only office open is the information one. They closed early due to the electrical outage. We're here as a precaution."

Frank didn't engage in conversation but wondered, *Precaution for what?* He rang the bell at the information counter. No one appeared. He waited until the second hand of the wall clock passed three times and rang again. Sheila finally appeared. Surprise registered on her face, but the way she held her lips and stared warned Frank that something was off.

"How can you help you, sir—I mean, how can I help you?"

He fished for the right words. "Um, just here to check on a citizenship application."

Sheila put her finger to her lips. "The computers are down, so I can't help you. Everyone is gone. Please come back on Monday."

Nonchalance wasn't his forte, and Frank scrambled to reply. "I guess I picked the wrong day to inquire. Looks like the electricity just came back on."

"Yes, but it takes a while for the reboot."

As she talked, Sheila jotted down a note and handed it to Frank. He glanced down to read it. "Okay, well, I'll come back on Monday. Have a good rest of the day."

Frank rushed out, ignored the guards, and ran around to the back of the building. The black sedan was parked there. He silently thanked Sheila for warning him. She didn't say why Joseph was here or why she was the only employee to remain in the courthouse. If Joseph wasn't with the police, who was he with?

He didn't have to wait long for the answer. The back door opened, and Sheila popped her head out. When she spotted him, she put a rock in the doorjamb and came over. "Joseph is in big trouble. My boss is inside with a Mr. Ferguson. He's some kind of special agent. I knew you were up to something."

Frank didn't apologize. "Why are you telling me this?"

"Well, you are the only one I can trust."

"Sheila, you have to be careful. I'm not that powerful. You know my past."

"That is exactly why I trust you."

Frank didn't understand her logic. "Okay, what's going on?"

"My boss was ambushed by Mr. Ferguson. Made him promise not to call the police. I'm suspicious. But Joseph seems okay, and they ordered food, so I'm just waiting."

Frank was afraid to ask the next question. "Did you see a gun?"

Sheila's eyes popped out. "No, of course not. Joseph and Mr. Ferguson were talking, not yelling. I didn't hear what they were saying, but they both seemed more worried about my boss."

Frank's body sank against the wall. "Remember the night you came to my hangar at the airport? You said something about your boss being suspicious. Was that just a ploy to visit me, or was he fishing for information?"

Sheila threw up her arms. "Damn you, Frank. Listen to me. I don't give a rip about that other night. I'm telling you that I don't trust anyone but you to get your friend help." She turned and headed back inside.

Frank touched her arm. "Could you leave that rock there? At least I'd have a way in later if need be."

As Sheila entered the building, she found a smaller rock, less obvious to anyone looking. Frank heard a helicopter. He recognized the insignia: King 5 News. By the time he had circled the building, a crowd had appeared outside the courthouse. He shouldn't have been surprised. Miguel was among them.

Miguel stood between Joseph's recruits, the bartender, teacher, and postmaster. Each held a sign written in bold green letters: "People's Movement: Face the Problems, Find the Solutions, Do Something." Miguel's sign was more pointed: "Our Community Is the Source of Our Power." Behind them, Frank noticed kids from the high school, some of the farmworkers, and trailing at the back of the group, Mr. and Mrs. Henderson.

Frank hoped the group's presence would work in Joseph's favor.

He slipped into the crowd beside Miguel and said, "You look like you're in your element. Did you know that Joseph is holed up inside?"

Miguel shrugged and pointed to the top window. Joseph was standing with his back to the window, but his silhouette was undeniable. "Wish I could say I was clairvoyant, but usually the simplest explanation is the easiest. I was hanging by the police station, eavesdropping. They were scrambling with the arrests at the farm with those Russians, then the bootleggers. But nothing was mentioned about Joseph's arrest. I got suspicious."

Frank stared up at the shape in the window. The longer he looked, the odder it seemed. He remembered when he was a child and afraid that his sister would sneak into his room to scare him. He'd stare at the edge of the door, watch as the edge waivered. The mere act of staring caused the wobble, but as he looked up at Joseph's silhouette, it didn't move. "Miguel, I don't think that is Joseph. I mean, it's the right shape, but you know he'd never stand that still for so long. We've been tricked."

Frank didn't wait for Miguel's reply. He ran to the back of the courthouse. Sure enough, the black sedan was gone. The back door was shut tight, the small rock neatly placed by the garbage can. On the way to his truck, he jiggled the front doors. No luck—the courthouse was closed. The hair rose along his arms. Joseph had disappeared, and what had happened to Sheila?

By the time Frank found his truck, he was out of breath. Miguel leaned against the passenger's side and pointed. When Frank opened the door, he found Sheila crouched in between the seats with a coat over her head. Miguel slipped into the front and put his feet on the dashboard. Neither spoke as Frank drove off.

They'd traveled a few blocks, when Sheila whispered, "I know you know I'm down here. Is it safe to come out?"

"That depends on why you're hiding."

"Don't you go making fun of me, Frank. And tell your friend here to give me some space. I took a risk. This better be worth it."

Miguel dropped his feet from the dashboard and scooted over. Sheila removed her covering and scrunched in beside Miguel. "You were right, my boss turned Joseph in. Claims he's a Russian spy with no United States documentation."

Frank held on to the steering wheel with clenched fists. Gasping for breath, he pulled over at the first open parking spot. A full minute passed before he could speak. "That's insane. No one is more loyal to the United States than Joseph. What in god's name happened at the courthouse?"

Sheila went silent. Tears followed.

Frank sank deeper into his seat, closed his eyes. He couldn't imagine a worse scenario than Joseph's incarceration, and for what—being a spy and an illegal? What had Joseph imagined would happen?

Miguel finally broke the silence. "Sheila, Frank didn't mean to upset you more. Please tell us why you are hiding in Frank's truck and where everyone else is."

Sheila stared at Frank. Finally, he chimed in, "It's okay, Sheila. I'm just worried. Joseph is the closest person I can call a friend. He isn't a spy. You risked your life because you trusted me."

"Don't get mushy on me. I did what I needed to do. Joseph looked me in the eyes. My gut told me that he was honest. He paid attention to me, saw me as an ally immediately. I saw how my boss twisted all the information that he had discovered. He made up a story and called the authorities. But that Mr. Ferguson challenged him. Asked my boss who he spoke to, where he got his information. He interrogated my boss while Joseph sat in another room. I listened and realized . . . I don't know what I realized."

Frank took her hand. "Go on. What happened next?"

"I gave my car keys to Joseph, and I slipped outside and found your truck."

Miguel piped in. "So you don't know where Mr. Ferguson and your boss are?"

"I didn't wait around. I went out the back door. My boss's car was still in the parking lot, and so was the black sedan."

Frank started his truck. He knew where he'd find Joseph. The rest he didn't bother to think about.

# CHAPTER 42: *Sow Chaos*

Huddled in a small staff room off the main floor of the children's cancer ward, Hannah sat with Luis, Rosie, and her parents, all transfixed on the television screen.

Every news outlet carried a story giving various renditions of the electrical outage throughout Skagit County and the community protests at the hospital and the courthouse. But King 5 News ran an in-depth television program on the capture of a local Russian spy and his connection to what they called DDOS, distributed denial-of-service, attacks from Russia beginning in the early 2000s. Through a government informant, others had been identified and sought for their participation in the present disruption of service. According to their sources, an elderly man identified as an accomplice had succumbed to a heart attack and was unable to speak.

The airwaves spread a sense of fear in Hannah. She tasted a metallic sourness, felt the ripples of lies crackle in the air. Her parents held hands, Rosie looked out at the hospital hallway, and Luis, although he sat by her side, had disappeared to somewhere she couldn't reach.

Hannah turned off the television. "We can't just sit here doing nothing. I can't believe that all of the good Joseph did could be twisted."

Rosie reached over and took her hand. "That's the problem with being humble. Joseph never touted his successes. His silence allowed others to twist his actions and bury his accomplishments. Truth is never served by silence."

Her mom, still holding her father's hand, looked around the

room. "I kept silent too long, and so did your dad. I was wrong to hide behind Jenna's death and not speak up about injustices on the farm. Joseph is a good man, a good neighbor. Different, but not a spy. Your father knows the truth. Anyone can be targeted."

"And yet we're hiding in a hole in the wall." Hannah put her hand over her mouth. "I'm sorry. I didn't mean to make everyone feel worse." Hannah squeezed Luis's hand. "Luis, I know how much you care about Joseph. He's been my ally since I was little. I'm the one who got involved with those Russian boys—I didn't know."

Luis shook his head. "No, *no*, we've all got this wrong. I thought at first the news was saying Joseph was dead. But he isn't—he's alive and a target. Russell must have died. Rosie, you must sense that. Russell was the one who warned us of the electrical problem. He's the one with the heart attack."

Confused, Hannah looked over to Rosie. "Is that why you've been so sad? You seem weary."

Rosie smoothed a hospital blanket that lay on her lap. "I do have the chills, but it's more than that. I felt a loss, but not that of Joseph's dying. Russell has been very ill, and he warned me to take care. He sensed more than his own death." Rosie gave a half-moon smile. "That sly old man, always found a way to work through the confusion. He's no spy either. Russell saved the valley once before. Joseph is made from the same cloth. The two must have cooked up a scheme. Now we just have to find Joseph and clear his name."

Hannah heard a commotion outside of the staff room. Nervous, she instinctively stood in front of Luis.

"Hannah, stop. You don't need to protect me. I'll open the door."

The light from the hallway blinded Hannah. Once her eyes adjusted, she nudged Luis over to get a better look. A sea of faces greeted her. Shelly and Robin, in the front, and behind Robin's wheelchair stood the same students that had gathered outside the hospital earlier in the day and older faces she recognized from the community.

Each held their cell phones.

Shelly stepped forward. “We’re here to help. Robin, tell Hannah and Rosie your plan.”

Hannah noticed how exhausted Robin looked. Her eyes had dark circles, and her skin had the familiar flaky reaction of a transplant patient. Hannah kneeled by the wheelchair. “Robin, you’ve been working so hard. What idea do you have?”

“I was thinking about our protest because the other kids couldn’t be in the research project with mushrooms. That was wrong—how they decided not to help poor kids. We stood by each other. We need to stand by Joseph. All the kids on the cancer ward are texting their friends. And, well, you know how it works. Some of the kids know you, and their sisters and brothers know you. We can spread the word about his capture. Joseph saves lives.”

Hannah heard her mother in the background whispering to her father. The two walked out of the room. Her father knelt on the other side of the wheelchair. “Robin, you don’t know me, but I’m Mr. Henderson, Hannah’s father. You’re so brave to think about others. I like your idea. Your mother teaches dancing, right? Hannah likes to dance. Maybe we can make a ruckus with our voices and dancing.”

“Yes, Mr. Henderson, Joseph wants us to speak up. He wants us to live. I know you’re trying to do something fancy, but we can’t wait. It isn’t just about saving us from the side effects of chemo. It’s bigger than that. I’m just a kid, but I can tell when someone is being bullied. Talk to Hannah’s friends, they’ve got a plan.”

After Robin made her point, her body sank down into the wheelchair. Shelly gave her a water bottle, and Rosie rushed over. “I think you, young lady, need to go back to bed. We’ll take you back now, and I’ll get you settled.”

As they left, one of the students walked up to Hannah and said, “I don’t know if you remember me. I was in your computer science class last year.”

Hannah did remember him, though she couldn't think of his name. "You're the smart one, right? You were always creating your own programs or trying to hack other programs. You even got into trouble with the teacher."

He shrugged. "A bunch of us got together and created a program to track outages and weird stuff. Maps around the United States, big cities, border towns, trains, ports, and the electric grid. I heard what you said about Joseph. He's smart, but he misses lots because he's off the grid and doesn't know computers. My friends and I can help."

Luis stepped in. "How can this program you created help? They've accused Joseph of being a spy. He isn't a citizen, so he's like lots of us without documentation. He'll get deported or sentenced as a traitor. We can't even get the government to recognize the Dreamers. You think they'll save someone who made the dreams of others come true?"

Before the boy could answer, Mr. Henderson pulled Luis aside. "Save your anger. I have an idea. Connie can work with that young man. She's got teachers and officials involved. We should go back to the farm and get Rubio and the farmworkers I'm training. Now's the time to offer another vision. These workers will be owners and citizens."

Hannah walked down the hallway. She listened to the hospital hush of healing whispers. Everyone had their job, working to make life easier for the patient. She wished her own government had taken the Hippocratic oath to *do no harm*. It would make life simpler than enforcing the Constitution. Everyone would be considered equal and allowed treatment and to thrive. No one would be expelled from the country for their differences.

She sat down by the nurses' station. A wave of weariness spread through her limbs as she thought of Robin, Rosie, and every patient in the hospital. Why hurt Joseph when he did so much good? Why expel hardworking people? Hannah returned when she spotted Rosie leaving Robin's room. "Rosie, how's Robin?"

Rosie tried to smile, but her eyes didn't match her lips. "That little girl holds the world in her heart. We can't let her slip through our fingers."

"That won't happen. I won't let it."

Rosie cupped her hands around Hannah's face. "My new friend, then join with your family, Luis, and all these people. Make a stink, make sense, and find the path. I know that misinformation only works when people are afraid."

Hannah relished the warmth of Rosie's hands. She closed her eyes, and a jolt of understanding went through her. "Rosie, what are you afraid of? I felt it in your hands. Something's wrong. Can I help?"

"Don't you worry yourself. I'll be okay. Russell warned me to pay attention to a storm brewing. He has history in his bones and wisdom in his essence. I'll miss him. I sense it's time I return to Puerto Rico."

Not knowing what to say, Hannah embraced Rosie. A sense of determination and sadness swirled within their arms. Rosie turned and Hannah caught up with Luis and her father as they were leaving. Her mother remained with the boy from her class and the crowd.

## CHAPTER 43: *No Man Left Behind*

Joseph drove around town, circling the streets as if they were mazes that would suddenly open a new path. Released but still imprisoned, he knew of no direction that would make his fate clear. Mr. Ferguson's directive to disappear created more deception. He'd never be free of lies.

He'd seen it written on Sheila's face. Her own boss was a snitch, but worse an instigator and a traitor, willing to compromise rules for money. He never would have known that citizenship laws could be broken, even before the immigrants applied. Another gift of insight into how easily what he thought sacred could be corrupted.

After all his effort to come forward, Joseph refused to be silenced again. Mr. Ferguson had no right to negotiate with his life. With the news of Russell's death announced on the radio, Joseph headed upriver to Russell's home. No one would be searching for him in Sheila's car. And even if they were, he knew he had to pay his respects.

Joseph arrived at Russell's house without incident. Cars lined the driveway. JoAnne sat in her wheelchair in the doorway. The designated greeter, or the guard? Their eyes met, and with her tight lips and tears, he surmised that it was the latter. Before he even entered, he reversed his steps. Better to find Spencer.

Behind the house, by the stacked wood, Spencer sat with Ralph. The two appeared to be smoking a cigar, but by the length of the ashes, Joseph knew they'd taken the cigars as a pretense for a refuge to hide. Joseph sat on the chopping stump. "Can I join you in a smoke?"

Ralph raised his eyebrow. "Only if you don't inhale. We need to make the cigars last as long as the crowds are here." He handed Joseph a cigar and lighter.

Joseph's words came out in fits. "Russell, he . . . ah, he's really gone?"

Ralph and Spencer nodded. After an awkward silence, Spencer offered his thoughts. "Don't blame yourself. Russell was ready to go. You made him a hero again. He liked that. Now all we have to do is remain true, like he would."

Joseph didn't look at Spencer and feigned interest in Russell's garden. "Russell had a green thumb for corn. Better than you, Ralph. I'm sure he could have grown grapes that would have rivaled yours, Spencer."

"It's okay, Joseph. You don't need to make small talk. Spencer and I are ready to help. Russell left a long list of how to rally his buddies. We can contact them if you need us to verify the extent of the Russian hacking and infiltration into our electrical grid. You'll need all the leverage you can get. Otherwise we'll lose you too."

"Mr. Ferguson would rather I'd lie and hide than expose the government's inadequacies. They care more about protecting the Russians' infiltration into our secrets than protecting people's freedom. I don't care if I'm deported. I'm hoping we can help all the migrants, the Dreamers, and the ones who never did anything wrong. I won't be shut up."

Spencer smiled. "What's the plan?"

"The way I figure, we must follow the law's intent and take the blinders off for everyone to see. Pride and greed . . . My father came here to work on the railroads, died doing it. He came because the United States needed workers. It's all economics. People become disposable when the money dries up."

Spencer tapped his cigar. A line of gray ash fell to the ground. "What does that mean? We're wasting our time, if you want to prove constitutional philosophy. No one cares. Most people take their rights for granted. Give me something more, Joseph."

Joseph continued, "Russell wasn't a skeptic. Look at JoAnne, in her wheelchair, still protecting our rights, just like she did in WWII. The two of them have been my allies and mentors. Let's show the officials what they already know but don't practice. All our civil servants—firemen, police, postal service, teachers—they swore to uphold the Constitution. Give me that list from Russell."

Ralph unfolded a piece of notebook paper with Russell's penciled scrawl. "Just tell me something. If the ICE agents come for you, what do you want us to do?"

"It won't be ICE that comes after me. I think Mr. Ferguson doesn't want me locked up. He'd prefer I *not* make an issue about the safety of the country. He wishes that I wasn't an asset. Funny how that works. Seems that migrants have to be special, *perfect* to get citizenship and asylum, but if you're too knowledgeable and create cures and inventions, you become a problem." Joseph took the paper and studied the names. "In answer to your question, whatever you do, don't be heroic."

Everyone looked up when they heard the thumping of JoAnne's wheelchair as she came down Russell's ramp. "I heard that, Joseph. I don't know whether to cry or scream. Russell believed heroism was about doing what was right, even when it wasn't convenient. He never sacrificed his morals. Neither will we. Enough said. And get that somber look off your face."

Joseph saluted. He could only imagine JoAnne when she was a pilot in World War II. Despite his frustration, he smiled. "Has everyone left? I couldn't tell if it was a wake or an intervention."

"A little bit of both. No one asked about you. Federal agents traced the outage to our area but couldn't figure out what was going on. Russell's radio cronies laid out what had been happening with the pings and the weird cell towers. The agency claimed that they never got Russell's complaint but said they would look into it."

"They left just like that, no more questions?"

JoAnne shrugged. "I'm sure they're hanging around somewhere in the woods. They don't know what they're looking for, but certainly you'd be a prize. I think you're more a threat to them now than they are to you."

Spencer wheeled JoAnne closer to the group. He squeezed her shoulders.

Joseph knew that the two had traveled through life with their own burdens and yet they remained hopeful. "I didn't mean to offend, but I won't let others suffer." Joseph figured they'd have to agree not to agree on this point. Russell and his friends all had served the country. They were more patriotic than selfish and realized what was at stake. "Okay, ignore my comment. You're all just as stubborn as I am."

JoAnne laughed. "I already have. Russell filled me in on the situation before he passed. I took the liberty of sending out a call to arms. Our friends from the airport know you well and have concurred about meddling in their airwaves. Ditto for the ambulance service. Russell told the EMTs the story with his last breath. Also, I've rallied the ham radio troops and contacted the veterans. I still have a few connections with people who know how to get through the feds' red tape. I told them to meet in town. I hope you don't mind that I told Frank you were here. He's going crazy looking for you with Sheila."

"I should thank you, but there are no thanks in this." Joseph started toward Sheila's car. "Where in town did you tell people to meet? I'm not so worried about my own deportation, but of the destruction of my research. Who knows what will happen to the mushroom experiments and, worse yet, if my design for a superlight wing falls into the wrong hands?" Joseph sounded braver than he felt. "I am a thorn with principles. Seems that the Russian oligarchy used me as a distraction, so they could wreak havoc with our systems.

Now I'm on their radar. I refuse to hide from our laws, but the Russian government is vindictive."

Ralph rushed forward. "Don't leave in Sheila's car. Come with me. I'll drive you back into town. Spencer will drive Sheila's car."

JoAnne chimed in, "You're not leaving me behind. I'm going with you, Spencer."

Joseph slipped into Ralph's truck and let his friends play musical cars. His worry switched to Hannah and the children with cancer. Despite all his good intentions, he realized his actions were selfish. "Ralph, let's go back to the hospital. The kids might be traumatized after witnessing my sudden exit. If I'm going to make a difference, I need to show them the way."

"Are you sure? Don't you think the Russians will make a move?"

"They already have. By making me hide, they got rid of me. All they want is to control with fear. That's the difference between a dictatorship and democracy."

Joseph sank into the seat and closed his eyes. His thoughts spiraled, like the double helix of DNA. How could he unwind the coil and stabilize the crosslinks? It was as if the genes of the country he loved had mutated.

. . . . .

"Wake up, Joseph, we're at the hospital."

Joseph woke with a start. "Did you speed to get here? I snoozed the entire trip." He sat up straight and observed the flow of traffic and the now-empty parking lot. "Ralph, no use searching for trouble, it'll find us. Let's get inside. I need to speak with Mrs. Henderson. I have a feeling that she has been just as efficient as our JoAnne."

Ralph didn't move. "You want me to come in with you, Joseph?"

"I forgot about you being allergic to hospitals. You don't have to come in, if you'd rather wait out here."

"No need to," Ralph said. "Looks like Mrs. Henderson is the pied piper with a parade of teens and teachers following her."

Joseph chuckled. "That woman could create a tornado and then clean up and serve dinner. Sure glad she's on my side now."

All the kids waved. Mrs. Henderson directed the group over to a table outside of the hospital. Joseph caught up to them and said, "You've been busy. What's going on?"

Mrs. Henderson pointed to each student as she introduced them to Joseph. "I've rallied the younger set to save our future. I thought we needed help beyond what you asked me to do. These kids may not have the same passion or experience as the tavern owner, the postmaster, or the teachers, but they speak the language of technology."

Joseph studied the earnest faces. He saw in them what he saw in Luis, an innocence and determination. "Good. I can use the help. I'm out of the loop with computers. My way is too slow."

He sat down as they showed him a collection of dots spread across the nation where key electric grids had been hacked. Superimposed on top were military contractors, water utilities, and strategic ports of entry. After looking over the digital map, Joseph sensed something missing. "Can you find out where the money is? There has to be another trail that reveals what is happening."

Mrs. Henderson interrupted, "I may be able to help with that. When I talked with your friend, John, from the post office, he mentioned that the wiring of money to families had changed. The patrons seemed pressured, and the addresses were concentrated. Can someone trace money orders if I pull some strings?"

Joseph warned, "Nothing illegal. We have to convince the federal government with data they can't refute and the public can view."

"How dare you think I'd do something illegal!"

"I didn't mean to offend you. Just making sure . . ."

Before he finished his sentence, Mrs. Henderson laughed. "No worries, Joseph, I do have a sense of humor."

He tried to be jovial, but a cloud covered the sun, and a breeze came up. The shift of weather reminded him that nature was unpredictable, as were humans. Convincing bureaucrats didn't save lives. "Mrs. Henderson, I've got to go upstairs to see Rosie, Robin, and the other patients. If you see Frank, give him the results. If not, I'm sure JoAnne sitting over there in her wheelchair can get the data into the correct hands."

"Before you go . . . my husband, Luis, and Hannah went to the fields. He's worked so hard in training the workers to take over the farm. Who knew that paying forward would be so dangerous? Thanks for trusting me. I'll keep you informed if you'll do the same for me."

Joseph blushed at her warmth. "Yes, his plan to train the employees is better than being cynical. Give them the skills and they'll thrive." He continued, "I'll keep you in the loop."

Mrs. Henderson shooed him away. "Go, Rosie can use your help. I'm just worried for Hannah and Luis. They have such good intentions. Just like my husband."

As Joseph departed, he realized her despair went deeper. "I wish I had found a cure for Jenna, but cancer never leaves us, the patients or their caregivers. All we can do is knock it back. But you aren't just worried about cancer, are you?"

Her laughter gone, Mrs. Henderson reached for Joseph's hand. "I have faith, but finding kindness seems to be an uphill battle. I don't want to lose this one."

## CHAPTER 44:
## *As the World Turns, So Does History*

Hannah placed her mother's bright African-print skirt on her bed. She'd found it in a dusty trunk with clothes from what her mom called her "hippy period." Hannah couldn't imagine her mom as a hippy, but lately she seemed more motherly, freer. *Anything is possible.* Scrambling to pull the performance together these last few weeks had been easier than she thought. Everyone wanted to donate something for the dance performance. Shelly had given her full access to costumes from the studio, but Hannah wanted the outfits to reflect the community as well as the music.

Abuelita had loaned her castanets, a black scarf with tropical birds, and masks used in traditional dances. Robin insisted on giving her dance slippers, when she discovered their feet were the same size. Even Stella, who picked blueberries with Hannah, offered her earrings. The men on the farm wanted to participate, and Rubio gathered together a traditional violin, maracas, and embroidered black velvet vests that they wore for special occasions. Luis would look elegant.

Hannah packed her suitcase and headed out the door. "Mom, I'll see you and Dad at the park. Don't be late." Out of habit, she paused at the bottom of the stairs. Her mother rushed out from the kitchen and gave her the once-over.

"Oh, Hannah, don't worry. Your father promised he'd be back in time for us to go together. If he isn't back from the beach, I'll go on my own. He wouldn't miss your performance, and besides, the show was his idea—a way to launch the farm's new path."

Hannah was worried, not about the performance, but about the town, Joseph, and the future. She smiled when her mom kissed her forehead.

As she drove past Joseph's driveway, she tooted her horn. She didn't expect to see Luis, but this would nudge him to hurry. Joseph for sure would take his time.

She could hear Luis's voice in her head. He always cautioned her on jumping ahead with what-ifs. As they practiced their dance routine, he often repeated, "Stay in your lane. Don't anticipate, just be ready." Now, to keep her worries in check, she focused on the car ahead of her. No passing, no hurrying as the route would eventually bring her from the cabin into town. Instead of going into the worry lane, Hannah counted blessings. Joseph wasn't in jail, and the trial project with mushrooms had been approved by the FDA. Now Robin and the other kids would have the medical help they needed for free.

So much was still up in the air. All that mattered was that her family and friends were safe.

. . . . .

Luis braced his back by bending his knees and lifted the statue on its end. Miguel ran the rollers underneath as Joseph directed the two. Once the stone sculpture was wheeled outside and placed in the truck bed, Luis sighed in relief. "Joseph, this weighs a ton. I hope Mr. Henderson's truck makes it out of here okay."

"Yes, his truck is bigger and newer. Sometimes that is better, but don't quote me on that. I never dreamed the sculpture would take me so many years to carve. Now my truck is battered like me. Jeff will need the truck later. Said he'd pick it up at the park. I've arranged helpers to unload at the other end."

Luis still couldn't get up enough nerve to call Mr. Henderson *Jeff*. But apparently Joseph now considered him a friend. "You two seem close."

Joseph wiped his chalky white hands on his coveralls. "Do I detect a slight bit of jealousy? Isn't it a good thing to get along with your neighbors?"

"No, no, no, I mean, yes. I'm just not used to you being friendly." Luis realized that he'd put his foot deeper into his mouth. He looked at Joseph. "You're laughing at me?"

"Not at you, but with you. Jeff is now your boss again and your girlfriend's dad, so I see your dilemma."

Luis climbed into the truck bed. Miguel wrapped Joseph's freedom statue with foam as Luis tied ropes to keep it steady. Then Luis said, "My dilemma isn't with Mr. Henderson. I don't want to get my hopes up. I'm on my way to citizenship, thanks to sponsors. But my parents, well, getting a green card now might be impossible."

As he jumped down from the truck, Luis heard Hannah's double toots as she drove by. "We can talk later. Hannah is on her way to town, so I've got to get going. Lots to do before tonight."

Miguel gave the statue one quick shake to see if was steady. "Are you coming with me or driving your own vehicle?"

Joseph and Luis answered in unison: "Go ahead."

They watched as the truck lumbered down the driveway and out of sight. Luis packed up the extra ropes and headed back to the shop. Joseph called out, "You weren't thinking we'd go into town together, were you? I mean, I can give you a ride, but I've got to meet Rosie and do some finessing."

Luis answered with the shake of his head, but Joseph glanced down the driveway and back at his work building. Luis asked, "Are you worried about something? I thought you were out of DHS's eye. What finessing do you have to do?"

Joseph busied himself at the entrance to the cabin. "Did you notice I patched the hole by the door? The light you saw there was from the pump house. One small line of light, but no hiding place."

"You're changing the subject. Are you going to tell me?" Luis readied himself for one of Joseph's lectures, but instead Joseph sat on the stoop by the front door.

"Don't be angry with me. I'm leaving. Not for good, but I'll be gone for an undetermined amount of time. I want you to live here while I'm gone."

Luis sat down beside Joseph. He fought back tears. "Are you sick? You've lived here your whole life. Why leave unless the government is deporting you?"

"I may be old, but I'm not ill. No, I'm not being deported. Trust me, it'll all be fine."

Luis had no comeback. He couldn't question the word *fine*. Joseph controlled the conversation, and there was no bend with this explanation. "I'll stop asking you questions, because I know you won't answer. I'd rather you give me one of your philosophical talks. All this makes me uncomfortable, Joseph. Promise you'll let me know if you're ever in trouble."

Joseph gave Luis a hug. "I'll see you at the park. I'd tell you'd to lock up before you leave, but we never do that, do we?"

Luis didn't laugh.

. . . . .

By the time Frank arrived at the park, most of the tables for the auction had already been set up, under Sheila's supervision. Since her ordeal with Joseph, she had jumped into organizing and helping with all the paperwork for green card sponsors and citizenship. She was nowhere in sight, but Joseph's committee of helpers waived him over.

Frank studied the community table. A poster of Skagit Valley hung in the center of the display. Written in both Spanish and English, it showed the fields with overlays of crops. Tulips, daffodils, potatoes, peas, blueberries, cabbage, and other vegetables. The season changed with overlays, and with it the employment. Arrows showed the produce destinations—not just locally but around the world. Dollar signs marked the economics associated with the labor and the profit. A list of workers—from the fields, mechanics, drivers, managers, stores, and processors—explained the vibrancy of the valley's labor. Frank chuckled. "Looks like a teacher put this together."

A group of students beamed and explained how the teachers in all the high schools got together and made the project their educational focus that would count toward extra credit for the next fall semester—social studies, economics, math, language. They'd even met the state-mandated criteria.

Their enthusiasm was addictive, but Frank couldn't help his skepticism. "So, what happens after today? How will all this information help?"

Sheila walked up behind Frank. "Shame on you, Frank. Where've you been that you haven't heard. You and Joseph started this. Living upriver is a problem if you can't keep up with the news. The kids are set to meet with the legislature in Olympia. We've got senators and representatives who want to listen."

"I've been busy working on another project." Frank turned toward Sheila. "I'm not used to all this activity. I guess I have to come into town more."

The core committee members jumped in to save Frank from more embarrassment. John, the postmaster, offered the simplest of explanations: "Joseph set us loose on working out the details. Once Mrs. Henderson got involved, she thought the next step was to bring the issues to the state legislature. Locally we can do something, even if nationally they can't decide on the Dreamers."

Sheila offered Frank her hand. "Follow me for more surprises."

He went along until they were out of earshot of the students. "I've got stuff to do, Sheila. What's this about?"

"Looks like Hannah's classmates have discovered a pattern with the hacking, electrical grid, and money laundering. It's raising eyebrows with DHS. They have been summoned to go before a committee in Washington, DC."

Frank didn't know what to make of this. He formed a tentative smile. "You like this, don't you, Sheila? I'm glad you aren't suspicious of me anymore. If DHS can connect the money to the Russians and a plot to hack into our power sources, it'll help Joseph's case. This explains why Joseph is so testy." He squeezed her hand and turned to go. "I've got to set the stage for Russell's funeral service. Then get Joseph's statue set up."

"Go, I'm meeting Mrs. Henderson at the sign-up station for citizen applications. Maybe I'll see you later."

"Maybe."

. . . . .

Hannah tried to calm her nerves as she looked out at the audience. She tapped her fingers to the music of her routine. Luis stood at the opposite end of the stage, his eyes focused on the audience. Her parents sat in the first row with Robin and Shelly. Behind them sat the healthiest of the children from the cancer ward. Rosie had insisted that the cancer patients be up front and separated from the crowds by a clear plexiglass barrier. Once the doctor's fear of infection had been resolved, she conceded to the children's attendance.

It had taken longer than anticipated for the crew to create the stage props. Luis had insisted on making papier-mâché replicas of the rocks from Chuckanut shores where they danced. Steps and landing spots had to be incorporated so that the choreography worked smoothly and they wouldn't break through. The real miracle had been the background scene with Joseph's more-welcoming rendition of the Statue of Liberty and Miguel's miniature wood-drift worlds. Her father, Joseph, Luis, and Rubio had worked late into the night making a wooden carousel that could be seen rotating from the back of the park. It was her father's series of paintings that took her breath away. Her sister's portrait, the paintings of the farm fields and the bay with waves breaking on the sand, all brought the valley together.

It was almost time for the dance. She listened to JoAnne and Spencer as they finished their eulogy. JoAnne ended with words Hannah could apply to her sister as well. "Russell is here in spirit, leaving us with hope, with his spunk, and old-fashioned ways. He never left the past behind but used the insights of its lessons." Hoots and applause came from the back of the park, where the ham radio club sat. Hannah heard Ralph consoling Sharon.

Rosie took the mic. "Russell was an old soul and inspired new souls. He rests in peace because he saw the best in all of us."

As Rosie moved off the stage, the carousel turned. A hush fell over the park, and a bald eagle flew overhead. A slow drumbeat signaled Hannah to enter. Luis came from the other side. The curtains rose to reveal a conglomerate of musicians gathered from school bands, orchestras, and performers from around the area.

Hannah clapped the castanets and moved to rhythms of native drumming, as Luis took the counterbeat and the music picked up into a mamba, then a salsa. The two danced together across the stage, releasing into leaps on the painted rocks. Hannah took a deep breath as she leaped into the air and dissolved into Luis arms.

Suddenly a frenzy of Russian music brought forth an array of dancers dressed in vibrant colors. With a flair and a sly smile, Vladimir and Yuri took Hannah's hands, and they circled together, raising their arms as a canopy. Luis danced below and pulled Hannah through. A clicking of heels and stomping introduced a Scottish theme, and the local Highland dancers streamed from either side of the stage. Bagpipes slowed the music down as the native drumming began again. Native dancers encircled the group. In the last moments, Hannah took a striped red-and-white scarf from her costume, just as Luis swirled the blue scarf from his waistband. They bent in between the other dancers with lunges and twirls until they had formed a red, white, and blue flag over the top of the group. Gold stars fell from above. Hannah took Luis's hand just as the crowd went crazy with applause.

. . . . .

Luis searched the stands and crowds for Joseph. He thought that Joseph would want to see the town's reaction to his sculpture. Maybe Joseph knew that the TV crews would be back. All the attention tired Luis. He didn't blame Joseph for wanting to disappear.

Even in jeans, Luis felt conspicuous. He spotted Hannah with Robin and Shelly. She waved him over. Remembering Hannah's lecture on germs and low immune system for cancer patients, instead of shaking Robin's hand, Luis bumped knuckles. "Robin, nice to meet you and your mom. Hannah has told me so much about you."

"Yeah, she said a few good things about you too. I have to go rest now, but maybe you can dance at our studio with Hannah."

Luis smiled. "That would be nice. I'm sure your mom could teach me a thing or two."

As they walked away, Hannah tapped him on the shoulder and whispered, "Look over at the parking lot. That's Mr. Ferguson with Vladimir and Yuri. I thought something was up."

"I didn't want to say anything before the performance, but Joseph is going away for a while and won't say where. Maybe it's connected." Luis scanned the park, looking for Miguel, Frank, and Rosie. "Something's up. Everyone except your parents has disappeared."

Hannah took his hand. "There's not much we can do about it right now. Let's go over to the new Henderson Farm Co-Op stand and congratulate the staff on their ownership. We can worry about the others later."

# CHAPTER 45: *Stones Speak*

Luis sat alone at the kitchen table. Joseph had been gone for over a month. Silence kept him company as he ate the last of the greens from the garden and a cheese sandwich made from Sharon's bread. It seemed that every few days a new loaf would appear, as if by magic. He was grateful.

He barely saw Frank now that he was working full time at the Henderson Farm Co-Op. He studied at night to pass the grueling exams that Rubio had created with the Washington State University Agricultural Extension Program. Not all the farmworkers knew English, and he'd offered to translate the curriculum and tutor them so they could be partial owners instead of employees. Luis had a new definition of change: work, plus thought, plus vision, plus heart, equals transformation. Joseph would laugh at his equation.

Not quite ready to study, Luis placed his one dish in the sink and headed out to the shop. The path still accumulated stones, what Joseph called greeting cards. Luis called them stories. It was the upriver mail system making permanent marks. The last note came in the form of a fossil. Luis couldn't be sure, but he thought Miguel had left it for him before he took off with Rosie, back to Puerto Rico. They'd left in a hurry, Rosie talking about a virus and a storm—a premonition. Two weeks later, Luis read in the paper about the Zika virus and a hurricane that had devastated the island. Rosie's picture was front and center, caring for her partner Jesus, the local hero.

Luis walked barefoot over the fossil. It was smaller than a quarter but held the impression of a palm leaf, a feather, and a fish scale.

Luis made up its story. He believed the history of the earth was at its center—plant, bird, and fish pressed together to document and stand witness. Or it could be Ralph or Frank making him feel welcome. Either way, the inclusion in the pathway spoke to him.

Luis opened the door to the shop and settled into Joseph's sculpting corner. Joseph had left a small piece of sandstone sitting on the counter and a note on top of his knives and chisel: *When you're ready to talk, touch me, feel my essence. I'm here forever. Put yourself in, and together we'll speak.*

Tonight, like every other night this past month, Luis had waited, wondering when the stone would be ready. He turned the light off as he heard Hannah pull into the driveway. He shook his head; he hadn't heard the stone's secret.

Hannah greeted him halfway along the path back to the cabin. She handed him an envelope addressed to him. "This just came to my dad, via someone who knows Mr. Ferguson."

Luis walked into the cabin and turned on the light. Hannah held her breath as Luis opened the letter. "Joseph has accepted a special position in research with the World Health Organization. His first posting will be in Puerto Rico. He will be considered a citizen of the world, with accompanying paperwork to allow him access to disaster areas." Luis dropped the note. Tears fell as he took Hannah's hand. "Come outside with me. Let's dance along the stones."

They took off their shoes. Barefoot, they felt the impressions, the stories, the greetings. Luis sang in a made-up language of movement, *I'm here, I'm in, I feel, we speak.*

## ABOUT THE AUTHOR

Abbe Rolnick grew up in the suburbs of Baltimore, Maryland. Her first major cultural jolt occurred at age 15 when her family moved to Miami Beach, Florida. To find perspective, she climbed the only non-palm tree at her condo complex and wrote what she observed. History came alive with her exposure to Cuban culture.

After attending Boston University, she lived in Puerto Rico, where she owned a bookstore. RIVER OF ANGELS flows from her experiences there and is the first novel in her Generations Series. She continues with COLOR OF LIES, the second novel in the series, bringing the reader to the Pacific Northwest where she presently resides. Here she blends stories from island life with characters in Skagit Valley. The third in the series, FOUNDING STONES continues with characters from her two previous novels.

Her recent experiences with her husband's cancer inspired Cocoon of Cancer: An Invitation to Love Deeply. (2016) It's a love story that shares intimate tips for caregivers and family.

Tattle Tales: Essays and Stories Along the Way (2016) is a compilation of twenty years of writing.

An avid world traveler, Abbe can be found with her husband Jim in Africa, Southeast Asia, South America, Sri Lanka, the Middle East, and other exotic countries when they aren't at their home amid twenty acres in Skagit Valley, Washington, or visiting with her grown children and grandkids.

To learn more about her writings, Abbe's Notes and Abbe's Ruminations, visit her website, **www.abberolnick.com**.

Abbe welcomes questions and requests for speaking engagements. She'd love it if you posted your reviews of her writings on Amazon.com and Goodreads.com. Spread the word virally and by word of mouth to all book lovers.

## FOUNDING STONES
## Reading Group Question and Topics for Discussion

1. Joseph, Hannah, and Luis each have been abandoned. Each carries a past that ties them down. Discuss their loss and their history and how this binds them and sets them free.

2. Immigration is a complex topic. Discuss reasons for people to emigrate to another country. Do you know anyone not born in the same country as you? Where do your ancestors come from? Can you see their influences?

3. Joseph is fixated on stones. What do they represent to him? Why does he believe each has a message?

4. Hannah is coming of age. How does she find her voice? Why has she kept silent in the past?

5. Culture is often separate from one's everyday life—something shared on occasions. Luis, even though he is away from his family and their influences, still exhibits his Ecuadorian heritage. How does his heritage come through?

6. Russian history follows Joseph, although he has never set foot in that country. How is the past connected to the present? Joseph feels pressures—are they real or self-inflicted?

7. In a world that uses technology, can being off the grid make a difference? What skills does Joseph have that allow him to endure during difficult times? What limits does his education and his lifestyle impose? Who are the educated? How does Joseph blend the worlds?

8. Do you think that Mr. and Mrs. Henderson were correct in protecting Hannah from the problems at the farm? How did the loss of their other daughter influence their behavior?

9. Music, dance, and art are universal languages. How does this bring the community together? How did they save Hannah?

10. Rosie has been in all three of the books from the Generation of Secrets series. She plays a minor role in Founding Stones. Why is she so important? What does she bring to the story? Who in your own life returns, either in the flesh or in spirit, to help you move along?

11. Frank is loyal to Joseph. He is just coming into his own skin, even though he is in his seventies. What stops an individual from progressing to maturity? Hannah and Luis, in their teens, take each hurdle as a stepping stone to growth. Who in your life has not moved on?

12. What power do we have as individuals to make changes that affect other lives? When do we move beyond our own security? How do we make a pathway to be inclusive and balance the rights of all?

# MORE BOOKS BY ABBE ROLNICK

---

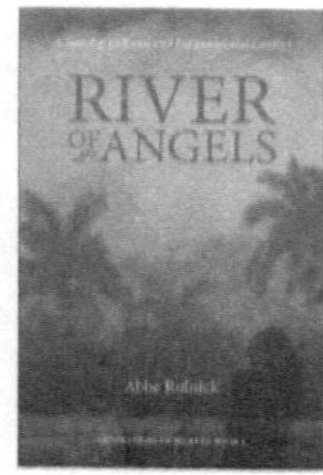


***River of Angels, Generations of Secrets, Book One***

When a prostitute is beaten on a Caribbean Island, no one realizes that this seemingly minor event will light a fuse to blow apart the old, corrupt social order. Pursuing healing for the wounded young woman and for other poor workers, members of the community become targets of ruthless entrepreneurs planning to reap big profits while despoiling the island's riches.

. . . . .

*"Rolnick weaves a story of tangled relationships and intrigue on a tropical island . . . where everyone struggles."*

*~Chuck Robinson, Co-Owner of Village Books, Bellingham, WA.*

*"The sights and smells are rich in themselves, but the characters are what make this book come to life . . . with cultural nuances, facts and stories . . . All are treated with a combination of respect, curiosity, wonder, and affection that ensures they will endure."*

*~Joan Arioldi, Whatcom County Library Director*

# MORE BOOKS BY ABBE ROLNICK

***Color of Lies, Generation of Secrets, Book Two***

Lies, even the little white lies told to protect themselves and each other from the past, suddenly conspire against them as the valley's secrets unravel. Threatened with exposure, the perpetrator resorts to more malicious behavior, and her victims must join with community to stop her and save the valley. All must face truths to halt the accumulation of more that one kind of toxic behavior.

. . . . .

*"Color of Lies is a story of aviation, history, and the interconnectedness of people. It's also an effective environmental 'why do it' . . . Rolnick succeeds in pulling all these themes together with a tight plot that keeps the action moving forward to the ultimate denouement."*

*~Peter Stekel, author of Final Flight.*

*"Buried secrets, both literal and metaphorical, come to light when residents of a small town in Washington notice birds dying . . . Rolnick uses her setting well, making local landscape, industry, and history essential to the plot . . . A well-researched novel that highlights community."*

*~Kirkus Review*

# MORE BOOKS BY ABBE ROLNICK

***Cocoon of Cancer: An Invitation to Love Deeply***

A book of inspiration, *Cocoon of Cancer: An Invitation to Love Deeply* is for those diagnosed with cancer, their caregivers, families, and staff. This collection offers an insider's look at the way life changes forever when the word *cancer* is uttered. The essays and poems reflect an attitude of wonder, defiance, acceptance, and beauty through the painful journey.

Sometimes raw, letters to and from friends voice the unspeakable. The scientific voice of Jim, the patient, comes through when he has the energy to speak. His wife and caregiver Abbe witnesses and documents the signs of distress, gains, losses, and the new equilibrium that forges deep love. More than anything, this is an invitation to feel and find comfort.

Abbe also offers invaluable insights with her *Caregiver Tips, Questions I Still Ponder*, and *Questions for the Reader to Ponder.*

. . . . .

*"Cocoon of Cancer is a poetic, poignant, and scientifically accurate memoir. Abbe's Caregiver's Tips add insights to those who will identify with similar thoughts and feelings."*

*~Dr. Fred Applebaum, Fred Hutchinson Cancer Research Center, Seattle Cancer Care Alliance.*

*"Enlightening . . . I highly recommend this book for patients and families undergoing the sometimes confusing, often fearful, and yes, at times, even joyful process of cancer care."*

*~Dr. Bruce Mathey, Skagit Regional Cancer Center.*

*"This book will be a source of comfort, support, and information to couples entering the foreign world of high-tech cancer care while preserving their sense of family."*

*~Dr. Stewart B. Fleishman, Founding Director of Cancer Supportive Services, Continuum Cancer Centers of New York.*

# MORE BOOKS BY ABBE ROLNICK

***Tattle Tales: Essays & Stories Along the Way***

Abbe Rolnick—teller of tales, celebrant of life, world traveler—offers visions from the heart in this collection of short stories and essays. Explorations of whimsy and wisdom take the reader from the basement of a young girl learning about the Holocaust via a repairman, to a literal and psychological deep dive in the Caribbean, to the humble truths of a dung beetle in Africa, and all points in between. The author's keen perception and compassion light the way.

- Short Story Finalist, 2011 80th Annual *Writer's Digest* for, **Swinging Doors.**
- Short Story Finalist about Family, 2009, *Cup of Comfort,* **You've Got a Match.**

.....

*"The most memorable entries are those that skew toward fiction . . . 'Lace' is a particularly lovely example of Rolnick's mastery at conjuring images of such things as handmade lace and deep-sea diving, which highlight the allure of travel . . . Rolnick offers many observational gems to enjoy. Resonant reflections from a skilled literary artist."*

*~Kirkus Review.*

*"In Tattle Tales, Abbe Rolnick's joie de vivre is evident. These stories and essays take you to an inner realm where Abbe, the observer, contemplates an ever-changing landscape called life. Her enthusiasm and passion thread through each thoughtful piece."*

*~Mary Elizabeth Gillilan, Editor at Clover: A Literary Rag*

www.ingramcontent.com/pod-product-compliance
Lightning Source LLC
Chambersburg PA
CBHW021814110726
47902CB00006B/1769

* 9 7 8 0 9 9 9 5 2 9 1 4 0 *